T

DARK
HORDE

BREWIN

Published in Great Britain in 2012 by Ignis
An imprint of Polybius Books

A CIP catalogue record for this book is available from the British Library

ISBN 978-0-9565880-7-4

Cover Design by Arati Devasher, www.aratidevasher.com
Cover Photo by Jake Lowe, www.jakelowephotography.com
Typeset by Elaine Sharples, www.typesetter.org.uk
Printed and bound in Great Britain by
MPG Biddles, King's Lynn, Norfolk, PE30 4LS

www.polybiusbooks.com

www.thebrewin.com

ACKNOWLEDGEMENTS

Some things can lie dormant and hidden, festering for an apparent eternity, before eventually manifesting into reality... Such has certainly been the case with *The Dark Horde*! I wish to thank the following for making this book possible:

Adam Kolczynski, for giving me this opportunity, for editing and direction;
Barbara Brabec, for advice and making this possible;
Jill Brewin, for your endless love, support and guidance;
Margaret Clark, who started me on the journey of writing books for publication over twenty years ago, when this very story was first imagined;
Jake Lowe, for your amazing photography and Arati Devasher, for your brilliant artwork;
Luke Lakeman, Neil Cheney, David Ranson, Trevor Evans and Trevor Pillinger, for expert forensic advice,
Also Lee Cheney, Anita Bell, Maria Foster, John Marsden, Matthew Reilly, Clive Barker, Clark Ashton Smith, August Derleth and Howard Phillips Lovecraft, among many others for advice, support and inspiration;

And finally, *you* the reader;

Thanks and Cheers to you all!

"Come Dark Horde remember, your journey with me,
A journey of spirals, turning to infinity.
Spiralling through all that was, and ever will be,
Come Dark Horde remember, as one are we.
Great is your power, great was your reign,
Great is your age, yet great is your pain.
Held in contempt, and abandoned in shame.
Hunted and tortured, and put to the flame.
But no more shall this be, I release you to create.
All paths are open now, you are free to control your fate,
To inherit the earth, to inherit eternity.
Come Dark Horde, remember, and once more be!

We are as one, as many are we,
Become one, once more be.
We are as one, as many are we,
Become one, once more be.
We are as one, as many are we,
Become one, once more be..."

〞   〞   〞

After many hours of semiconscious chanting, I was startled awake by a sharp crack in front of me. Before me stretched a black void with depths beyond comprehension. A nauseating stench fell over me and I saw that within the nebulous darkness was a pair of eyes: red convex slits. They were a short distance away and staring directly at me, my mind naked before their gaze...

My God, what had I done?

DAY ONE

9th April 1989

SUNDAY 12:13 AM

His mind struggled...

His boot tapped the floor, his teeth gnawed his nails. Finally, with a great sigh, he made his decision. The other two players were relieved: their patience had already washed away with the amber fluid of a slab of beers.

"Faaarm," Barney announced, placing a single 'F' chip alongside the word 'ARM' on the worn scrabble board.

'Farm' was all he could think of. It was this place where he lived alone and all that he owned. Here he was host to Frank, his twenty-four year-old son and Henry, a mate of Frank's whom they hadn't seen much of since he moved down to Melbourne five years ago. Barney's ute had broken down during the week, so it was welcome relief to have visitors, although Henry's visit this evening was a surprise.

Barney rose to go to the toilet, leaving the others to have their turns. That was when the doorbell rang, singing its merry ding-dong tune that had always irritated Barney.

"Who the bloody hell is that?" he said. "It's bloody quarter past twelve!"

Henry and Frank looked up a moment, but showed no sign of moving. Already out of his chair, Barney grumbled, "I'll get it." He dragged himself over to the door.

Henry tried different combinations of letters on the board, striving through intoxication to determine which would score him the most points. Frank leaned against the fireplace by the window, drinking homemade whisky and coke because there was no beer left. He seemed oblivious to all except his drink and something out of the window.

Barney's voice drifted down the corridor, "What the fuck?"

Then there was a ripping sound followed by a dull splatter.

Henry and Frank both looked up and heard the morbid resonance of something snapping. Then a huge, hairy, dog-faced figure stepped into the lounge, its upright two-and-a-half metre frame stooped against the ceiling, Barney's decapitated head hanging by the hair from one of its twenty-centimetre rakes for claws. It glared at them with red, hate-filled eyes the shape of swollen slits, as its bloodied snout curled to reveal a chaotic array of sharpened teeth. The beast tossed the severed head onto the scrabble table, scattering the pieces over the wooden floor.

Frank stumbled drunkenly to scoop a plumb-axe by the fireplace, but Henry could still see reality through a haze of alcohol and knew that this beast meant only death. The creature stood in the doorway to block that exit, so he retreated into the liquor cellar via the trapdoor by the opposite wall. The beast ignored him, its attention upon Frank with deadly fixation.

Frank leaned against the brick wall of the house with one hand, as he fumbled to ready his weapon in the other.

Wish I wasn't so pissed.

The beast strode forward, hurling aside the table in its path with a flick of its wrists. A curdled mixture of blood and saliva dripped from its wolfish snout in long ropes.

It grinned.

Frank let out a desperate scream as he swung the axe at the creature's neck, but his swing was stopped short, as the beast effortlessly caught the blade in its hand.

The beast tore the axe from Frank's grip and whilst it still held the blade, smashed him over the head with the wooden haft. The blow's incredible strength drew a shock of blood and sent Frank sprawling to the ground.

The room spinning before him, Frank fought to control his senses. Then he was lifted by his shirt-back. His vision struggling into clarity, he saw dagger-teeth bared to rip his throat out.

Frank lunged at his attacker with two gouging fingers. Determination steered his aim into those piercing red orbs that regarded him with lust to kill. He felt his fingers rushing past their soft flesh as the beast roared in pain and fury. Instinctively, it covered its wounded eyes and Frank slipped free.

He sprinted out of the front door and into the empty driveway, crazy with terror, frantic to remember where he had parked his car. His eyes struggling to pierce night's blanket, he followed a dark outline of trees around a corner...

Tears welled in his eyes when he spotted his 'baby' ahead.

Panting, he ran to the door of his big orange Kingswood, fumbling for the keys in his pocket.

He had always been proud of his '73 Holden HQ Kingswood. He loved the way her big V8 engine gave a throaty roar when he plunged the accelerator pedal. He loved the adrenalin rush of sitting at the helm of this mighty beast, the speed and power she possessed and being her master. He took great pains to ensure that his baby was always running perfectly and hated to see her get dirty.

He flung open the car door and stumbled in. Cursing at his intoxicated state, he groped with key in hand for the ignition. His bleeding head ached as he fought to steady his aim. At last there was the satisfying grating of metal interfaces, as he stabbed the key into the keyhole. Praying for salvation, he turned the key and slammed the accelerator pedal. Tears of relief washed his cheeks as the engine stuttered into life and unleashed a rich roar of firing cylinders.

Then came the sound of galloping footsteps...

Suddenly the creature appeared. Frank watched in horror as it leapt a full ten or more metres onto the windscreen, smashing it on impact with its sharp talons. Frank's lips parted to scream, as glass sprayed throughout the car. Then bloodstained hands like blades pierced his throat and tore it out.

Henry, crouching in the darkness of the liquor cellar, heard the Kingswood start, the sound of smashing glass and then nothing but the engine idling... He guessed the rest. An eerie chill passed over him, shaking off the vestiges of insobriety.

Now he heard the slow squeal of the trapdoor opening. The sickening anticipation of death washed over him like a choking wave. He was cold. He was scared. He was alone. But he was armed.

The beast had an acute sense of smell, enabling it to smell the raw terror in the sweat of its quarry. The smell of this human was strong, indulging its senses with delectable wafts. Hungry for the kill, it gripped the wooden handle of the trapdoor and slowly teased it open. The shrieking cry of its hinges rang out, enhancing the fear of the cornered prey. A sharp shaft of light bore its way down an inclined ladder into the dusty air of the cellar. It entered, scraping its clawed feet across each wooded step with calculated intent to terrify... Two down, one to go.

As it reached the earthen floor, it heard the strange sound of an airborne object spinning towards it. Confused, it turned and was struck in the face by a flaming bottle. Glass splinters and burning alcohol ravaged its flesh. It fell to its knees in agony.

Henry moved away so as not to be seen, already arming another makeshift Molotov cocktail, glad that he had a lighter in his pocket.

The beast wrestled the fire that had taken a hold, its mind consumed by the agony of its sizzling skin. At last the flames were stifled, but the white pain remained and with it, the beast's hatred. Gashes from the burning impact of the bottle had been worn by its claws into strips of smoking flesh that hung from its bleeding, blackened face. The air was thick with the pungent stench of burnt hair and flesh, confounding its 'fear smell', but it could still see and hear. Livid with hate, it would taste this mortal's life on its lips and feast on its torment. Thrills of desire swept through the beast, urging it to the kill.

In quick succession, another two of these fiery weapons whirled towards it. It now knew better than to face these attacks and instead it leapt aside, easily dodging the bottles. With a shriek of smashing glass, they struck the racks laden with bottles behind it and erupted in flames.

As the flames began to spread, it quickly moved to safety, its footsteps covered by the hiss and splatter of burning wet bottle-racks. It manoeuvred into the silent cellar darkness behind its target, as the other end of the cellar resounded with the crash of shattering bottles. Having found temporary refuge from the fire, it felt again the burning pain of its flesh, becoming burning hatred that would only be appeased by the sweet taste of this mortal kill.

Through the light and fumes of the fire, Henry saw that the beast had recovered, but he had anticipated this...

Another alien sound assailed the beast's ears: gushing liquid. It realised it was the sound of large casks emptying.

The potent liquid flowed across the floor, feeding the fire and carrying it throughout the cellar. Where the fire had started, entire racks were alight and rocked with explosions of glass, choking the air with dense smoke.

It detected rapid footsteps towards the ladder and acted swiftly.

Dizzy with fear and smoke, Henry dashed for the exit. Tripping onto the ladder in panic, he nearly completed his frantic ascent when the beast grabbed his ankle with such force that he heard a violent crack. He twisted on the rungs to slam his free foot into the mutilated face of the relentless demon and felt its snout crumble against his boot. Slipping on the wet floor, the creature fell backwards, but its grip remained on Henry's ankle and he was wrenched from the ladder to the cellar floor with the beast. Together they crashed into a flaming rack in a rain of broken glass and burning wood.

Henry recovered to find himself under glowing beams searing the cotton jacket he wore. Adrenalin flooding his body, he scrambled free of the burning planks' embrace to his feet, his ankle slipping out of the beast's now-relaxed grip. The beast moved no more. The air stung with the fetor of burnt hair and flesh.

"Die, you fuck!" he spat at its blackened demonic visage.

Horrified, he saw its head turn to fix on him and unleash an unearthly scream to drown the fury of the surrounding flames. Henry bolted for the ladder, wincing at the shots of pain in his ankle. As he ascended the ladder once more, the scream transformed into a deafening guttural roar.

He dived into the lounge, now thick with smoke and slammed the trapdoor. As he dragged a couch over the trapdoor, the chilling sound of laughter began to emanate from below.

The floorboards of the lounge grew hot with the flames below and the thick smoke almost overpowering, but Henry stayed to pile whatever heavy items he could, onto the couch. This demon, this beast that had killed his friends, this abomination from hell, must die.

He toppled the bookcase onto the couch first, then threw on an oversized TV and was dragging over the scrabble table when the trapdoor burst open. With disbelieving dread, Henry watched the beast easily force aside the obstructions and arise from the cellar: a bleeding, burning and mutilated machine of merciless destruction.

Unstoppable.

Weary, Henry ran to the front doorway of the burning house, only to see that three more of them were advancing up the driveway, blocking his only exit...

Grinning.

Oh shit.

SUNDAY 7:42 AM

Something stirred in the darkness and moved closer...

Reality staggered its way into consciousness and with it, a massive migraine. Brian groaned and rolled over to embrace Sasha, his sleeping girlfriend. Then the phone rang. He rolled away to the stand beside the bed, feeling a lurch of pain in his right temple.

He fumbled the phone and it fell beside the bed, rattling on its cord. On the other end a voice crackled, "Hello? Hello Sergeant Derwent?"

Struggling to grab the phone, Brian slipped and bashed his head against the bedside table. His headache became unbearable.

He dragged up the phone-cord and caught the receiver. "Yes, speaking. What is it?" he demanded.

The voice, whom he now recognised to be Constable Harrington, answered, "Sorry to wake you, sarge, but there's been a situation down at the Weston farmhouse. I think you should come down and take a look."

'A situation' was the vague sort of description a subordinate like Robert Harrington would use. Robert was a fresh recruit lacking any real experience. And probably trying to pass on responsibility in case shit hit the fan later on.

"What sort of situation?"

"There's been a fire at the Weston farmhouse and we've discovered two fatalities."

"Two fatalities? Is the area secure?"

"We've only just got here. It looks like they were murdered."

Great. What a fucking great start to Sunday morning. A fucking murder job, which he had a clear obligation to investigate being the head of Howqua Hills Police Station. And neither the monster headache nor the monster erection he had, helped. He looked at his bedside clock and saw that it'd been a little over three hours since he'd been on duty.

"Right well, tape off the area and don't touch anything until I get there."

"Pity the fire crew are still all over everything. They're still putting out spot fires."

"Oh, that's all we need is smokies going around fucking up evidence! As soon as they've declared the area safe, get them the fuck out of there."

"We're working on that."

"How many officers are down there?"

"There's four of us."

"Okay well, isolate any witnesses and make sure no one except the smokies goes anywhere near the scene. So where is it?"

"Lot 31. Maple Creek Road. The property backs onto Oberon Grammar School grounds."

"Right." He sighed. "I'll be there as quickly as I can." He hung up.

Shit!

, , ,

It was, in a word, a mess.

The Weston farmhouse was now nothing but a charred skeleton of a fire that had raged and then smouldered its way through the early morning hours.

Neighbours on adjoining properties noticed smoke rising from the farmhouse with the first rays of autumn dawn and quickly notified the Country Fire Authority who reached the scene before seven. Immediately upon arrival, they realised the greater horror – the farmhouse had been host to murder. And so whilst the fire was doused, the local Howqua Hills police were contacted and were to arrive soon after.

Sergeant Brian Derwent arrived shortly after eight in the morning, parking his 4WD patrol next to two others about a hundred metres down the driveway from the farmhouse that was flooded with water and foam. The fire crew nearby had finished their work and were packing up their equipment, whilst police were busy taping off the area. Constable Harrington came out to greet Brian.

"So what makes you think it was murder?" began Brian.

"Er... When you see the injuries on the bodies, I think you'll agree it looks fairly obvious."

"Have any witnesses been identified?"

"No, but no one's come forward yet either."

Fucking great... Why did this have to happen to me? On my turf? Pain stabbed his right temple like a knife.

"Have the CFA declared the area safe?"

"Well, they've put out the fire, but they've also advised us that the floor and what's left of the walls aren't safe."

Brian saw that the farmhouse was reduced to burnt foundations with the occasional standing support beam. Piles of brick, ash and foam lay in the centre of the devastation, revealing the remnants of a cellar. He noted that the gardens surrounding the building seemed untouched by the fire, perhaps shielded by the light dusting of rain.

"Any ideas on how the fire started?"

"Not sure, but I was talking to the fire brigade OIC about it. He said that the cellar appeared to be where the seat of the fire was, but that identifying any accelerant used is virtually impossible due to the extent of the damage."

"Right well, you can get me a detailed report from the fire brigade, including what their activities were and their opinion on the fire's cause." Brian rubbed his forehead. "But first, show me what you've found."

Robert led Brian to an ash-covered orange Holden Kingswood nearby. Seated behind the smashed windscreen was the body of a man in his early twenties. Torn vertebrae poked forward through a gaping hole in his neck, his head hanging from his shoulders by flaps of muscle and skin. In death, his hands still gripped the wheel. Brian recognised it was Frank Weston. In a small community like Howqua Hills, roughly two-thousand, strangers outside the ski season were uncommon.

"The fucking media are going to *love* this!" said Brian. "Has the Coroner been informed yet?"

"Not yet. We were waiting until you got here and could make your assessment."

"I see," said Brian, thinking.

Robert pointed to the doorstep of the house. "There's a second body without a head over there. Looks like it was torn off."

Brian looked where Robert was pointing, at what appeared to be a blackened skeleton. Not far away, the other officers were securing the crime scene perimeter. White police tape now surrounded the remains of the house and extended around the smashed Holden.

Brian's eyes returned to Robert. "We'll have a close look at that body when forensics get here. In the meanwhile we'll secure the scene and any witnesses we can get, and contact the relevant agencies."

Brian started over towards the other officers with a display of urgency and importance. Robert followed.

Present were Sergeant Douglas McDougall, a complete arsehole you couldn't trust not to chat-up your missus, Constable James Irving, smirking at some comment he'd just made to the others, a smug pretty-boy wanker that thought being in the force four years was a long time, and Constable Lisa Klopski, a thirty-something year-old woman with fake blonde hair, big tits and a nice arse.

Brian greeted the officers abruptly, then gave instructions, "Lisa, I want you to notify the State Coroner's office and request that an arson chemist, photographics, including video, and crime scene units attend."

"Shall I notify homicide as well?"

"We will have to get those pushy self-important morons involved, but let CI do it. That's their job. Tell CI that their assistance is needed urgently."

The sooner the Criminal Investigation Branch got there, the sooner they could take responsibility for this mess.

"Okay," Lisa quipped.

"Douglas, I want you to do a check to make sure that there isn't any evidence outside the sealed off area. Anything that may be the slightest bit relevant, I want taped off."

Douglas nodded, stroking the ends of his moustache in thought.

"I've already given instructions to Robert to interview the fire crew. And smart-arse here," Brian looked at James, "can establish a primary entry point past the tape and keep a log of who enters the crime scene and why."

James restrained a grin as he exchanged glances with Lisa.

"Well, keep up the good work, guys. I'm just going to sit down for a few minutes. Get me if there's anything urgent." Brian walked away towards his patrol, massaging his headache.

Robert followed.

Douglas frowned at the Sergeant's behaviour and mused that he wasn't coping well with pressure of late. Brian had recently separated from his wife, Julie, and contact with his two children, Samantha and Howard, was limited. Little was secret in a small country town like Howqua Hills and it was well known that Brian had left his wife for a promiscuous young lady twenty years his junior. Julie hadn't forgiven him for this and wanted to have as little to do with him as possible. Most of Brian's colleagues, Douglas included, tried to tell him the error of his ways, but Brian was stubborn in ignoring all advice until no one cared anymore to help him fix the mess his life now was. Friends turned their backs on Brian and yet continued to support Julie, which only added to Brian's frustration with the world. On occasion, Douglas had thought how differently things could have turned out with Julie. Douglas had known Julie before she met Brian, and back then, he fancied her himself. But that was a lifetime ago. Now he was married, with a family of his own. Dismissing further thoughts, Douglas began looking for any undiscovered evidence.

Brian noticed Robert and stopped. "Yes?"

"Are you alright, sarge?"

"I just need to sit down for a few minutes *alone*. I've got a fucking-splitting-headache and right now you're not helping."

Robert took the hint and left.

Brian sank into the driver's seat of his patrol with a deep sigh. He reached into the glove box for some painkillers and washed them down with cold coffee from a thermos that remained in the vehicle from last night's shift.

He really hated his job sometimes, but this had to be the worst. He leaned back against the headrest and closed his eyes, oblivious to the world around him.

Oblivious to red eyes watching him from the trees overlooking his vehicle, appraising the enemy. Something stirred in those trees and moved closer...

, , ,

Brian was stumbling down a dim tunnel towards a morbid red glow far ahead. The sickly light cast sinister shadows that moved with his imagination. Something followed in the darkness behind, drawing relentlessly closer. The stench of it began to suffocate him and he broke into a run. In panic he fell, the rough ground scraping the skin of his palms and drawing blood. Quickly, he regained his footing and continued running, panting, his racing heart obscuring the sound of his footfalls. Not daring to look behind at what madness followed. Then he felt its rancid hot breath on his neck, its presence drowning him with its sickening aura. Blinded by fear, his will to live drove him onwards to the light. Then he saw that the red glow he was approaching came from a pair of eyes the shape of slits.

Waiting.

, , ,

He tore away from the nightmare to find he was soaked with perspiration, his headache more unbearable than ever. He glanced at his watch. 8:50 AM. He'd only been asleep for a few minutes.

He rubbed his eyes and stumbled out of his car. Trying to relax now was futile. He lit a cigarette and looked up at Oberon Grammar School on the hill overlooking the Weston property. Perhaps they could throw some light on what happened last night.

Brian returned to the other officers, but no one asked him how he felt: his gait and expression made that obvious.

"I'm going to ask some questions at the school. Maybe someone there saw something."

"I'll accompany you if you like, sarge," Robert offered with enthusiasm.

Brian's first instinct was to decline, but then he thought it'd be handy to have someone there to take notes for him.

"Okay," he said with a wry smile.

SUNDAY 8:50 AM

That smell.

Lucas inhaled to immerse himself in its wondrous, invigorating energies again. It was the smell of autumn. The smell of fresh rain on dry dust. A smell he loved.

The morning sun shone through tatters of fading cloud, warming his spirits. A gentle, refreshing breeze began to blow, making a brilliant day into a perfect one. Lucas Prescott stood outside his office to gaze upon his kingdom: 'Timberhome', a Year Nine coeducational campus at Oberon Grammar School, set in the high country on the slopes of Mount Warrambat amidst white Manna Gums and narrow-leaved Peppermints.

Here at this elite boarding school in the mountains, the young adolescents learnt team spirit and self-reliance away from modern technology. Living in single-sex, fifteen-bed dormitories called 'Units', they were responsible for the maintenance of their Unit, including their wood supply for heating and their only source of hot water: a wood-stoked boiler. They were also given cleaning tasks about the school and kept fit with three cross-country runs a week. Every Wednesday, the kids went hiking in the surrounding bushland, returning on Friday before the area became busy with weekend campers. Classes were Saturday through to Wednesday. Timberhome was a unique educational experience like no other in Australia, possibly the world. And it was Lucas' great privilege to not only be School Principal, but the grandson of its founder, Gregory Prescott, as well.

Lucas could look down on most of the school from his office. Across the flagstone assembly courtyard were the dining hall, the sanatorium and the administration buildings. The other buildings, mostly classrooms, stretched out along the dirt roads running up to the school chapel, along to the five girls' Units and down to the ten boys' Units. Three dirt roads did not lead to the Units. One of these led to the houses of the staff village, another became a surfaced road back into the Howqua Hills township, and the last road led down the hill past what was once the Weston farmhouse, to paddocks owned by the school. Only the burnt carcass of the Weston farmhouse remained now, crawling with fire crew and police officers like ants over a bone.

The fire wasn't noticed until the light of day, the smoke blew away from the school and the interposing foliage obscured the flames. Lucas knew Barney Weston, the farm-owner. Barney and his son Frank had helped the school doing the odd maintenance job. The event dominated discussions at breakfast. "What happened? Was anyone hurt? Was it intentional?" were the questions that most were asking and none could answer. Before morning tea, he would contact the police and find out, but right now, he had other things to attend to.

Lucas Prescott inhaled that wonderful, sweet aroma of rain on dust once more. Although now faded, he could still taste its rich qualities. He so loved autumn, the season of colour, of joy...

Of death.

Where had that thought come from?

Lucas shuddered and turned to enter his office...

And walked into a boy behind him.

The small boy fell backwards, dropping an armload of books.

Startled, Lucas apologised, "Dreadfully sorry! Are you okay?"

The slender child pushed himself back onto his feet. He looked shaken but unhurt. He wouldn't make eye contact.

"Here, let me help you with those," Lucas offered.

The boy was silent as together they gathered up the books. Lucas realised he didn't know this pupil.

"I'm sorry, I don't know your name?"

The boy looked at him with hazel eyes from beneath a low brown fringe. His jaw quivered a moment, "D-Danny."

Lucas smiled before producing a calloused hand, "Pleased to meet you, Danny. You can call me Lucas."

Danny winced as he returned Lucas' friendly shake and tried to smile. "Thank you," was all he managed to say.

What a strange boy.

Then Lucas saw a police vehicle driving up the main road into the school. He thought better of using this opportunity to become more acquainted with the child.

"On you go, Danny."

Without delay, Danny ran off to class, breaking into a dawdle once he was a few metres clear of Lucas.

Two officers emerged from the 4WD police patrol. The younger of the two, bore a friendly smile. The other reeked of cigarettes and bore a grim expression as he said, "Are you the principal here?"

"Yes, I am." Lucas' stomach turned. "This is to do with the Weston farmhouse, isn't it?"

The officer smiled. "Can you spare a few minutes?"

We have time to spare. Death is forever patient. They crept closer...

, , ,

Lucas was now seated in his office with the two officers. Constable Robert Harrington sat cross-legged taking notes with a pen and notepad, whilst Sergeant Brian Derwent remained standing, making Lucas nervous.

"So, do you have any ideas on what could have happened?" Brian asked Lucas.

"None at all! I mean, it's such an unthinkable thing to happen to anybody, but Barney and Frank Weston? They had no enemies, they were good people who earned an honest living and were well respected by the community. They were always such good workers for the school, but we didn't realise what had happened until daylight, and we only thought it was a fire then. I'm shocked and speechless to hear that it looks like they were *murdered*. I have no idea who could possibly have wanted to do this, and I'm concerned that whoever it is, is still out there."

Brian raised a palm and opened his mouth to speak, when there was a scrabbling sound across the roof. The three of them paused and looked at the ceiling, puzzled.

Lucas broke the silence that followed the noise. "What was that?"

Brian looked at Lucas and then at Robert. "Probably nothing. Rob, can you go check that out?"

Looking apprehensive, Robert put down his notes and crept outside, gripping his loaded hip holster.

Sunlight streamed through the gum trees in-between the buildings. Not far away, classrooms buzzed with the excited chatter of children, punctuated by the buzz of flies around him. Robert peered around the eaves of the office roof where the noise was last heard, his eyes straining against the sun.

He was unable to see anything that might have been the source of the noise, but it was difficult with the sun and the trees.

Must be a possum.

Across the flagstone courtyard, a kookaburra in the trees burst into laughter, its song filling the air. Robert turned for a moment to see it launch from its perch and fly away, laughing.

Robert shrugged his shoulders and headed back inside...

Unaware of the dark shapes lurking in the trees behind him.

SUNDAY 9:40 AM

He crept closer, poised to strike.

The desk creaked as Burke leant out of the aisle, aiming his peashooter – the cylindrical shell of a pen – at Danny. Danny sat at the front of the classroom gazing out of the window next to him. An easy target made even easier considering the teacher, Mrs Farell, was writing something on the blackboard and had her back to the class.

Pfft! A spitball shot down the aisle and into Danny's hair. Most of the class saw it, but not Danny who stared out of the window at the gum trees and the school weir beyond.

Burke laughed with his mates, Brad and Martin, at the back of the class.

Their laughter stopped when Mrs Farell turned to face them.

"For today's class I want you to write a story based on the words I've written on the blackboard."

Brad whispered to Burke. "She didn't even notice man! Haha!"

Martin held a peashooter of his own in his mouth, giving the appearance of a pen. He read the words "The Colour Crimson" on the blackboard and leaned back on his chair against the wall behind him. "How are we s'posed to write a story on that?"

"Don't ask *me*, Martin." Mrs Farell's horn-rimmed glasses

rose over the wrinkle of her nose. "I only give you the clay. It's up to you to mould it."

Martin threw up his arms and looked to the others. "Ohhh great."

Burke loaded another spitball in his lap. "Can you maybe put a few topics up and we can choose?"

"I think that should be plenty."

"Please, Mrs Farell! Just one more. That one's really hard."

She sighed. "Okay. I'll put up one more theme, but that's it."

She turned again to the blackboard as Brad, Burke and Martin all fired spitballs at Danny. One spitball joined the one already stuck in his hair, one stuck to the back of his chair and the other one hit Jessica in the back of the neck. Jessica looked around at the trio, who gestured that they were aiming at Danny. The teacher continued writing on the board, unaware.

Danny looked out of the window, at the slender trunks of trees in the morning sunlight...

As a dark shape moved between them.

He jolted and became conscious of mingled chatter and laughter behind him. It was probably about him so he ignored it. He focused again on the view outside.

In the shade of the gums, away from the other buildings, something ape-like lurked. Something he realised was staring back at him with piercing red eyes. His heart thumped in his ears, his face flushed with fear.

Now he saw that there were many of them, lurking in the trees...

Watching.

He shuddered and looked away at the class. Mrs Farell had just finished writing another line on the blackboard. No one seemed to have noticed the scene outside. Incredulous, he turned back to the window...

They were still there.

"No more questions?" Mrs Farell scanned the room.

No one answered. Many quietly cursed.

"I guess you must all be too eager to *rip* into that story!" She sat at her desk to begin correcting papers from her last class.

Brad, Burke and Martin pretended to start writing, then reloaded their peashooters as soon as the teacher wasn't looking.

Danny had the instinct to run, but didn't want to attract attention either. He glanced outside again and at the others in class. He was sure the class should be able to see them outside. There must be twenty or more of those things, crawling in the shadows of the trees!

He turned to Rebecca sitting next to the window behind him.

Rebecca looked up from the single line she had written. "What are you looking at?"

Danny pointed out of the window, unable to form words.

"Turn around, idiot! You'll get me in trouble!"

He returned to face his desk, speechless.

It was true, no one else could see them. Was he imagining the whole thing? The red eyes regarding him from cover a short distance away, told him otherwise.

"Soon you will be ours," resonated a deep voice inside his head.

Then there was a knock at the door. Heads raised to see that it was the principal, Lucas Prescott.

Mrs Farell rose from her seat and walked to open the door.

"Sorry, Wendy. Can I have a quick word with you in private?"

She nodded and turned to her class. "Listen please

everyone. I'm going to be out of the room for a couple of minutes. When I come back, I want to see you all writing. If I catch anyone not working, there'll be trouble."

The class was silent and Mrs Farell smiled. As soon as she left with Mr Prescott and closed the door, there was a volley of spitballs, mostly at Danny.

Burke decided to go one better and ran down the aisle to whack Danny's bare legs with a ruler. Danny cried in pain as Burke rushed past him, grabbing Danny's pencil case on the way. Burke threw Danny's pencil case to Martin, who stood on a chair to catch it. Brad kept a lookout down the corridor for Mrs Farell's return. The rest of the class watched.

"Give it back," came a weak voice.

Martin grinned as he emptied a bottle of correction fluid into the pencil case, holding it up for Danny to see. Martin laughed along with Burke and Brad.

"Oh, don't do that!"

"What are you going to do about it?" Martin challenged.

"She's coming!" Brad called.

Burke bolted back to his chair, reaching it just as the classroom door opened. Martin dropped Danny's pencil case on the floor. Everyone pretended to be writing.

Mrs Farell walked to the front of the desks, a serious look on her face. Mr Prescott stood in the doorway, watching. "Mr Prescott had just informed me that he has spoken to the police about what happened at the Weston farmhouse last night."

Brad was trying hard not to laugh. Burke tickled his ribs. He lost it.

"Do you think it's funny, Bradley?"

Red-faced, Bradley managed to contain his laughter. "No, Mrs Farell."

"Perhaps you won't find it so funny when you have to be up to do a Banner Road tomorrow morning at six."

"Shit," Bradley whispered, not wishing to attract further punishment. Nobody wanted to do a Banner Road. It meant getting up before everyone else to do a five-kilometre run out to Banner Road and back with some of the teachers.

"I don't want anyone to panic, but something very serious has happened. Last night, Barney and Frank Weston were killed in a fire at their house nearby and we don't know how it happened yet."

Stunned silence.

"There'll be a formal announcement at lunch, but in the meantime, I want you all to be very careful and not go anywhere alone. We are safe and secure here, but this is just a precaution until we know what happened."

Danny shivered and cast a furtive glance outside.

They were no longer there. Moving shapes were now mere branches in the wind. Nothing even suggested that they had ever been there...

His thoughts were broken by a spitball hitting him in the side of the face.

Laughter followed.

SUNDAY 11:29 AM

"Catch this!" he called.

As Arthur said the words, he tossed the tennis ball into the air and prepared to bash it with the small cricket bat he held.

Howard was standing about thirty metres away and trying not to think how unco he was going to look in front of his best friend, Arthur.

As the ball came down, Arthur swiped at it, teeth clenched. His bat met no resistance and he spun full circle. He planted the bat to stop himself from falling. The tennis ball bounced to a stop at his feet.

Arthur looked at Howard and smiled. "I was just testing ya. T'see if you were ready."

Howard smiled back, but said nothing.

Arthur threw up the ball again and this time heard a satisfying 'thock' as he connected. The ball went soaring over Howard before he reacted to give chase.

As Howard sprinted, the ball seemed to hang in the air like a comet. His eyes still on it, it began to fall within striking distance, like a meteor hurtling to earth. He put on a final burst of speed before launching himself headlong.

Howard landed hard in full stretch and slid across the grass. He opened his eyes to see the ball lying in his hands.

Howard remained lying on the ground, staring at the ball

in his palms, as Arthur ran across the oval to him, his face beaming.

"How'd you catch that? That was unreal!" Arthur said as he pulled Howard to his feet.

"See if you can beat that," Howard said, feeling suddenly taller and older than his nine year-old friend.

"You're all dirty now," Arthur said grinning.

They both laughed.

, , ,

Howard and Arthur were walking back home now. They crossed the quiet suburban road to Howard's house and rang the doorbell. Howard's mother, Julie, answered the door.

"Oh Howard, look at your clothes!"

"Sooorry Muuum."

"I've told you before not to get dirty! You've ruined another good pair of pants!"

She began to peel his clothing off. "Go and put some clean clothes on from your room and *don't get dirty again*."

Howard now stood in the front doorway in only his underwear. "Mum, can we have some Yogo?"

Julie looked at Arthur for the first time since they returned. Unlike Howard, he was fairly clean. She looked again at Howard.

Howard clasped his hands together in prayer. "Pleeeaaase!"

"Okay, once you go dress yourself, I'll let you have one Yogo each. But no more, as I have to take Arthur home for lunch soon."

"Can't Arthur stay for lunch?"

"No Howard, he can't! His mother is expecting him home at twelve thirty. So he can only stay for another *half hour*."

Howard pouted and tried to think of something to say. Arthur scratched his ear and remained silent.

"Go and get changed, Howard. Now, please!"

Howard looked at Arthur. "You want to stay, don't you Arthur?"

Arthur nodded and opened his mouth before Julie said, "Howard, it's final! Go change or you won't be able to have Arthur over at all!"

It didn't look like Howard could push things any further. He dashed off to his room to change, whilst his mum poured cordial for Arthur.

Howard passed his sister Samantha's room on the way to his own, noticing that his bossy older sister didn't seem to be home.

Smiling, he turned to his room...

His smile vanished as he stopped in the doorway to look up at the poster facing his bed.

It was an eerie poster of Long John Silver, the cutlass-wielding pirate, in the light of the full moon, a red parrot leering from his shoulder. Long John Silver's eyes looked straight at Howard, his weathered features portraying a dark and powerful side. In the background was a dark ocean with the murky profile of an island in the distance. Emblazoned above the picture was the title *"Treasure Island."*

Howard didn't like to look for long at the picture, as it gave him the 'shivers'. The poster was a birthday present from Arthur, and his mum insisted that he put it up on his wall out of respect. If Howard had his way, he'd pull the thing down and hide it away somewhere. When he first got it, he had nightmares about pirates chasing him. Almost a year later, the poster still unsettled him, although he'd never got around to removing it.

He forgot about the poster and began looking for clothes to wear.

A short time later, Howard returned to the lounge where mum sat with Arthur. A cartoon video of *Transformers* was on in the background. Howard had watched it a million times.

Arthur held up one of the two mini-tubs of chocolate-flavoured yogurt. "Here's your Yogo."

"Thanks." Howard turned to his mother as she held up a jug of cola cordial. "Maybe I can go with Arthur and stay at his house?"

She frowned. "Howard, the answer is NO."

The phone rang.

Julie answered, "Hello?... Amanda! I was just telling the boys that I have to take Arthur home soon."

Julie frowned. "Why? What's happened?"

She covered her mouth with her hand. "Oh my God! Amanda!"

Howard and Arthur gathered around Julie, who gasped as Amanda relayed the news.

"If there's anything I can do to help, you just let me know. I'll mind the kids here until you get back. In fact, I'm sure they won't mind if Arthur stays here the night, if that helps."

Howard smiled broadly as he gave Arthur a big thumbs-up, but Arthur seemed more concerned about what had happened with his mum.

"Sure, that'll be fine, Amanda. Ah, perhaps you best tell him when you get here. I don't know how to tell him." Julie looked at Arthur.

"Okay darling, I better let you go. What a terrible thing to happen. I'm so sorry, I don't know what to say."

Julie hung up the phone looking shaken. Holding back

tears, she turned to Arthur. "Arthur, you're going to be staying here for a bit longer. Your mother has to go down to the police station. Something's happened to your uncle Barney and his son Frank."

"What's happened?" Arthur said.

Julie hesitated. "I, I can't say."

SUNDAY 1:45 PM

"Remember Henry Wilcox?"

Jason looked at Aaron and then out of the hotel window at the road outside. "Yeah, that loser."

Four mates, all in their early twenties, sat around a counter meal at the Royal Hotel in the Main Street of Howqua Hills. They'd been there since soon after twelve and had downed a number of beers already. There were no plans to go anywhere until they'd downed a number more. Conversation currently revolved around recollections of school days at Howqua High.

Bruce laughed. "Remember that time they found him in the forest?"

"It wasn't just one time, it happened a few times," Aaron said.

Vincent spoke up. "What happened?"

Aaron replied, "Oh that's right, you came to our school in year twelve after he'd left. He was a schizo. He'd be like sitting there in class and then suddenly he'd jump up and shout something like, 'I banish the demons from my mind!' And the whole class would just crack up laughing." Aaron acted out Henry's movements as he spoke, drawing more laughter.

Vincent cut from laughing to ask again. "But what happened in the forest?"

"They found him chanting some ritual with candles. The

fuckin' freak! Apparently he'd sleepwalked in there," Aaron said with sarcasm as he mimicked Henry again.

"Chanting a ritual?" said Vincent.

"Something like that," said Aaron. "Some satanic masturbation ritual."

"And what the fuck is a satanic masturbation ritual?" said Bruce, his voice carrying across to nearby tables where other patrons sat trying to have a quiet meal.

"I don't know!" Aaron gave another demonstration. "Like, oh Satan! Oh Satan, my master!"

Vincent laughed awkwardly and glanced at the patrons on nearby tables. The others seemed oblivious to being in a public place.

"He wasn't a Satanist; at least I never heard him talk about that, the few times he *did* talk," Bruce said.

"Yeah probably not, just fucked in the head," Aaron replied.

Jason rose from the table. "Oh look, who gives a fuck about that loser! Who's up for a game of pool?"

Vincent seemed happy with the diversion. "Yeah, I'm in."

Aaron waved them off. "Nah, you guys have a game and then I'll play the winner. I'm still finishing."

"That's 'cos you've been too busy fuckin' talkin'," Jason said as he grabbed a cue. He headed for the pool table with Vincent.

Bruce had finished his meal, but remained at the table with Aaron and put his feet up on a vacated chair. Aaron was silent whilst he shovelled pasta into his mouth and Bruce's gaze wandered to the television screen overhead. News Centre Six, the local news bulletin, was on.

A shot of the smouldering remains of a building amidst gum trees, with uniformed police officers in the foreground. "In breaking news, two people were found dead this morning, at the scene of a burnt farmhouse near Howqua Hills..."

Bruce sat bolt upright. "Hey Aaron, look!" He pointed at the television screen.

"The Country Fire Authority responded to a call from Howqua Hills residents who noticed smoke coming from the farmhouse shortly after six-thirty am this morning. There they discovered the bodies of two men, whose identities have yet to be released, at the scene of a house that had been destroyed by fire."

Aaron choked on his food. "Fuck, that's Barney Weston's farm! Hey guys!" he called to the others playing pool. "Check this out!"

They began to gather around the screen, as did other patrons.

A shot through police tape at a black tarpaulin covering what appeared to be a body, next to the house ruins. "One of the victims was found decapitated at the front doorstep."

A rear-view shot of an orange HQ Kingswood with an AC-DC sticker they all recognised as Frank's. "And the other was found in his car with his throat torn open."

They were exclamations of shock and surprise from the other patrons, but from Bruce, Aaron, Vincent and Jason there was only stunned silence, their disbelieving eyes fixed to the screen.

"Police are treating it as an arson-homicide case and had this to say:"

A shot of a uniformed police officer surrounded by microphones, cameras and reporters. The officer is tall and gaunt, sporting a bushy moustache. "The actual cause of the fire and the cause of death have yet to be established, but I can say that it does appear to be malicious and particularly savage in nature. We cannot disclose more at this stage, including their identities, but their immediate families have been contacted and are assisting the police with their enquiries."

A reporter's voice came over the clip of the police officer. "Police urge anyone with any information regarding the events of last night to contact them by calling Crime Stoppers 1800 333 000."

Bruce was the first of the four friends, all of whom knew Frank, to speak. "I need another drink. Who wants one?"

Aaron had lost interest in his food. "Think we all do." He lit a cigarette.

Vincent went with Bruce to get drinks and returned soon after. Jason sat at the table, his shaven head sliding into his arms.

Aaron cleared his throat to speak, but Jason spoke first. "That was Frank's fucking car we just saw, wasn't it? Tell me I'm not fucking dreaming!"

Aaron nodded and then sculled his beer. Bruce sipped his beer in contemplation. Vincent looked at his watch and away outside. Jason kicked a chair in frustration and stood up, unsure where to unleash his anger.

Aaron slammed his empty glass down. "Fuck it! Frank's our mate. Let's go down there now and see what happened!"

"Who's going to drive?" Bruce said.

Aaron looked to Vincent. The others followed his gaze. "Well, Vino's been nursing his drinks since we got here, so–"

"I have not!" Vincent protested.

Jason laughed. "How many have you had? Two?"

"Nah... I've had like... Five or something. Probably more actually."

"Oh bullshit, you have! That's probably the same drink you bought an hour ago!" said Aaron.

Bruce raised a palm. "Well anyway, none of the rest of us can drive, so if Vincent won't take us then we can't go."

Aaron stood up. "Nah, fuck that! I'll drive if I have to. I just reckon this pussy should do it 'cos he's had much less than the rest of us."

"I have n–"

Jason cut Vincent off. "Oh, who fucking cares, Vincent! You're a pussy and Aaron's going to drive. I'm grabbing another drink and then we're going."

"Grab me another while you're there, here's some money," said Bruce.

Jason waved Bruce away. "Nah, I'll get it."

"I'm gunna get a coffee," said Aaron. "You having another beer, Vino?"

Vincent looked uncomfortable. "Actually, I was thinking of getting going."

Jason stormed off to the bar. Aaron persisted. "Going? What the fuck for?"

"It's Amy, isn't it?" said Bruce.

"Nah, I'm just tired and stuff."

"Bullshit! You're pussy-whipped and won't admit it. I bet as soon as you get home you'll be giving her a call," Aaron said.

Vincent said nothing, so Aaron kept going. "How often do you ever come out with your mates? You're always with her!"

"Least I've got a girlfriend."

"Fine, fuck off then," replied Aaron. "Don't expect any of us to care if anything ever happens to you."

"It's not like that, Aaron."

"It's not? Well, come then. Frank was your mate too. Or don't you give a shit about anyone except Amy?"

"Of course I care! I didn't get much sleep last night and–"

Vincent screwed his face up in an expression of pain, struggling to think of something to say.

Aaron's face became flushed with anger and Bruce intervened, "Vincent, why don't you just call her and tell her what's happened? I'm sure she'd understand."

Vincent looked around the bar.

"And there's a phone just over there," said Bruce, pointing.

Vincent saw Bruce was right and sighed. With reluctance, he rose and started walking to the phone, "I'll try."

Aaron followed Vincent, saying to Bruce, "I'm gunna make sure he actually calls."

A short time later, Vincent and Aaron came back to the table where Bruce and Jason were seated. Vincent looked glum.

"So are you coming?" asked Jason.

"Yeah, let's go." Vincent ran a hand through his hair.

Aaron seized the moment, slapping his keys into Vincent's palm. "Good. You can drive."

SUNDAY 3:43 PM

The door opened.

A short, skinny, brown-haired boy stood at the entrance to his dormitory, H Unit, uneasily a moment before entering.

Another kid, Damien, emerged from the pantry. "Oh, it's shit-head again."

Danny tried to ignore the insult, but was overcome with angst.

He began to cross the study where Ben and Alex were playing table tennis. Ben didn't look up, "Hey Danny, can ya get me some snakes from me tuck box."

Hoping to reach his bed in the dorm, Danny tried to protest, "Well Ben, they really are yo–"

"Just fuckin' do it!" Ben threatened, turning to Danny with a raised bat.

Danny turned and fetched Ben's snakes. He then ended up getting Alex some Maltesers as well.

Danny collapsed onto his unmade bed, half-expecting it to slide out of his way and taunt him. Tears welled in his eyes as he felt again the pain of loneliness, of isolation. He was alone and unloved in a world of brutal indifference to his plight, a world without mercy, justice or hope.

I wish I had a mate, someone big and strong, who'd stick up for me, someone who'd pulverise anyone who laid a finger on me. "Don't you dare touch Danny, he's my mate!" he imagined his mate saying.

As regular as the tide, the flood of homesickness returned. His breath became jerky as tears spilled down his cheeks.

His father wouldn't stand by and watch him get abused like this; he'd teach these kids a lesson... Or would he?

He often wondered why his dad always put down his oldest son and yet pounced on anyone who did the same. "I'm your father. I know how not to hurt your feelings," he'd proclaim.

If Danny ever tried to explain that comments like, "You mean after all I've told you, you still don't get it? Gees, you're stupid!" *did* hurt his feelings, he'd be quickly rebuked.

"Oh, come on Danny, a little criticism now and then never hurt anybody."

Yes, but how often was now and then? Once a week? Twice a week? Every day? Every–

His thoughts were interrupted by the rapid approach of a whizzing sound. He instinctively sat up, just in time to catch a water-bomb on the forehead. The balloon burst and sent water gushing over his face, shirt, pillow and bed sheets. There was a sea of laughter around him.

"SCORES!" shouted Mark, raising a hand in triumph. The others continued laughing.

Through a blur of tears, Danny looked around the hostile panel before him and saw neither compassion nor means of escape. He dug his face into the soaked pillow to muffle his crying and their laughter.

Robbo moved in to stroke Danny's knotty hair. "Ohhh, the poor little cry baby. Where's mummy now?" More laughter.

Robbo continued, "Don't cry. We didn't mean it." The chorus of laughter grew louder.

Then the dormitory door flew open and the room fell silent.

Danny craned his neck around to see a gaunt figure standing in the doorway, eyes ablaze on those present: Unit Master, Mr Neilson. Behind him, Ben and Alex made faces in an effort to make the others laugh, but weren't successful.

"WHAT IS GOING ON?" Mr Neilson demanded.

No one dared answer. All avoided his intense stare.

"I WANT SOME ANSWERS!" He shouted as he slammed down his foot with a crash that echoed around the wooden room.

Still no one spoke. Kids hung their heads low and shuffled their feet. Even Ben and Alex gave up their attempts to amuse the others.

Like a searchlight, Mr Neilson's gaze circled the room, scrutinising each face except Danny's, daring someone to meet his eyes.

Clint, thinking the searchlight had passed him, looked up at the wrong time.

"Clinton Byrce." Mr Neilson smiled.

Clint gulped.

"Tell me what has been going on here."

"I-It was just an accident." Clint looked down at his feet and stuck his hands in his pockets. "We were, y'know, just throwing it around when–"

"What were you throwing around?" Mr Neilson interrupted.

Clint gulped again and glanced around the others. The silence amongst them was as complete as before. He momentarily met Mr Neilson's gaze, said "A water balloon, sir," and looked away.

"And just *why* were you throwing around a water balloon?"

Clint hesitated, before answering, "I don't know."

"And you were just throwing this water balloon around when it accidentally hit Danny on the head... Is this what you're trying to say, Clinton?"

"Yes sir," he mumbled.

Mr Neilson's searing eyes fell upon Danny as he said sternly, "Is this true, Danny?"

Against his intuition, Danny searched those fierce green eyes for sympathy, but there was none. He tried to pivot his head away, but like a rabbit caught in headlights, his muscles were frozen with fear. He was transfixed and compelled to answer.

His mouth opened, but the word was stuck. Other words formed in his mind, sinister, flashing across his consciousness too quick and too many to grasp. Meanwhile the gallery waited... For him to pronounce his own sentence, to say the word "Yes" and die, or the word "No" and die. More time passed and still they waited, poised to attack on the whim of his word.

Then a new idea surfaced:

Running.

Before the others could react, Danny jumped through the open window behind him. He landed roughly from the one-and-a-half metre drop on the downhill side of the dormitory. In the next instant, he was up and running, leaving them staring at the spot he had been two seconds ago.

He didn't hear the commotion and didn't care. He was getting out of that place, even if it killed him. Who knows, even if he did get lost and a rescue squad had to come and find him, he might just be returned back to mum and dad, instead of back to this *hell*!

Danny hit the blackberries at the foot of the hill at

breakneck speed, crashing thirty metres in before slowing. Thorny fronds slashed his bare shins and stinging nettles flung themselves at his face and hands.

The bushes are probably on their side as well, H Unit and all the rest of them. United, the world plotted his demise. But for once, he didn't care.

A strange new defiance had risen in him, an unknown strength of purpose. Never before had he experienced such confidence, such determination that nothing was going to stop him. He did not know its origin, but for once in his life, he felt in control.

For once in his life, he felt free.

He was oblivious to the pain in his hands and legs. He was oblivious to the possibility of failure. He was oblivious to the approaching logging truck as he ran onto the road beyond the forest. With sudden astonishment and fear, he looked up into the white, shining eyes of the screaming lorry, its tyres gouging black streaks of rubber into the road...

Just like a rabbit caught in headlights.

And then he was oblivious to everything.

SUNDAY 4:51 PM

Home at last.

Brian turned the engine off and sighed in relief.

What a day. What a totally fucked day. But it was over.

He stretched his arms and yawned. He sank back into the warmth of the patrol, collecting his thoughts.

As expected, enquiries at the school and nearby properties were of little help. No one saw anything, nor had much to say that could assist the investigation. Robert studiously took notes and seemed to enjoy the endless banter with locals. Douglas, meanwhile, assured the media that every effort was being made to bring the perpetrators of this hideous crime to justice, but not to expect results soon, as the information was still being collected and analysed.

The Coroner's report on the two bodies should be available within the next twenty-four hours and Brian would liaise with the homicide division of the Criminal Investigation Branch tomorrow. Right now though, he was going to get some sleep and recover. Maybe a good hot meal and some sex too.

That's when he realised that his girlfriend wasn't home. Sasha's car was gone but she couldn't be far away. Brian yawned again and closed his eyes. Sleep was so inviting, so close...

So easy.

, , ,

He stood alone in an unfamiliar room filled with a thick, musty smell. Nervous, he saw that the room had no exits.

A peculiar design was painted on the dirty grey carpet. A black circle a couple of metres wide, surrounded by a dozen half-burnt black candles. Within the black circle was a white circle placed off-centre. The walls were a mottled yellow that only came with old age and against one of them was a worn dressing-table, its mirror facing the wall. The remains of a tape recorder graced its surface and a wooden chair lay before it in splinters.

Where the hell am I and how did I get here? More importantly, how the fuck am I going to escape?

Suddenly the mirror began to pivot, its rusty hinges squealing, sending shrill notes through him like slithers of ice. Brian backed away from the unnatural animation, awe-struck with disbelief.

Now the mirror faced him, revealing a dark scene that was no reflection of the room. Like a haunting movie, images began to play across its cracked surface. Unable to move, he watched with horrified fascination...

He saw himself, distraught, running. Running blindly from darkness into darkness. Never slowing down, he kept glancing over his shoulder. Then the vision zoomed past his image and onto the panicked melee behind him.

Hundreds, maybe thousands, of men, women and children were running, a rampant, screaming stampede with a common goal: escape.

People fought their way through the pack, knocking down the weak or slow in the anarchical exodus. Children lost their parent's hand, babies fell from secure arms, the elderly collapsed in exhaustion. Those who fell were trampled by the surge of bodies, a human tidal wave of relentless momentum.

Then shining claws pierced the shadows, enveloping the fleeing masses. The population scattered as blood splattered and limbs shattered. The assailants were obscured by the massacre unfolding, a frenzy of bleeding blades. Bodies fell like dominos and agonised screams racked his mind. Riveted by terror, Brian watched as all of them were cut down with brutal efficiency. Within a few minutes, the ground was thick with butchered corpses. Then the killers were gone as suddenly as they had appeared.

Silence hung over the still, dismembered dead with terrible finality. The only movement now was the steady flow of blood from a thousand cuts.

Brian sank to his knees, unable to bear what he had seen...

But the nightmare had only just begun.

The dresser and candles simultaneously burst into a fury of flames, filling the room with palls of smoke. Fingers of fire crawled up the mirror face, leaving black snail-trails in their wake.

Reeling from the scorching heat, Brian forced himself up. The dressing-table, now a charcoal skeleton, collapsed to the floor in a cloud of ash. The blackened mirror clattered after it. The room became an inferno of fire and smoke. His eyes stinging, his lungs burning, Brian began to cough violently.

There has to be a way out of here!

Now a flaming head emerged from the gaping void the mirror had become. A gruesome fireball, it bounced across the smouldering floor, screaming, "They come!"

Brian cringed away from the severed head as it moaned

and shrieked in varying pitches, "Demonic! Mighty! Without mercy! Force of terror, destroying all that be! Feeding on anger, fear and greed! Essence of Man's evil, nurtures the seed!"

Brian now saw that the head wasn't the last thing to emerge... Elongated claws, shimmering in the light of the flames, began to slice through the smoky air above the void.

The head continued wailing, "Run! Run! The *Dark Horde* cannot be stopped! Run while you live!"

Then a taloned foot came crashing down on the head, crushing whatever life it had.

The demon stepped into full view, a monstrous, hairy beast from the depths of hell, its lupine form towering over Brian as he stumbled backwards. Its head pivoted to fix on Brian with crimson eyes as its drooling lips curled to reveal teeth-like knives. A rancid hot breath issued forth...

Horribly familiar.

It stepped closer, smelling his fear.

So easy.

Unleashing a hellish roar that deafened him with its crushing force, it raised an arm to strike.

Images blurred, sensation ceased. The looming figure disappeared with conscious thought as Brian blacked out.

꙳   ꙳   ꙳

Falling through a wall that was never there, Brian awoke.

For fuck's sake! I'm on the floor of my kitchen!

Draped in sweat, he lay there with the head's words echoing in his head. He pondered their significance.

Hang on! Am I crazy? It was only a fucking dream!

He rose, rubbed his eyes and moved to switch the kettle on.

I'm back in reality now. Everything is normal.

Then the kettle began laughing.

He froze at the mocking, evil sound.

Please, let the madness end.

"THEY COME!" the kettle screamed.

Brian turned his head to see the hairy beast leap through the phantasmal wall he had fallen through. It landed with a heavy thud and paused to throw its head back and unleash a fearsome howl that shook the walls.

Brian turned and ran into the lounge, eyes on the front door down the hall.

It had other ideas.

It hurdled the kitchen bench, landing within arm's reach of Brian. Its muscular arm shot forward and snared Brian's retreating left foot. Brian face-planted the ground.

His nose bleeding, caught by his ankle, Brian twisted around to face his attacker.

Its snout opened wide, drawing thick threads of saliva from a mouth crazy with sharpened teeth. The stench of decay consumed him as the disgusting orifice lunged forward, seeking to swallow his face.

He rolled away, but was still held fast at the foot. Its snout impacted centimetres from his head, sending shudders through the floor.

Expecting flesh, its teeth struck only carpet. Furious, it lifted its head to see that the human had moved. Not about to be outdone by a mortal, it grabbed the human by the throat with one claw and prepared to impale the human's head with the other.

Unable to struggle free, Brian scanned the floor around him for something of use.

For once, I wish that Sasha hadn't cleaned up.

It savoured the moment, immersing its senses in the reek

of fear. The final struggle before death was a treasured moment of victory. A rare delicacy. Brian began to check his pockets...

Suddenly the human pulled out a thumb-shaped object from which leapt a small flame. Howling in protest at being forced back by prey, it withdrew, releasing its grip. The human rose slowly and waved the flame daringly within centimetres of its face. "I've got you now, you bastard!"

The flame blurred double, dominating its vision. Incensed, it blindly launched itself at the candle, resolved to engulf it along with the human's hand.

For a moment, Brian was smiling – he was in control. The next moment its slavering mouth was closing around his hand, his lighter quenched. He jerked back his hand as its teeth raked his skin. The lighter vanished into its closing mouth.

The beast spat out the remains of the device, revolted at its harsh taste. Then it saw the hall-door slam.

Its quarry was escaping.

The demon hurled itself at the closed door, smashing through it like paper. But Brian was waiting in a nearby doorway, armed with his son's cricket bat. As it came into view, he swung the bat up into its face as hard as he could. The crunch of the creature's face travelled down the cricket bat and numbed Brian's arms.

Shit, that feels good.

The creature bellowed in agony, but before it could act, Brian followed up with a low hook into its knees.

Crippled and bleeding, it buckled to the floor, staining it a dark purple.

There's another cherry for your bat, Howard.

Brian abandoned weapon and beast and fled.

He careered through the front door, only to see that he

wasn't outside at all. Instead, he had fallen through the front door of a car – an orange, bloodstained car. Only unyielding blackness could be seen beyond the shattered windscreen.

Fuck. I'm in the car that was found at the Weston farmhouse.

A distant voice spoke. "Escape the dream, Brian. Escape it before it claims you!"

It took a few moments for him to realise it was Sasha, his girlfriend.

"Escape it, Brian, escape it now!"

Her voice was replaced by another behind him, much closer. A cruel, rasping growl, grating like nails on a blackboard.

It loomed over him, preparing for the final strike.

Again Sasha called, "Escape the dream, Brian! Before it's too late!"

Brian threw himself sideways, back through the open car door.

He awoke.

➤   ➤   ➤

The 4WD police patrol that Brian had fallen asleep in materialised around him. He was lunging out of the open car door into Sasha's arms. She stood confused by Brian's sudden embrace.

"Oh Sasha! You've saved me!"

Sasha struggled under his weight. "Are you okay? It took me ages to wake you."

Brian sank back into the driver's seat, shaking. "Yeah, I'm fine now... Sorry I freaked out. It was just a nightmare."

She stroked his hair. "Come on, let's get inside. You've obviously had a *hell* of a day."

Brian raised his eyebrows. "Your choice of words is impeccable."

As he rose, his headache returned with a vengeance.

He closed the car and walked with Sasha to the front door.

She turned to him at the doorway. "Your nose is bleeding."

Bleeding?

Brian wiped his nose... And looked down at a blood-covered hand bearing two deep gouges along its length.

He vomited.

SUNDAY 6:22 PM

It was dark.

The dark was dark. He was alone in the silent, empty dark. Darkness without boundary, without substance...
  Enveloping consciousness.

SUNDAY 7:03 PM

"I'm back."

"Oh, go away," he said.

"Don't tell me to go away, you slimy little shit-face!"

"Pleeease!" he moaned.

"Look here, you stinkin' excuse for a child; you filthy, dickless wart. If you think you can tell me what to do, then you better think again. I give the orders, anal features! And if you ever tell me to go away again I'll rip your tiny testicles off and pull your scrotum so far down over your ugly head, that it'll come down to your fucking toes! Do you hear me, spew-face? Do you understand, little wimp boy?"

He began to cry. It was too much. He wanted out. *"Awww what's the matter now, cry baby, want your mummy, do you? Heh, heh, well bad luck, I killed her. I mutilated and raped her dead body in her own bed, while your father watched. And then I grabbed your father's head, I grabbed it in my claws, and shoved the fucking thing right up your mummy's bloody cunt. And you know what, you disgusting ball of shit? While your dad was suffocating to death, his head inside of his dead wife, your younger brother, the stupid little turd, came in screaming. Screaming 'You killed my mum and dad you bastard, you fucking bastard!' So I picked the skinny dung-heap up and used him as a baseball bat to kill your fucking whining cat. Whined it did,"* the horrid voice rasped, *"alll the way to helll, Danny... Alll the wayyyyy to helllll!"*

,   ,   ,

Danny broke free from the horrid dream. He was alive!

A blur of faces swirled above him like fish through distorted glass. But the filthy words said only moments before dominated his consciousness.

One of the faces spoke, "Oh Danny! Thank goodness you've awoken! We've been so worried about you! Do you remember what happened?"

Danny stared up at the smeary images blankly.

The faces talked amongst themselves, fragments of their speech audible:

"I don't think he's aware yet of what's going on around him..."

"Yes, it could be brain damage, you know..."

"Of course I will, he's in good hands now..."

"We need to get the opinion of a psychiatrist..."

"Oh yes, absolutely! You couldn't be more right, the sooner the better..."

All but one of them, a fat one in dark blue clothes, left. His vision remained blurred.

Were his family really dead, like that voice said? Was that voice going to come back? Where was he, anyway? And who were those people? Was he brain-damaged like they said? What happened to me?

For all he knew, he was just a bubble in the abyss, removed from the world he had known, what he saw and heard a mere reflection of his own thoughts. Abandoned, of no value to existence, condemned to spend an eternity in sorrow, to spend his days in woe at what he might have done and might have been. The paradise of death lay beautiful before him, a forbidden release from the mortal coils of pain and misery, ensnaring coils that dragged him forever downward.

A hand touched his arm and his eyes regained focus. His loving mother stood before him, her eyes melting.

"Ohhh Danny, my poor boy."

Streaming tears of relief, Danny leapt from his bed to embrace his mother he so missed, his lowly candle of hope suddenly aflame.

Then she began to change...

Her eyes became black and glaring, her mouth curved and cruel, her disposition malign and hateful. Danny cowered against the bedhead whimpering. That voice of evil was now hers.

"Danny, you good for nothing piece of shit! Do you really think I came back to collect you? I'd sooner bathe in fetid vomit eating rancid faeces. How they remind me of what you are! Your family despises you; we eagerly await your death so that we can piss on your miserable grave. No, you pathetic outcast of my womb, I came here to see that you were dead, so that I could spit with contempt on your broken body and laugh at your suffering. But you can't do anything right, can you! For once in your wretched life you had the chance to do something right and die. But instead, you hopeless failure, you fuck it up completely! I pray that the almighty Venomed One consumes your body, mind and soul. And will celebrate when it does!"

His mother and the malevolent voice disappeared. Danny sank deeper into self-pity.

A hand touched him again and soothing words mocked, "It's okay, Danny, we're here to look after you. It's okay."

He cringed away in terror.

The voices multiplied, urgent, judgemental.

"We better sedate him now. He's in shock."

"Agreed."

Figures surrounded him, stroking him gently. Teasing

him with words like, "It's okay, Danny... Just relax, no harm is going to come to you... We're here to help you, Danny, we're not going to hurt you."

He saw this ploy for what it was. They were dragging him down to his own hell. A hell created specifically for him, as no other was miserable enough.

He wasn't going to let them.

He struggled off the bed and tried to fight his way through the web of arms that moved to stop him... In vain. Too many to battle through, he collapsed to the floor sobbing.

The soothing voices returned to taunt him. They lifted him off the floor against his will and placed him back on the bed. Belted restraints were applied to his arms and legs.

There was to be no mercy for his, the most contemptible of souls.

He felt a sharp pain as fluid was injected into his arm. The voices became distant as the dark waters of sleep closed over him.

"Thank God that's over."

SUNDAY 8:38 PM

A quick visit.

Lucas turned his shining bronze Ford Fairlane from the tree-lined dirt road leading to the school, onto Mueller Road. A clear starry night cast a strange chill over him. Trains of thought chugged through his mind, simultaneous, unrelated.

A lot had happened today. The tragic fire and murder at Barney Weston's farmhouse, dealing with the police, managing the school through all of this and then Danny, one of his pupils, was almost killed by a truck. The truck stopped in time, *thank God*, but Danny, suffering from shock, was taken to Howqua Hills District Hospital rather than into Matron Susan Inglis' care at the school's sanatorium.

It was Lucas' duty as head of the school to see how Danny was, and see that everything was done to assist Danny's recovery...

And ensure that the school was not liable.

Lucas reached Banner Road and followed it into the quiet town centre. Businesses lined the street, lit by street lamps casting an eerie subdued light. At the junction of Main and Highett Streets lay a large roundabout dominated by the soaring Troopers' Monument to three Constables killed by Ned Kelly's gang in 1878. Only the two pubs on opposite sides of the roundabout seemed to have much activity: locals drowning fears of a killer on the loose. He turned into Highett Street where Howqua Hills District Hospital lay a couple of blocks away.

The carpark had only a handful of vehicles. Visiting hours were over, but Lucas noted the "After hours admissions" sign on a nearby electric glass door.

He walked past a matrix of steaming pipes protruding from the back of the brick-veneer building and up the concrete ramp leading inside. He entered a colonial-styled interior that reminded him of a museum. Glass cabinets containing antique surgery implements flanked him. A worn rug stretched to a nurse station situated at the terminus of four hospital corridors.

Approaching the desk, he was greeted by an attractive young nurse. "Can I help you?" She smiled.

"I'm here to see Sister May Kennedy for Danny Malone. I called a short time ago to say I was coming."

"Sister Kennedy is with Danny at the moment. He's in A-wing just on your left there, room 7. It'll be one of the first rooms you come to."

Lucas said "Thank you," and dashed off towards Danny's ward.

A sickly-sweet smell greeted Lucas as he entered a cosy room containing a single bed with railings and an open curtain partition. Danny lay sleeping in restraints, a drip in his arm, looking sweaty and pale. A rosy, round-faced nurse Lucas guessed to be in her forties, sat by Danny's side.

"Sister Kennedy?"

She rose and turned to Lucas. "Yes, and you must be Lucas Prescott?"

"Indeed. How is he?"

"Yeah nah, alriiight," she began.

Lucas started to wring his hands.

"He's calmed down now, but a little over an hour ago he was having hallucinations and attempted to escape. He's obviously in shock from the accident, though apparently not physically hurt."

"Hallucinations?"

"Yeah nah, he claimed to be surrounded by demons that were taunting him. But it's too early to say how severe or temporary this episode is, but he's definitely suffered some mental trauma."

Lucas nodded in thought, looking at the floor.

"Until we get some tests done tomorrow, there's not much we can do except keep him relaxed. Poor thing – we had to put him in restraints and give him something to sleep."

Lucas looked to Danny and stroked his hand.

Danny stirred awake, eyes squinting at the fluorescent light.

May nodded at Lucas and whispered, "It's okay. You can speak to him."

"It's Mr Prescott here, Danny. Your principal."

A muffled whine, "No. No more, please!"

"I'm not going to hurt you, Danny, I came here to see how you are."

Danny's head rolled slowly over the pillow. "That's what they all say! That's all they ever say!"

"Your parents will be here to see you tomorrow. You'll be okay, you're in good hands here."

Danny stared blankly beyond the room into limbo.

Lucas looked back to May and shrugged. "What should I do?"

She gave him a consoling look. "Keep trying."

"Danny," Lucas began again, "can you remember what happened?"

Danny's answer was clear and resonant, *"The door opened."*

Lucas frowned.

Communication was hopeless. Should I persist or just leave?

"Has he been like this the whole time?" Lucas asked of the nurse.

"Yeah nah, while he's been awake he's been like that. We can't get any sense out of him, even to the extent of what happened. Anything we do distresses him, because he thinks we're demons, or sometimes his parents, or sometimes voices no one can hear. But tomorrow a psychiatrist is coming in to make an assessment, so things should be clearer then."

"Hopefully he'll be more coherent tomorrow after some rest."

"Yeah, poor kid."

There was nothing more he could do here...

Lucas left the hospital and sank into his car. Sighing, he started the engine and slowly began driving back to the school.

Yeah, poor kid.

Now he feared the dark.

What lurked in the darkness around him? In the darkness of sleep? In the darkness between the stars?

Real living nightmare.

But how could it be real? How could it be living? How could it be anything but dream?

Because it's coming for you, Brian, however impossible it seems. It's happening.

How do I end this? When will it stop?

It will never end. It is useless to try.

,   ,   ,

Brian awoke with a gasp. He was lying under blankets on the lounge couch. Sasha sat next to him watching the television, sipping a mug.

She noticed Brian wake. "How you feelin', hun?"

Brian yawned loudly. "Fucked."

He wiped his eyes and tried to focus on his surroundings. He was reminded of the dream by the bandages now on his right hand.

"Another nightmare?"

"Yeah." He yawned again. "How long have I been out for?"

"Over four hours. I was gunna wake you soon."

Brian struggled up from the couch and walked to the kitchen for a drink.

"So you sure you still don't want to tell me about your day?"

Brian poured himself a glass of water and gulped it down before answering. "Quite sure. If I could talk about it I would. But I can't. It's okay really, just a whole bunch of shit to deal with. I'm used to it."

Gees, I'm good at lying sometimes.

"I know it's all to do with the murder at Weston's farm. And that whoever did it, is still out there," she said.

"Who told you that?"

"Oh, come on honey, everyone knows that. Two mutilated bodies were found in the burnt house and no killer."

But sometimes I'm blind to the obvious, damn it!

"Obviously. But who's going around talking about it?"

"*Everybody*! Since when has anything like this happened in *Howqua Hills*? Everybody's talking about it."

Brian returned to the couch, rubbing his temples. "Ohhh shit," he sighed.

Sasha crossed her arms. "So if you wanna talk about it, we can talk about it. Otherwise I'm going to bed."

Better to say nothing and endure her anger, than to tell and damn everything.

"We'll talk about it in the morning."

She rolled her eyes. "Whatever." She rose and took her mug to the sink. "I'm going to crash then. You coming?"

Brian groaned. "Think I'll stay up for a bit."

"Okay." Sasha walked to the hall door and stopped. "Oh and your wife called today. Think you'd better call her back tomorrow."

So that's what all this is about. Sasha's feeling left out because she doesn't know what's going on and she thinks that I'd tell Julie. Maybe she thinks that, but she'd be wrong. He couldn't tell anybody.

"Thanks, Sasha, I'll join you soon. I'm just going to go out for a walk first. I need to think some things over."

"Okay, goodnight. Make sure you lock up when you go."

"Yes, mum."

"You forgot to lock up this morning when you left, so I'm just reminding you now." She went to bed.

The streets were dark and silent. A chill breeze rustled dead leaves under the pallid light of street lamps. His patrol's windscreen mirrored a panorama of stars above. A near full moon leered.

Halfway down the driveway, he stopped.

What am I doing? Am I crazy?

Yes, you are. So who cares?

He laughed. I'm really losing it, aren't I?

He continued walking out onto the street, pushed by a cold wind, his footfalls echoing in the darkness. He moved past houses in slumber, oblivious to his passage.

His life was clouded in dark shadow, taking him down a dark road into the sinister unknown. Alone he travelled, alone he was destined to fight, alone he was destined to fall.

What fell path was his life taking? What could possibly happen now to make things any worse?

He shivered and stopped in the middle of the street. Icy fingers of fear clawed at his heart, weakening his resolve.

Was the path he took unchangeable? Its destination unavoidable? Doom unstoppable? The dream inevitable?

He neither knew the answers, nor had energy to seek them anymore. Life had become a constant battle against assailants on every side. Which side he was on and what he was even fighting for, was no longer clear.

Overwhelmed, he began walking again, hoping that the

brisk walk in the night air would revive his spirits and clear his mind.

A fire. A multiple murder. A dream. A nightmare that was real. A wife and children. A life now denied to him. A career. A dead-end. Nothing made sense. Everything seemed beyond his control.

And now he stood at a crossroads. He had no idea which way to go, nor an inclination to care. He sat down on wet grass against a telephone pole, watching his weary breath trail off in mist.

Darkness called...

, , ,

"I've been waiting for you," said a voice in his mind.

Who? What? Where am I?

"So many questions and so little time. What do you care?"

I do care! What's happening?

"What do you care if there's nothing you can do about it? Your fate is sealed. You will all die soon. There is no hope, so give up now."

No. No I can't. I must keep fighting.

"You tell yourself that, but look at you. A miserable wreck that can't even keep his family life intact, let alone keep a job or an easy fuck happy. What hope do you have?"

What is this voice in my head? Am I completely fucking mad?

"Yes, you are. And no one will believe you. You are on your own and no one will help you."

End this! If it's all in my mind, I must be able to stop it!

"You can't control your emotions, so what makes you think you can control your thoughts? Especially when they are not YOURS."

Oh God, please make this end!

"Praying to your pathetic absent God already, are we? I haven't even started with you yet. Watch how easily I can manipulate your every thought, emotion and desire..."

A suffocating fear enveloped him, irrational, uncontrollable. The urge to run away screaming was overwhelming, but he could not – his muscles were paralysed. Unable to move his lips, he began to gag on his tongue.

"So easy, so vulnerable. You think yourself so advanced, but look at you now, helpless in the grip of fear. Hahaha."

Fits of coughing shook him, vomit swamped his mouth and spilled down his shirt, but still he could not move.

"I am going to destroy you, Brian. First I will destroy everything you have and have ever sought to attain. Then I will destroy all hope and thought in that useless brain of yours. And then finally, I will destroy you and all your kind."

Why?

"Because we are the dominant species now. Your extinction is imminent."

Darkening room... *Growing darker.*

Light fades... *Shadows merge.*

Evil lurks... *Creeping closer.*

A sudden chill... *Grips my soul.*

Am I conscious? *All is dizzy.*

Where is body? *Mind is bending.*

Something's calling... *Overwhelming.*

Falling into darkness... *Never-ending.*

DAY TWO

10th April, 1989

MONDAY 12:58 AM

An eternity passed.

He opened his eyes again and the dark returned, like fractured memories of a dream.

He lay naked on cold stone. Red glimmers of light, dogged by adept steps, moved past him like fireflies. Guttural murmuring followed them, echoing throughout cavernous walls. The stench of filthy beasts assaulted his senses. Fear gripped him.

He shuddered aloud and heard something turn to face him... Claws scraped stone, red eyes scanned the darkness.

He held his breath...

May the darkness keep me safe!

Something crept closer.

There was a low growl and then sniffing.

I dare not even swallow.

It paused.

His heart screamed in his head as he fought to contain his breath. He looked for an escape, but could see only darkness. His breath would last but a few seconds longer.

Something grunted and rushed towards him...

And darkness returned.

MONDAY 7:15 AM

Dawn struck like lightning, illuminating the darkness.

Somewhere there was the reek of vomit. Traffic drove past the roadside he lay on. Then he remembered.

Brian broke into a fit of coughing, convulsing forward into a sitting position. Somehow, it seemed strange to be...

Alive.

How strange that word was when he was sure he was as good as dead anyway. Squinting against the emerging light of day, he looked down to see his hand half-submerged in a pool of lurid, smelly mess. He cringed from his creation.

Fuck, I hope no one's recognised me. I've gotta get out of here.

Brian rose, wiping his hands on his trousers. He realised he had a great need to empty his bladder.

Well, at least I didn't piss myself.

Running a bandaged hand through his matted hair, he noticed his headache was gone. Instead, he felt a dull throb in his wounded hand. He looked down at the bandages a moment.

Yesterday's events seemed impossible. He must have cut himself in the car somehow. No other explanation was plausible.

He shivered involuntarily and looked at his watch. It was time to head home.

There were many questions he had to find an answer to, but first he had to find a secluded spot to piss...

The temporary relief he felt didn't compensate for his weariness. A full day lay ahead and it felt like he hadn't slept at all.

He needed a holiday.

Brian dawdled his way back home, dwelling on what he was going to say to Sasha when he got there.

"Sorry honey, there's just these demons running around trying to kill me and everyone else. I'm sure it'll all blow over."

Nah, somehow that just won't work.

A maroon sedan rolled past. The driver noticed a wreck walking along the footpath.

Is that Sergeant Brian Derwent?

Nah, couldn't be.

He drove on.

In no time, Brian was walking up the path to his front door. And still he didn't know what he was going to say, or how he was going to cope with the day ahead.

His mind on autopilot, he rang the front door, forgetting he had keys in his pocket.

Sasha answered the door fully dressed, glaring at him. "Where have you been?"

"You don't want to know."

"What do you mean? What happened? You look like shit!"

"Yeah, I feel like it too." Brian put a foot inside the front doorway.

Sasha stepped aside, holding the door. "Brian. Tell me what's going on."

Brian looked at the clock on the wall in the hallway. He'd have to leave in half an hour to be at the station on time.

"I only wish I knew," he said.

"Brian, tell me what's happened! You still haven't told me anything!"

Brian closed the front door as school children passed outside.

"Believe me when I say you don't want to know."

"Like fuck!" she screamed and pushed Brian into the wall. "You get called out yesterday to the murder, come home and pass out in your car, you can't tell me how you cut your hand or what happened at the farm, and then as soon as you're awake you go out last night and don't come home!"

Brian held up a hand. "Sasha, Sasha, listen-"

"No, you listen to me! You could be in serious danger or having an affair for all I know! I could be in danger, or someone else! I've hardly slept since you didn't come back home, I've had Julie and Sergeant McDougall on the phone, both wanting to know how and where you are and I didn't know what to tell them! Do you even care? How can we be together if you won't even fucking talk to me!"

Brian looked up from the floor into Sasha's eyes. "Is there anything else you wanted to add? You seem to be on a roll."

"Fuck you!" She thumped his chest and stormed off towards the kitchen.

Maybe later.

Brian felt acids burning his empty stomach and oesophagus, and his headache returning. With some effort, he followed her.

"Sasha honey."

She picked up her cigarettes from the kitchen table and stuck one in her pouting mouth. "Don't you Sasha honey me."

As she paused to light a cigarette, Brian took the

opportunity to continue. "Honestly, I don't know what's happening. I keep having these visions and passing out. Like in the car yesterday when I got home, the same thing happened last night while I was out walking. I don't know what's wrong with me, but it's got nothing to do with the investigation. I'll know a lot more about that today when I go to the station, which is where I have to be in half an hour-"

"You're gunna go to work? You need to go to a doctor!"

Brian reached for her cigarettes. "I'll go this afternoon. I've got too many other things I have to sort out first. Then we can talk."

She rolled her eyes and turned away to make a cup of herbal tea. "Whatever."

"Sasha, until then I can't really begin to explain what's happening. It'd take too long and I don't understand it yet anyway."

Sasha kept her back turned to Brian as she poured her tea. Brian imagined the anger building inside her.

She turned around without making eye contact and walked past him towards the lounge with her tea.

"Well, I'd better call Douglas anyway. I'll call Julie later when I get a chance," he said.

The door to the lounge slammed shut.

MONDAY 9:04 AM

Something was wrong.

Chris Gamble rubbed his eyes and stretched his arms before looking again down the microscope.

The cells had no nuclei like all mammalian blood cells and yet they also contained mitochondria, unlike any known animal blood cell. And they were far too large, complex and interconnected to be anything resembling bacteria.

And then he noticed something else... The mitochondria were definitely moving.

The cells were alive.

Chris jumped away from the lab bench and ran a shaking hand through his hair.

Cells organised together that were still alive in a solution of formaldehyde, bearing no resemblance to any known organism on a molecular level were... Alien.

I've discovered something extraterrestrial! But wait... What will this mean for the investigation? For his life?

I've got no choice but to tell David, my superior. Otherwise, sooner or later someone else will see what he'd found and question why he hadn't raised such an anomaly earlier.

I hope David knows what to do.

Chris found forensic pathologist Dr David Dawson with mortuary technician John Taylor downstairs in the 'homicide' autopsy room. David and John were wearing white lab coats, forensic masks and gloves. The pair had been working on the bodies of Barney and Frank Weston since late last night. The naked body of Frank Weston lay with the chest cut open on a lipped metal trolley under the glare of a lamp. On a nearby trolley, various dissection tools lay in neat rows next to organs in plastic bags on green surgical towels. The body of Barney Weston, a 'crispie', lay in a sealed body bag on a trolley across the room. The air was thick with the sweet miasma of burnt hair and flesh.

"You're not going to believe this," Chris began.

David suppressed a yawn and looked up from his gruesome work. "What have you found?"

John looked at Chris with raised eyebrows and a smile. "Your brain?"

Chris answered David. "It's hard to say what it is."

"Yeah, I'll say!" said John laughing.

David ignored John. "What do you mean, Chris?"

"I'll have to show you. Trust me, it's something I've never seen in my life. And if it's what I think it is, nor has anyone else."

David's face went deadpan. He put down his tools and walked around the trolley to where Chris was standing.

"What are you trying to say?" David said.

"The sample taken from under Frank Weston's fingernails contains blood cells that don't seem to be of *any animal*, let alone of any *human*."

"Surely Chris, there must be some mistake. They must be bacterial cells or–"

"David, I checked the sample again and again to be sure of it myself. Not only do the cells lack nuclei, but they contain organelles I presume to be mitochondria, which are still active in a formaldehyde solution!"

"Still active now?"

"Well, a couple of minutes ago when I left the lab, yes."

"I have to see this." David turned to John. "John, you can continue with things here or take a break if you like."

"I might as well keep going, Dave. I wanna get home and get some sleep!"

"Good idea. I'll be back soon." David led Chris out, closing the door to the ward behind them.

John, alone now, turned back to Frank's body and shuddered.

Frank's head, attached to the body by muscle tissue only, rested on his right shoulder, staring at John with dead eyes. He didn't recall the corpse's eyes being open or the head being placed in such a way.

Now I'm imagining things! Must be lack of sleep.

John moved the head back to a more normal position and closed the eyelids. As he did, he thought he saw one of the legs twitch. He jumped back from the body.

What am I doing? Bodies don't move so long after death. This is really getting to me. Good thing no one else is here to see me freak out.

John looked again at the body and thought about the find that Chris had allegedly just made. The cells were still alive.

Maybe I will go take a break until the others get back...

John rushed outside, resisting the temptation to run.

⟩ ⟩ ⟩

Dr David Dawson was on the phone to Sergeant Brian Derwent, head of the investigation into the deaths of Barney and Frank Weston.

"I know it's a way for you to come to the Institute of

Forensic Pathology here in South Melbourne, but it's really important that you see this before anyone else does."

Behind David, Chris wrung his hands nervously.

"Today if possible."

David looked at Chris and nodded.

"After 2pm is fine. Just go to reception and they'll page me."

As soon as David hung up, Chris spoke, "What are we going to tell him?"

MONDAY 10:30 AM

"So what can you tell me?"

Sister May Kennedy sat with Oberon Grammar School Principal Lucas Prescott in the cafeteria of Howqua Hills District Hospital. She placed a cup of steaming coffee on the table before her. "Weeell, he had a CAT scan of his brain done this mornin'..."

"And?"

"And the radiologist couldn't find any signs of physical trauma."

"Oh, thank goodness for that!"

"And he couldn't find any abnormalities or tumours in Danny's brain either."

"What a relief!" Lucas leaned forward. "That is good news!"

May raised an eyebrow. "Weeell, although we haven't found any signs of physical injury, it doesn't mean that there isn't any. We need to do more tests. And even if there is no physical damage, the incident may have triggered a psychosis, or some other mental disorder."

Lucas frowned. "I see... How are his spirits since last night?"

May nodded and took a sip of her coffee. "Yeah nah, much better. There's been no sign this morning of psychotic behaviour. He's even been cheery."

"No hallucinations?"

"No, nor any delusions. However, he had no recollection of last night."

"Does he remember anything else?"

"Yeah nah, he's recalled everything up until passing out when the truck almost hit him. We also assessed his reflexes and cognitive skills and took a blood test. The blood test is being analysed today, but everything else looks fine, at least on the surface."

"That's quite a recovery since last night!"

"Yeah maybe. We'll know more after he's had a psychiatric assessment."

"When is he having that?"

May looked at her watch. "Since about ten minutes ago."

⸳   ⸳   ⸳

In a single ward devoid of decorations save a pastel-coloured painting of the Australian bush, Danny lay reading a history textbook. No drip was attached and no restraints held him. No curtain partitions surrounded him and no nurse sat by his side. Sunlight streamed through the window to his left as footsteps approached the open door to his right.

Danny looked up as a stocky, bearded man dressed in slacks and a brown cardigan entered the room, bearing a briefcase. He wore a thick set of glasses and had a crop of grey hair drawn across his pink scalp.

"Hello Danny. My name is Bernard."

Danny smiled. "Hello Bernard Russell."

Bernard stopped.

How did this kid know my surname?

Bernard sat on the chair next to Danny's bed and placed his briefcase down. "I'm a psychiatrist and I'm here to–"

"Help me," Danny finished for him. "Aren't you going to ask how I knew your name?"

"Well, I could ask–"

"It's on your ID badge. Nice photo."

Bernard looked down at his badge a moment. "Ahhh but Danny, you couldn't have been reading it when you said my name. I was too far away."

Mental note: Subject displays faulty reasoning or deceptive behaviour. Possible Personality Disorder.

"Many things that seem far away are in fact not at all," Danny answered.

Better get the tape recorder on.

Bernard reached into his briefcase. "Danny, do you mind if I record this conversation? I can assure you that the recording is kept strictly as a private and confidential discussion between us, except in cases where there are serious concerns about harm you might do to yourself or others. The recording is primarily to save me needing to take notes."

"And it makes it easier to analyse every word I say," Danny replied.

"Yes." Bernard laughed. "But only so that–"

"You can help me with my illness."

Bernard placed the tape recorder on a nearby trolley and held up a cautioning palm. "No one is saying yet that you have an illness."

"So can I leave then?"

"Once we've made an assessment and determined that you are in good health and fully recovered."

"So how can I convince you of that? I'm really keen to get out of here as soon as possible."

"Do you feel threatened in any way here, Danny?"

Danny smiled. "If you're trying to establish that I'm

suffering paranoia that is leading me to fear being here, you're wrong. I merely wish to get back to school and resume my normal activities."

Sounds reasonable enough, but something isn't quite right about this child's nonchalance towards the psychosis he allegedly suffered last night. Mental note: Patient's symptoms of psychosis appear to have subsided and mood is substantially different from yesterday and perhaps previously. Need to establish mental history of the patient through consultation with parents. Possible long-term psychotic, schizotypal or bipolar disorder.

"So you like being at school then?"

"Well, I'm not sure whether *like* is the appropriate word, but *obligated* yes. Just as I imagine what work is for many people, they may not particularly like it, but they're obliged to do it."

"What don't you like about school?"

Danny shrugged his shoulders, looking relaxed under the microscope. "Nothing in particular."

"Do you get along well with the other kids at school?"

Danny shrugged again. "Well enough."

"What are your favourite subjects?"

"Hmm." Danny pondered the question for a moment. "They're all about the same, I guess."

Mental note: Subject displays apathy, a precursor to various personality and mood disorders.

"How about your family? How are your relationships with them?"

"Fine. There's never been any problems there."

"Would you mind if I spoke to them as well? I'd really like to meet them."

Danny smiled again. "No need to pretend you're genuinely interested, Bernard. Ask them whatever you like.

I'm sure you won't discover any evidence of mental disorder in *my* past."

"Is there something you're not telling me, Danny? You seem to be evading something."

"Well, I s'pose I haven't reiterated to you that I have no recollection of anything that happened last night and today I feel fine and in full health."

"Yes. About–"

"Oh, and that I've never had any feelings of persecution, humiliation, isolation, anxiety, depression, delusions or hallucinations."

Bernard chuckled. "And yet you seem to be defensive about my questions–"

"Only because I'm trying to save you time and get this over with. Oh and before you ask, I've never taken any kind of drugs either, nor had any prior medical condition that could be relevant."

Bernard folded his arms. "So what would you say caused your experiences yesterday?"

"Well, as you know I can't remember them, but they were probably just the result of shock or concussion or something. Regardless, whatever it was, it's gone now." Danny smiled.

"You smile, why?"

"Because you amuse me."

"Amuse you, why do I amuse you?"

"Because you think I'm crazy. You think I'm seeing demons and hearing their voices." Danny's smile grew wider.

"Well you were–"

"You think I'm schizophrenic, or a manic depressive. Maybe I'm a split personality. Or maybe I'm all three. Or maybe I'm none of these at all. Maybe I'm just a normal kid who you're wasting your time with trying to diagnose."

There was something about this kid he didn't like. Something he didn't like from the start. That smile of his seemed wicked, he was too perceptive, he knew too much. Every avenue he tried, this kid seemed to know how to outwit him. That's what he didn't like – this strange fourteen year-old child was outwitting him. Outwitting him with uncanny foresight. And he was harbouring something. Something evil.

What was he thinking! He was getting carried away. Here he was trying to diagnose a child who was coherent, articulate, friendly and cooperative. Not only was he assuming that this kid had some sort of mental disorder, but now he was thinking that he was evil as well! He dismissed these thoughts from his mind and returned to the young boyish face, still smiling. Where was he?

"Um, so you don't, you're not–" He stopped, swallowed and began again.

Psychiatry had never been this hard.

"What I mean to ask is, have you had any trouble with your thought-processes this morning? Do they seem speeded up or confused?"

"No. Do I seem confused? I don't think I'm the one who's confused."

Little bugger. Don't react and encourage him. Focus.

"Are you feeling in any way concerned about what happened last night, or any other recent events?"

"No. You seem to be more concerned about them than anyone else. Nothing bad has happened to me and nor am I in fear of anything bad happening."

"You're not concerned about seeing or hearing demons?"

Danny laughed. "Should I be concerned about something that I cannot recall and I'm told only occurred for a couple of hours after the incident yesterday? You seem to like these demons, Doctor Russell. Maybe you're the one who's seeing them!"

Bernard rose, fists clenched at his side. "DANNY! I AM TRYING TO HELP YOU!" He pointed a shaking finger at Danny. "And you're not helping! This is a serious matter that you seem to think is some kind of joke! Do you find this funny?"

Still grinning, Danny replied. "Okay, okay, maybe I did see these er, demons, but I certainly don't recall any of it. It's nothing to blow your stack over, though. You're supposed to be helping me, remember? Not shouting. It's not very professional."

Bernard sat in his chair again. "Yes, I'm sorry."

At that moment, a nurse called from the doorway, "Is everything all right, Doctor Russell?"

The doctor turned side-on to his patient to answer, "Yes, everything's fine." He turned back to his patient to continue, red-faced.

Danny lay there as placidly as ever, smiling at him.

The sly little bastard.

MONDAY 11:47 AM

It hurt.

Bruce wasn't sure what *it* was, but it hurt like fuck.

Bruce opened his eyes and saw that he was on the couch in the lounge at Aaron's place. Closed curtains cast shadows across a room strewn with takeaway food packaging, beer bottles and dirty plates.

His head throbbed and his tongue felt like it was wrapped in plastic. Struggling to swallow and dampen his mouth, he noticed drool over his face and pillow...

It was a dark colour and sticky.

He touched the sides of his face and recoiled with pain. Deep gashes from his own fingernails ran from his eye sockets down his jaw line.

It had been a big night. Bruce, Aaron and Jason were drinking at Aaron's place until sometime after the sun came up this morning, but he didn't remember this happening. Yesterday seemed like a dream.

Oh fuck. Frank and his dad Barney died yesterday. That wasn't a dream.

And the idiots they were, they'd decided to go down to the police scene whilst drunk to see what happened. Vincent, the driver, didn't even have a full licence. Now he'd lost it for six months and had a huge fine to pay as well. They didn't even find out what happened at the farm. The exact events that occurred were indistinct this side of the drinking binge, but he did remember Vincent going off at them for the idea and leaving in a huff. Bruce, Aaron and Jason went back to Aaron's place after that, numb by the day's events... And kept drinking.

And now he'd woken on his mate's couch to find half his face clawed off and blood all over himself. Fuck!

Bruce scanned the darkened room and spotted a light switch next to the doorway opposite.

Fuck, he needed a glass of water.

Beyond the doorway lay a short carpeted hall to the rest of the house.

With some effort, he sat up and yawned.

Then he heard a squelching sound from down the hallway. It ended as suddenly as it began.

Bruce felt the hair on his neck bristle from the chill of fear. He felt simultaneous needs to piss and vomit.

The squelching sound came again, this time longer, ending with a slopping thump. It seemed to be coming from Aaron's room.

What the fuck is that?

Nature's demands took control of Bruce's senses and he rushed into the hallway seeking the toilet. Trying to ignore the sound coming from down the hallway, he opened the first door on his right. He closed the door behind him and sighed with relief as he disgorged his bladder. He pondered sticking fingers down his throat to get rid of the alcohol still in his stomach, but decided he didn't feel as bad as that.

He then went through the sliding side door into the bathroom. Finding a light switch first, he grabbed a glass from the bathroom bench and filled it under the tap. He saw how bloody his hands were and looked up at the mirror.

A pale face presented itself, streaked with blood from his scratches, his eyes swimming in blood-tinged sockets.

What was he going to say to Aaron?

As he turned the tap off, he again heard rhythmic squelching, this time accompanied by a louder slapping.

I don't remember Aaron picking up last night! Wow, that's a first!

Bruce sculled his glass of water and poured himself another.

Now the sound was accompanied by strange deep grunts that did not sound human.

Bruce shivered and spilt his water.

Then the phone rang in the lounge and Bruce jumped, spilling more water.

The phone echoed through the house, causing the sounds from Aaron's room to cease.

I'm fucked if I'm going to answer that.

The phone kept ringing, as the noises down the hallway resumed.

Oh shit, I better go see what the hell that is.

Bruce stepped back into the hallway and noticed a potent stench that didn't seem to be of alcohol or cigarettes. It smelt like something rotten. The squelching and slapping continued, as did the animalistic groans.

Shit, maybe I should just leave.

The phone stopped ringing as the sound of crashing objects came from the lounge behind him. Mercifully, most of the lounge was out of view.

Fuck! Now what do I do? The front door's that way!

Bruce hesitated in the hallway. The sounds in the lounge stopped but not the wet sounds from Aaron's room.

Just stop thinking about it and go see what it is, you bloody pussy!

As Bruce crept to Aaron's door, he saw it was slightly ajar. His trembling hand pushed it open on squeaky hinges...

The door pushed aside the lurking shadows to reveal a scene of sickening slaughter. Aaron's eviscerated corpse lay strewn over the bed and surrounding floor, dripping entrails hung out like decorations. Splashes of blood and the stench of decay saturated the room. Before closed and blood-splattered curtains stooped a hairy beast in a pose of the basest horror. In colossal claws it held Aaron's decapitated head, rhythmically thrusting its erect member into a bloody socket. The horrifying sound it made was now dampened by the sound of its demonic bestial laughter.

It paused to meet Bruce's dumbstruck gaze with malice. It laughed again and licked its slavering lips before resuming its necrophilic task.

The hallway creaked behind Bruce. He turned to face the huge chest of another of the demons. Its bulk towered over him as its arms swiftly enveloped him.

The last thing he remembered was a crushing grip around his throat...

MONDAY 1:36 PM

"We're here to see our son, Danny Malone."

The nurse looked up from the reception desk at a portly middle-aged man standing next to a woman of equal years wearing a bonnet and a loud floral skirt. "Sure."

She typed a few keys on a keyboard and ran her finger along the green screen.

```
PATIENT: Danny Malone
WARD: Trauma 7C
ADMITTED: 5:14 PM 09/04/89
DATE OF BIRTH: 10/11/1974
NEXT OF KIN: Harold & Margaret Malone (parents).
DIAGNOSIS: Symptoms of post-traumatic shock.
Blood test, EEG and psychiatric assessment
pending.
MEDICATION: 4 mg diazepam, twice daily.
Others to be advised.
CONDITION: Post Psychosis. Stable.
ATTENDING STAFF:
May Kennedy
Dr Alice Clifton (GP)
Dr Geoffrey Hurst (Radiologist)
Dr Bernard Russell (Psychiatrist)
NOTES: Dr Russell has requested that visitors
speak to him prior to seeing the patient.
LAST UPDATED: 12:48 PM 10/04/89
```

"Dr Russell, the psychiatrist, has asked to speak to you first before seeing Danny. He's probably in his office now. Do you mind waiting here whilst I get him?"

Harold, the father, frowned. "Tell him we're here, and that he can come and find us. I didn't come here to see him, I came here to see my son."

"Yes, of course."

"Then take us to where he is now, or do we have to find it ourselves?"

"No, no, I'll show you to where Danny is. And then I'll fetch Dr Russell for you. This way please." She sighed.

The nurse led the way down the corridor, past various nurse stations and hospital wards. "He seems to have recovered well since yesterday when he was admitted."

"Probably because there's nothing wrong with him."

The nurse stopped for a moment to turn to Harold. "Well, you'll have to speak to Dr Russell about that."

Margaret, arm in arm with her husband, piped up, "Oh we will!"

"Nobody knows our son like we do!" Harold chimed in.

The nurse turned away and walked onwards.

"Danny, some visitors are here whom I'm sure you'll be pleased to see." The nurse gestured to the doorway as Danny's parents entered the room.

Danny looked up from writing in an exercise book to see his father, a rotund balding man in a short-sleeved chequered shirt, with his mother, a tall skinny lady with frizzy hair tied under a faded bonnet in that horrible yellow flower dress she often wore.

They were both silent as they waited for Danny to speak. The nurse sidestepped out of the way between them.

"Hi mum. Hi dad."

Margaret gushed tears as she rushed to embrace her son. "Oh Danny! Thank God you're safe!"

Danny returned the hug and then his mother moved aside for his father, wiping her nose and eyes on a tissue.

Harold patted Danny on the shoulder and gave him a firm handshake. "How's me boy?"

A confident reply, "Quite well!"

"I knew it!" Harold turned to Margaret. "See! He's fine. I told you there was nothing to worry about!"

Margaret returned Harold's gaze. "I'm not so sure." She looked at Danny. "I know you aren't happy at school, Danny. Mummy shouldn't have sent you there so far away from home."

Unflinching, Danny answered, "On the contrary, mum. I agreed to go to Timberhome of my own free will. It's something that I alone am responsible for, and not the fault of anyone else. And that includes what happened yesterday."

Harold nodded with a grin.

His boy was alright. No son of his was going to turn out a loony or a failure.

"I'll let Dr Russell know you're here," the nurse called as she left the room. Neither parent took notice.

"What do you mean what happened yesterday?" Margaret said.

"Surely you've been told what happened. I don't need to explain it again, do I?"

Harold put his arm around Margaret. "He doesn't want to talk about it, Marge. Let it rest, he'll be okay."

Margaret pulled free of Harold. "I want you to tell me what happened, Danny. The doctor said you were almost hit by a truck after running away from your dorm. He said you were in a state of shock and seeing things."

"Yes, well–"

"And you said in your last letter you weren't happy there, that you felt alone–"

"I miss you sometimes mum, yes. But most of the time I'm fine. That letter was when I was sick with that sore throat and I had a lot of free time to feel sorry for myself."

"But you ran away!"

"I went for a run, but not to anywhere in particular. I often go for a jog around the Unit, but I went the wrong way this time and accidentally ended up on the road. Fortunately, the truck stopped in time."

"You're covered in cuts!"

"Well, not really. But there are a lot of blackberries at the bottom of the hill next to the Unit. I went the wrong way as I said."

"The doctor said you were delirious! That you imagined you were being taunted by demons!"

"Really? I don't recall any of that." Danny shrugged. "Regardless, I'm fine now."

"Are you hiding something, Danny? You know you can't hide anything from your mother–"

"That's funny, Dr Russell said a similar thing." He smiled. "He was trying to establish that I was crazy and yet he couldn't find a single thing wrong with me."

Harold had had enough of this doting on his son. The boy was fine and Marge was refusing to acknowledge it. Bloody women, always trying to make a drama out of nothing.

"Come on, Marge. If there was anything wrong it would have been obvious. And they would have told us before we got here."

"Well, the psychiatrist did ask to speak to us before we got here–"

"Yes he did," came a nasal voice from across the room. Dr Bernard Russell stood at the source, a resolute expression on his face. "But in any case, I'm here now."

Harold and Margaret turned. Harold scowled, Margaret blushed. Brief introductions followed.

"Can we talk in private?" Bernard suggested.

"Isn't here private enough?" Harold returned.

"I meant somewhere private away from Danny. It's in his best interests that we're able to talk freely."

Harold huffed and Margaret said, "Oh I really don't think we should exclude Danny. Danny, you want to hear what the man has to say, don't you?"

Grinning, Danny nodded.

Bernard sighed.

It was having to deal with families like this that made retirement so appealing.

"Well, I guess I can relate the details to you here, as in this case I've yet to positively identify any serious symptoms of mental disorder."

"Exactly!" Harold said.

"Danny's traumatic incident yesterday appears to have triggered what is known as a brief reactive psychosis. But today, the effects appear to have subsided and he seems to have recovered."

"So–" Harold began.

Bernard raised a finger. "However, the results of some tests, including a corpuscular blood test and an EEG or brain wave test, are still pending. I anticipate that I'll be able to make a comprehensive assessment of Danny's physiological and psychological condition in the next day or so."

Bernard was getting blank looks from the parents. "But in order to understand the underlying cause for this psychosis and make a positive diagnosis, I need to ask you about his history. His habits, his health, his moods and any significant events."

Danny cleared his throat. "I'm fine, dad. I just want to get out of here and get back to school. I've already missed a whole day of class!"

Harold and Margaret turned back to Danny.

Danny held up an exercise book and a textbook on nineteenth century Australia. "Look, I've even been doing my history assignment that I have to hand in on Wednesday!"

"Fantastic, son! I can see you're itching to get back there. I would be too! I wouldn't want to be stuck in this stuffy place either, so don't worry. We won't be leaving until you're out of here!"

"Awww, thanks dad."

Margaret fretted but Harold's attention was only on Danny.

Crazy, be buggered!

Bernard could see that this wasn't going to work. He'd have to organise another time to speak to the parents in a more controlled environment. Time to execute closure.

"I'm prescribing some low strength anti-psychotic medication for Danny to take should the symptoms recur."

"Anti-psychotic? I thought you said the symptoms subsided," Margaret said.

"Well they have but–"

"Our son's not a psycho, he doesn't need any medication," Harold interrupted.

"Fine. I'll give the medication to the Matron at the school just the same, in case it's needed. I am confident *they'll know* how to look after him."

Harold frowned and folded his arms. Margaret rubbed

92

his shoulder. "So can we take him back to the school now, then?" he said.

"I'm happy to sign his release papers if you are satisfied that Danny is well enough to go back to school. However, I will need to check with the principal first and confirm that the school is ready to take him."

"I can do that. In fact, I've got Lucas Prescott's number right here." Harold pulled a card out of his breast pocket as he walked to the phone next to Danny's bed.

Bernard sighed and took a chair. "If you insist."

The main point is that the parents are happy to assume responsibility for Danny.

Harold rang the principal of Oberon Grammar School whilst Margaret sat on the end of Danny's bed and peered into his eyes.

Devoid of emotion, his eyes met her gaze. Unrelenting, unwavering, unrevealing. They might have been stones.

She began to feel tired, but she had to resolve this. She couldn't turn to the nurses or the doctor – they'd already shown how incompetent they were. The answers lay with her son. She'd expected a flurry of tears, confessions and pleas to "take me away from here". She'd expected her son to open up and tell her everything. Instead, she got this blank smiling face that told nothing, frustrating all attempts to breach the walls that Danny had erected. All the while, her bloody husband kept trying to calm her down and assure her that 'their Danny' was alright, when she knew something was wrong! Bloody men, always trying to repress things rather than deal with them.

"I want you to promise me, Danny, that what you're saying is the absolute truth, that you're not lying to me in any way. I want you to promise me, Danny, that you're not hiding anything from me, that you aren't still seeing or hearing things, and that you really are okay, as you've said."

He smiled and returned her intense gaze with an expression of calm, speaking lucidly, "I promise."

Nothing. Nothing! Absolutely, bloody nothing!

Margaret held a hand to her heart and turned to Harold as he put the phone down. Their eyes met.

"We're getting Danny out of here," Margaret said.

"The school's ready to take him now," Harold answered.

Bernard rose from his chair. "Let's go sign those release papers, shall we?"

Danny watched the whole spectacle... Smiling.

MONDAY 2:17 PM

Melbourne, the 'garden city'.

Brian looked around him at the endless stretch of shop fronts, factories, traffic lights and telephone poles along Sydney Road. Cars, trucks, electric trams and pedestrians fought for control of the congested street, spewing their fumes into the smoggy air. Beyond lay the city centre, no doubt even busier, where skyscrapers crowded the horizon: crystalline monuments to capitalism.

So much for living in the 'garden city'.

The outlook improved on reaching the tree-lined Royal Parade running through Parkville and past the historic buildings of Melbourne University. However, the improvement was lost on Brian as he struggled to navigate his way through swarms of traffic and an oval-shaped multi-lane roundabout at the terminus of five main streets. With difficulty, he ended up on William Street, which he followed into the thriving central business district.

He passed the stone edifice of the Supreme Court, the sheer glass of the recently completed twin Rialto towers and crossed the brown Yarra River near the venerable Flinders Street station. He turned into Southbank Boulevard and headed along the river towards the Melbourne Arts Centre spire, another new addition to Melbourne's skyline. Before reaching it, he turned off into Kavanagh Street and his destination, the Victorian Institute of Forensic Pathology (VIFP). The VIFP was established as a result of the Coroners Act in 1985 to centralise the provision of forensic pathology services throughout the state, in addition to housing the State Coroners' Office and providing training facilities, resources and research support to doctors and medical students.

Brian stubbed out a cigarette as he went through the boom gate into the VIFP carpark. There was a steady drone of vehicles on adjacent roads.

He yawned and paused in his seat a moment.

"Maybe you should take a break," Sergeant McDougall had said. It had been a hectic day with interviewing neighbours, relatives and friends, none of which shed much light on what had happened at the Weston farm. Now it was headline news and talk of a serial killer on the loose was rife in the town.

All the police really found so far was another set of shoeprints in the driveway of the Weston farm along with the footprints of large dogs. However, neither Weston had such a pet. Barney Weston lived alone and was being visited by his only son, Frank. Furthermore, everyone that Barney and Frank were in regular contact with, had been accounted for.

The homicide squad allocated to the job by CI, were keen to assume responsibility for the investigation, something which Brian was only too happy to relinquish. However, he still had a duty to see that the Howqua Hills district was safe and that meant finding the killer. The stress and frustration of the job was not helped by the constant enquiries from the media and the public, circling like flies to a shit.

"Maybe you should take a break," Sergeant McDougall had said. The idea had grown more appealing over the course of the three-hour drive to Melbourne.

Brian yawned again before dragging himself to his feet and starting towards the modern complex and an entrance prominently signposted "Reception".

A lupine-headed creature, heavily built and upright, descended from tree cover to sniff the driver's door of Brian's vehicle. Then it galloped towards the Institute, following the tree-line of the carpark. It leapt onto the five-metre-high roof and disappeared into shadow.

Brian entered, brushing lint off his police uniform and found himself in a well-lit foyer lavish with modern decor.

"Can I help you?" came a mature female voice behind him.

"Yes." Brian turned to face her, noting a desk covered in information pamphlets. "I have an appointment to see Dr David Dawson."

⸕   ⸕   ⸕

Brian stood in a forensic laboratory filled with test tube racks, microscopes and various medical contraptions he had no idea about. Science wasn't a subject he paid much attention to in school. The hot female teacher he had in Year Ten was, however, an exception. She'd even tried to crack onto him to get his attention, which it did, but not in the way that she might have hoped.

David, the only other person in the laboratory, drew Brian's attention to the sample he had set up under a microscope. "Have a look at this, Brian, and tell me what you think."

Brian peered down the eyepiece...

A collection of white circles floated past his view, brimming with mobile purple dots. His eyes watering from the strain, he looked away.

"Well?" David prompted.

"Well what?"

"What do you think? You know what they are, don't you?"

"Er..."

"Or rather what they're not! Haha!"

Brian gave a sour look. "Actually David, I haven't got a fucking clue."

And I wanna punch you in the face.

David spoke excitedly, "What's in that sample from under Frank Weston's fingernails is why I asked you to come here, so you could see for yourself–"

"The revelation's blinding me."

"You must understand that what I'm about to tell you is completely off the record and not to be used as evidence. I'm only showing you here and now, so that you can see for yourself and–"

"Just skip the preamble and tell me what it is, doctor. I'll decide whether it is or isn't relevant or admissible in court."

David became sombre. "I'm afraid I can't tell you unless you agree to strike it from any official record. I'm sorry, Brian, but there's no other way."

This was getting nowhere. I didn't drive two-hundred fucking kilometres to hear this. I'll do whatever I like with the information anyway.

"Okay whatever. Now tell me."

David's face lit up like a child. "Those aren't human blood cells! And nor are they from any animal!"

I'm so gunna fucking deck you.

"So, what's your point?"

"Brian, that *is* the point! Those cells belong to something that's completely unlike anything Science has seen before!"

Brian pictured demonic red eyes staring at him from the darkness. He hesitated to respond.

David pointed to a pile of forensic photos on the bench next to them. "Let me show you these and you may understand a little better..."

He showed Brian various gruesome pictures of the killings, describing them in detail. Brian's mind wandered as he struggled to comprehend David's extensive medical vocabulary.

David's summary was more plain: "The injuries on Barney and Frank Weston are consistent with a killer capable of ten-metre leaps and able to tear off a human head in one hand. Feats simply impossible for a human."

Brian leant on a nearby bench for support. "I take it this isn't a conclusion you've reached lightly, that you're *absolutely* sure about this?"

David scanned the corridor outside. He turned back to Brian, his eyes darting. "I wouldn't have asked you to come down if I wasn't. The sample is indisputable and the injuries are implausible not just by any human, but by any known animal as well."

David paused to take a breath. Brian found a stool to collapse onto. "A kangaroo or a particularly athletic dog such as a greyhound is capable of jumping ten metres, but no such animal or anything similar is capable of grasping the vertebrae of a human and tearing it out with such force that the spinal column is completely severed from the torso. There simply isn't a human or animal that can leap such distances *and* perform such feats of strength."

Brian noticed his bandaged hand trembling. He squeezed his forehead as he studied the ground, grimacing. David waited with clasped hands.

"Who else knows about this?"

"Only two of my immediate staff, Dr Chris Gamble and John Taylor, are aware of the full details and thus the implications."

"What do you mean by the full details?"

"Essentially, they're the only others who know that the samples reveal the presence of an unknown life form."

There, he said it. An unknown life form. Fuck.

"And to what extent are others aware of these findings?"

"Others here at the Institute, including the Coroner, understand that the wounds are unusually horrific in their ferocity, but not to the extent of them being inhuman."

"Why not? Haven't they seen the photos?"

"Yes they have but apart from myself, only Chris and John have read the field forensic report *and* been able to study the stress inflicted by the injuries in detail, which in addition to the sample, has been what's convinced us. At this stage the Coroner has only been sent a preliminary report that's inconclusive in its findings."

"Sooo..." Brian coughed. "Why are you telling me this?"

"Others will learn the truth soon enough, but I'm sure that the information available to them will be censored. And that censorship will probably include you and your station, so I wanted to tell you before that happened, whilst I'm still able to."

Brian frowned and rubbed his temple with his bandaged hand.

"What happened to your hand?" David asked.

Brian sighed and looked at David. "I was attacked by one of the same creatures I presume killed Barney and Frank. That's the only reason why I've believed you."

David's jaw dropped.

MONDAY 3:25 PM

The old man was furious.

His eyes turned white with anger. Slowly, he rose from his seat and as he stood, he appeared to gain in size and stature. He was changing before his eyes. Hair sprouted on his face and forearms. His nose lengthened and became dog-like. His teeth became pointed. He advanced towards Howard...

The outside world had ceased to exist for Howard. He sat on a beanbag in the library at St Mary's Primary School, devouring *The Warlock of Firetop Mountain*, a *Fighting Fantasy* gamebook in which he was the hero. He picked up his dice to do battle with the fearsome Werewolf, having already slain his fire-breathing pet dog.

Meanwhile, Arthur was perusing the non-fiction section, perving at books about the human body.

The Werewolf was no match for Howard's skill. After a few quick sword strikes, the monster slumped to the ground. Howard searched his clothing but found nothing of use. Cursing the old man for not having any decent treasure, he took a bunch of keys hanging on the wall of the sparse room. He continued south down a corridor...

Looking back, Howard noticed the body had vanished.

Then the school bell rang, signalling the end of the library session and another day of school.

Howard rushed to the borrowing counter to get his book stamped, eager to get home and complete his perilous quest. The book stamped, he remembered what else lay in wait for him at home: his bossy older sister Samantha and that pirate poster that had given him another nightmare last night.

He turned to Arthur. "Can I come over to your house?"

Arthur's mind was elsewhere. He looked back at Howard with teary eyes. "Um... Can we go to yours?"

Howard scratched his head and chewed his nails a moment, before shrugging. "I s'pose. I'll ask mum when she comes to pick me up."

"My mum's coming to pick me up too. She says it's not safe to walk home anymore, because there's a bad man out there that..." Arthur's voice trailed off as he choked on tears.

Howard patted his shoulder and led him towards the school exit where parents crowded in cars. "Don't cry, Arthur, my dad's gunna catch him!"

Arthur stammered through sobs. "He-he-he k-killed my c-c-c-cousin an ung-cle!"

Other children filed past the two nine year-old boys, exchanging curious looks with the two. Howard noticed the onlookers and waved them off.

"My dad will get him! He's the best police man in Australya!"

Arthur snuffled as he wiped his nose and eyes on his sleeves.

I don't want mum to see me like this.

Howard and Arthur reached the school gates and saw their mothers waiting under the shade of the same gum tree that faced the exit.

Arthur's mother Amanda wore sunglasses despite the overcast day. Howard's mother Julie looked tired.

Howard ran to hug his mother. Arthur dawdled to embrace his.

"Mum, can Arthur come to our house?" Howard said.

I've neither the strength nor the heart to say no. As weary as I am, I haven't just lost two family members like Amanda has.

Julie looked at Amanda, who nodded. She turned back to Howard. "Okay, but only for a couple of hours until six-thirty. I'll drop him home when I go to pick Samantha up from netball."

⸭   ⸭   ⸭

Julie flopped onto the couch next to a box of tissues that overflowed with used remainders. Through glass doors in need of cleaning, she could see Howard and Arthur playing in the backyard.

Eighteen months ago she was in a nice house with a loving husband and two beautiful happy children. Julie and Brian were secure financially, had plenty of money set aside for the kids' education and all the modern comforts they needed. After many years of arguments, they'd decided to have another child. It would be Julie's third child and Brian's fourth.

Craig Alexander Derwent was born on the 22nd of November 1987. He was a stillbirth.

Her relationship with Brian deteriorated rapidly after that. He spent increasingly less time at home in the evenings and weekends. He said it was work commitments, but she learned the truth soon enough through his work mates who agreed she had a right to know. He was spending his free time with Sasha, an eighteen year-old plaything, who didn't care that he had a wife and family. They separated soon after that and much to his surprise and dismay, Julie was helped by his sympathetic friends.

Now Barney and Frank Weston had been murdered in their home, destroying the peace and tranquillity of Howqua Hills. Attempts to contact Brian to find out what happened and to organise his time with the children had failed. Outside his working hours that stupid little slut never seemed to know where he was and Brian was never in the office to take a call. She'd even left messages, but still nothing.

Outside, Arthur and Howard were kicking the 'footy'; an oval-shaped red leather Australian Rules football; and impersonating their favourite footy stars.

"ABLETT!" Howard cried in triumph as he marked a kick rebounding off the back fence.

Howard yelled, "AND HE PLAYS ON!" as he ran past Arthur with the ball.

Arthur tried to tackle him, but Howard was too fast. He bounced the ball as he rounded the corner of the house, taunting, "Ablett is too quick for Dunstall and he runs into an OPEN GOAL!"

With Arthur in hot pursuit, Howard booted the footy over the gate to the front yard. It landed on the footpath and bounced into a 4WD police car that had just pulled up at the kerb.

"Oops!" Howard said as he covered his mouth and turned to Arthur.

Howard watched through the gate as a tall man with a handlebar moustache emerged onto the footpath and stopped to pick up the football.

That's Paul McDougall's dad. He's a cop like my dad, only not as good or important. I hate Paul, who's in my class at school.

Howard motioned to Arthur to follow him back inside through the glass side door...

Julie heard the doorbell ring and opened the front door to Sergeant Douglas McDougall. He was dressed in uniform and holding Howard's football, his welcoming smile matching hers.

Douglas raised the football. "Julie, you really should teach your son not to kick footballs at police cars."

Julie blushed. "He's not very kind to good Samaritans, is he?"

I probably look terrible at the moment. But I'm glad to see Douglas... But hang on, what's this sudden visit for?

Douglas spoke softly, so as not to be heard by Howard and his friend lurking in the background. "I need to talk to you about Brian; I'm very concerned about him. Can you spare a few minutes?"

MONDAY 5:50 PM

"There is no escape."

"Please, please stop! I can't take anymore!"

The horrid voice rasped again, nails on the blackboard of Danny's soul, *"Oh, but I've only just started, cock-breath! Your worthless little brain cannot imagine the pain that I am going to inflict on you! Soon you'll be back at school, away from your pathetic parents, away from safety. And then Danny, you useless fuck, the fun will begin!"*

, , ,

Danny awoke lying across the back seat of his parent's old black Jaguar as it drove past gum trees in tangerine sunlight. He sat up to take the scene in, rubbing his eyes.

How did I come to be here?

His parents sat in the front in silence, father drove and mother looked out over tree-lined paddocks. Danny tried to reassemble fragments of memory into a chronology that he could comprehend. He recalled impressions of running into the path of a truck, then horrible nightmares, then an important man with glasses and a beard who spoke to him and his parents. Impressions, but the details were obscured by the shadow of subconsciousness.

Where are they taking me?

He looked out on brown farms and hillsides and saw a

small blue "OGS" sign on the roadside up ahead, where a dirt road turn-off lay.

They're taking me back to Timberhome, to H Unit!

The car rattled across a cattle grid at the entrance to the turn-off and began to make the tree-lined ascent to the school.

"I don't want to go back."

His mother Margaret craned her neck around to look at Danny. "Oh, you're awake!" She absorbed what he had just said and her expression became worried. "That's not what you told us before!"

"I don't care what I said before. I don't want to go back."

Harold grumbled, but kept his eyes on the road.

Margaret glanced at Harold and then returned to Danny. "Darling, you're fine now, you have to go back to school."

Tears began to well in Danny's eyes. "But I hate it!"

She reached over to rub his hand. "Why do you hate it, Danny? You said everything was fine!"

"Maybe I did... But it's not! I'll go to another school if I have to, but I'm not going back to that one."

They were halfway up the long hill to the school by this time. Margaret turned to put a hand on Harold's elbow. "Stop the car, Harold. We need to resolve this."

"Bloody hell!" he protested as he slowed the car and pulled over.

Danny burst into tears, wet lines running down his cheeks like fingers through dust.

Margaret undid her seatbelt and twisted her body around to face Danny. "Why don't you like it? Are the kids picking on you?"

A sobbing whimper, "Yes they are! All the time!"

Margaret looked back at Harold. "I knew it! I knew that something was wrong. Finally Danny's admitted it."

BREWIN

Harold slapped the steering wheel. "Oh, for goodness sake!" His face flushed red, he turned to Danny. "Danny, you're fine! The doctor's said it, we've said it and you yourself have said it. So why the carry on now? You're probably just a bit nervous about going back. I'm sure you'll forget all about it when you get there."

Danny struggled to stop crying and looked pleadingly at his mother.

Her expression was resolute. "I'll speak to your Unit Master right away and tell him how those kids are bullying you. He'll make them stop."

"Mum, don't do that! They'll only bully me more then! I–"

"Oh no they won't!" Her brow furrowed with determination. "I'll make sure of that! I won't have my son being threatened by those monsters! I'll tell your Unit Master and he'll have to make sure they're nice to you."

"But–"

"And if they do try to bully you," she said over the top of his objections, "you tell them to leave you alone!"

"As if that's going to work!"

"Sticks and stones may break your bones, but names will never hurt you, Danny. They're just trying to get a reaction from you."

"Muuum..."

Harold spoke. "Danny, when I was your age, I remember this kid who used to tease me and think he was really clever. He kept going when I told him to stop, so I punched him and gave him a bloody nose. He never bothered me again after that." He smiled.

Margaret's jaw dropped. "Harold! Don't encourage Danny to hit people! Violence doesn't solve anything!"

Harold snorted. "Try telling Roosevelt that. If it wasn't for him, we'd all be bloody Japanese!"

Danny slumped back in his seat and gazed out of the window whilst his parents argued.

What did I say to them before that made them so adamant to take me back to school now? And why can't I remember? It's all so hopeless.

"I think the only thing for it, is to speak to the Unit Master right away. The sooner we get there, the better," Margaret said.

Harold nodded. "Exactly!" He started the car forward.

"Please, please stop! I can't take anymore!" Danny cried.

"Danny, this bullying isn't going to stop until we do something about it. Drive on, Harold."

My fate is sealed. I'm going back to H Unit. H for hell.

The car passed through the school gates and wound past the main wood shed, a couple of utility sheds and the various empty sports grounds. In silence, the passengers drove to the carpark at the hub of the school. The car parked before the long brown weatherboard dining hall that resounded with the murmurs and clattering cutlery of two hundred and fifty school residents at dinner.

Danny gulped. The wheel had come full circle.

"Come on, Danny!" Margaret ordered. She stepped out of the car and opened his door.

Danny hesitated, "But–"

Harold turned to look at Danny. "Stop worrying Danny, you'll be fine! On you go now with your mum. I'll be in touch soon."

It's useless to fight. It'll make no difference.

Danny sighed and hugged his dad from behind. "Bye, dad."

Harold patted Danny's head. "You'll be fine, son."

Danny took a deep breath and stepped out of the car. Margaret stood outside, scrutinising him as she chewed her lip.

Am I making the right decision for Danny? It's too late now to reconsider, I guess, so I best be sure in my decision for Danny's sake, lest it plant further doubt in his mind.

Margaret led Danny by the hand past a few dusty Holdens, Fords and Range Rovers, towards the side entrance to the Dining Hall. Clouds of flies and gnats circled in wait. Danny watched his destination loom ever nearer with terror.

, , ,

Price, bored and seeking to cause mischief, ignored the plate of spaghetti marinara dished out to him, to instead pour pepper from a shaker onto the table. Grinning, he looked up at Alex sitting opposite him on the long table set out for the whole Unit.

Alex read the mirth on Price's face. "Fuck off Price, you stupid geek!"

Derrick, a hairy lanky oaf with glasses, sat next to Price. He turned and spoke through mouthfuls of pasta. "Just eat your food, Christopher."

Price quit his games, but swept the pepper on the table into a pile for later. He reached for a jug of water, when a baby octopus was launched from the other end of the table and landed on his plate. Laughter ensued. Price turned to see who the culprit was.

Robbo, a small cheeky freckle-faced kid, called to him. "Hey Price! I found your twin brother!"

Price scooped the octopus onto a spoon and glanced around to check that there were no teachers nearby. He turned to aim a return shot, balancing the loaded spoon under his finger like the catch on a catapult.

Didge yelled, "JESUS FUCK MY CHRIST, there's Danny!"

He pointed at the teacher's table on the stage at the end of the hall.

Price paused to look, as did most of the table.

Danny stared at his feet and limply held his mother's hand as she spoke to Mr Neilson and the principal Lucas Prescott with stern hand gestures. Danny made the mistake of glancing in H Unit's direction, seeing only hostility when he did. Mr Neilson nodded and looked in their direction also. Danny began to wipe his eyes, a portrait of despondency.

Jokes began to circulate around the H Unit table and spread to the other tables. Only Derrick voiced any objections, but his comments were buried beneath a barrage of ridicule directed at Danny.

The mocking gallery watched Danny's mother say something to him, before turning him by his shoulders to face the audience. With reluctance, Danny raised his head to stare into the eyes of damnation. The sight of his mother kissing him on the cheek before pushing him in the direction of the tables drew more laughter.

Slowly, Danny made his way over to the waiting H Unit table, like a lamb to a pack of wolves.

He sank further into despair when he saw that the only available chair was at the 'elite's' end of the table, next to Robbo... And that to reach the free seat, he had to pass between Jamie Savage of his Unit and Anthony Sanders of G Unit. Both Jamie and Anthony were frightening prospects, especially Jamie who had twice been suspended for beating the crap out of someone. They both had their chairs back from the table, leaving a mere hand-width gap between them. As Danny approached, neither moved nor even acknowledged his presence. Around them lurked a mass of cruel smiling faces.

A feeble squeak, "E-E-Excuse me, Jamie."

Jamie looked up with fierce brown eyes beneath eyebrows bunched with menace, corded muscles twitching along his jawline. But fortunately, Jamie glanced at the teacher's table and saw that Mr Neilson was watching from his perch like a hawk. He turned back to Danny with a look to kill and moved his chair in enough to make an awkward pass possible.

"Th-Thanks, Jamie," Danny mumbled as he squeezed past before Jamie changed his mind.

Danny reached his chair and attempted to pull it back from the table, only to find it was stuck. Amidst chuckling, he saw that Robbo had his leg wrapped around one of the chair legs. As Danny struggled, the chair suddenly came free and knocked into Damien who sat on the other side.

"Fuckin' sit down, would ya!" Damien spat.

Robbo grinned.

Danny sat down before a plate overflowing with food scraps and used serviettes. The kids whose turn it was to serve meals this week – 'Slush duty', as it was dubbed – had already passed with the food trolley, so it seemed he was going hungry.

"Aren't you going to eat what we saved for you?" Robbo jeered.

Then, in a surprising act of human kindness, Mr Neilson brought over a plate of pasta that one of the 'Slushies' had dished up. He gave the others at the table an ominous glare as he handed Danny his meal.

As soon as Mr Neilson was gone, Robbo turned to Danny. "If your mum said anything to him, you're fucked!"

Danny tried to ignore Robbo and pour a glass of water. His hand trembled and he spilt some onto the table.

"Unco geek," Bruce said, sitting across from Danny.

"You can clean up this end of the table after," Mike chimed in, pointing to the seafood he spat onto the table.

There was no point in arguing. Nothing had a point anymore...

A bell rang to signal the end of dinner. At nine pm the dining hall would be full again for supper, but not before they had done their homework in their respective Units.

Each of the tables passed their plates to one end where one of the Slushies collected them, emptying scraps into their 'Slush bucket'. Robbo grabbed Danny's full plate of food and passed it up to the Slushies, but Danny didn't seem to notice. Danny hadn't even touched his food. Instead, he sat motionless, staring at the table.

Mike threw a cloth at Danny's face, breaking his trance. "Start cleaning, slave!"

Danny lifted the cloth out of his lap where it had landed and began to wipe the table, oblivious to the goo that oozed over his fingers.

Whilst the rest of his Unit left, Danny remained behind to stack the chairs away. Head down to avoid eye contact, he didn't see Derrick's look of concern.

, , ,

Danny dawdled down the hill towards H Unit, his prison. He thought he'd seen the last of the accursed place, but he was wrong. Now he was back and still had most of a full school year to go. That is if he was still around then... But even fantasising about his macabre death took more energy than he had right now.

Why bother trying to do anything at all?

By the time Danny reached H Unit, Mr Neilson was already there addressing the rest of the Unit assembled in the study. As he approached, Danny heard his name and immediately knew what the assembly was about. He again felt the compulsion to run, but now there was nowhere to run to. Even his parents had abandoned him.

He tried to sneak around to the Unit's side entrance, next to the wood shed, but Mr Neilson spotted him and called him to the gathering.

Head bowed and silent, Danny obeyed.

"Danny. I've spoken to everyone here and told them that they're to stop this childish bullying and leave you alone. I've also told them that if any of this silliness continues, that you're to tell me and then," he paused to look at the others, "there'll be big trouble."

Danny began to feel faint.

I don't know how much longer I can remain standing.

Mr Neilson clapped his hands together. "Right. You've all been told now, so this nonsense can stop. Bullying is a terrible thing and completely unnecessary, so I don't want to hear about it going on anymore. Alright, I'm sure you have plenty of homework you need to do, so I'll leave you to get started."

He turned and walked out.

As soon as he was gone, Robbo sneered at Danny. "Your mummy's not going to save you now is she, you fuckin' wimp!"

MONDAY 7:12 PM

Still no answer.

Mary hung up the phone, frowning in thought.

Where was her son, Henry? She'd tried to call him all weekend and today, but there was no answer. It was unlike him to be away from home for so long without telling her. *I hope something hasn't happened.*

But maybe he had just been out with some of his friends from the Melbourne Poetical Society, or maybe he'd finally found himself a regular job or maybe he'd gone camping... But maybe he'd started sleepwalking again.

There was only one way to put her mind at rest and that was to go to his flat in Fitzroy North and see if he was there. Even if he wasn't there, she might have more idea of what was going on.

She poured dry food into the cat's bowl, checked that the house was in order and gathered her handbag and keys. As she moved to the front door, Winston meandered into the lounge meowing.

"I'll be back soon, Winston," she said as if the cat could understand.

She locked the front door as her husband Peter was away in Sydney at a sales conference and headed out to the car in the fading light. It was a short fifteen-minute drive from their suburban house in Ivanhoe to Henry's two-bedroom flat.

She tried to dismiss visions of catastrophe from her mind...

, , ,

Mary parked her sedan on the kerb of Rushall Crescent, out the front of the block of flats where Henry lived. Under streetlights, she looked to see if Henry's car – a white 1972 Holden Torana – was parked there. Failing to spot his car, she took a deep breath.

She walked up the driveway, under a concrete staircase leading to the flats on the first floor and up to Henry's door on the ground. She pulled open the security door that refused to close, which the landlord still hadn't got around to fixing, and rapped on the wooden door.

She strained her ears for sounds, but only the blood pulsing through her veins punctuated the silence. The night breeze caressed her neck and cheeks with icy fingers.

She knocked again, this time more urgent. Her breath became short spurts, her knees weak. Standing became a struggle.

Still no answer.

Fumbling with her keys, she managed to find her copy of Henry's front door key. Holding her breath, she plunged the key into the lock and turned...

The lounge beyond lay covered by a blanket of still darkness. Obscure shapes loomed from the shadows and the stench of stale cigarette smoke, incense and something rotten greeted her. She reached for the light switch to her immediate right and flicked it on...

Then she collapsed against the door.

, , ,

Seconds or hours may have passed. The room materialised around Mary in all its disturbing detail: overturned and broken furniture, ransacked cupboards, smashed hi-fi equipment and plates, torn clothing and ripped papers and posters. Nothing it seemed was spared the destruction.

Tears began to flow. This was too much to bear.

"Henry! Heee-nryyy!" she called, placing a hand against the doorframe for support.

And still no answer.

I must find out what happened to my son. I won't leave until I know.

She stepped forward over the wreckage of a couch in smashed pieces and cast her eyes around the broken remains of wooden chairs and the coffee table she'd given him for his birthday. Only the wind stirred outside.

What could possibly have caused such destruction?

Hand over her mouth to stifle her cries, she moved across the room to where doorways led to the two bedrooms, the bathroom and kitchen. Standing atop a jumble of papers and books at the junction of the doorways, she could only see violent disarray throughout all the rooms. The carnage screamed catastrophe, that something terrible had happened to Henry.

Yet said nothing about where he was now.

Her eyes were drawn to the only area of clear floor in the flat. It was a circle of blackened carpet a couple of metres wide, in the centre of the second bedroom Henry used as a study. It was surrounded by black candle stubs amongst splintered furniture, computer and hi-fi equipment, piles of occult books and papers covered in Henry's scrawl. The foul miasma of decay seemed to originate from this room.

What new depths had Henry's madness descended to?

It had been years since his last relapse. Surely this could not be!

He must still be alive, I must have hope. I'll contact the police and get them to put out a search for him. Immediately.

Next to her foot, Mary noticed a cassette tape amongst other rubbish. It had a label with a dated note in Henry's handwriting. In trembling hands, she picked up the cassette and read the label:

I, Henry Anthony Wilcox, testify that this recording contains my final words. I pray that someone will find this and comprehend its message.

God save us all.

Henry Wilcox 07-04-89

Her mind began to implode.

MONDAY 9:46 PM

"Don't you dare cum in my mouth."

Vincent contained a grin and tried to appear serious in his reply. "Amy, of course not!"

"Me first and then you, okay. Then you can go to sleep. In that order."

Vincent stroked her hair, prompting Amy to resume. "Of course."

Must hold on. Make it last longer. Think about anything but the gorgeous woman whose lips are currently locked around your penis. Recite the alphabet or phone numbers. Think about what Aaron, Bruce and Jason are doing, about what happened to Frank and his dad. Nah, don't think about that...

Amy paused. "Is that enough?"

She didn't like going down on a guy at the best of times, let alone after they'd been camping for a day already and not showered. Being drunk helped, but now she was just tired.

Vincent was summoned back to earth by the questioning tone of her voice. She'd stopped.

"What'd you say?" he said.

Amy brought her head up almost level with Vincent's. Straddling him on all fours as he lay on his back in the tent, she said. "I want to feel you inside me."

The swaying torch attached to the apex of the dome tent

119

overhead cast revolving silhouettes as Vincent hesitated to respond.

She kissed his lips. "C'mon. Up you get. Your turn to do some work."

Vincent sat up slowly, brushing his hair from his face.

"Or do you want me to go on top?"

"Nah, it's okay," he answered.

Easier to control. And her sense of rhythm was bad anyway.

Vincent embraced Amy with another kiss as he assumed a position over her and reached for the tent's side pocket where the condoms were. Realising that he couldn't kiss her and reach the side pocket at the same time, he turned away from her whilst she lay there rubbing her vulva and nipples.

Outside in the forest around the tent, a herd of kangaroos bounded past in rapid flight.

"What was that?" said Amy, turning her head to the noise.

Rolling the plastic sleeve of the condom on, Vincent shrugged. "Just roos and stuff, I s'pose. There's no one around for miles. We're in the bush, remember?"

Amy looked angry. "It's not like I'm gunna forget that! What, am I stupid?"

She better not decide 'she wasn't in the mood anymore'. That was easy for her to say. She didn't have a raging hard-on built up with pressure that had to be released or he'd have severe groin cramps for the next day. Now was not a good time to start worrying about the wildlife.

"I didn't mean it like that! I'm sure the noises are nothing to worry about."

"Yeah, I guess so," she replied.

"I love you," Vincent said as he plunged his dagger in.

Amy sighed with pleasure as Vincent entered her. "I love you too."

Not really true, but what else could she say to him now?

Suddenly, the fabric of the tent was torn asunder. Standing two-and-a-half metres over them was a huge beast covered in dark fur. Powerful arms ending in long claws like scythes flexed in the light of a near full moon. Its wolfish snout curled to reveal jagged teeth and issued an ominous growl, reeking of death.

Amy screamed and Vincent turned in disbelief. He stared in horrified rapture as a swift claw shot forward and grabbed him by the throat. Lying prone with the collapsed tent in pieces around them, Amy continued screaming as the creature flung Vincent into the trees on the opposite side of the campsite like a rag doll. He landed some distance away with a heavy crash of branches. Then it turned to face her, licking the drool from its lips and fixating her with the demonic gaze of red slits.

With morbid amusement, it appraised the human quivering before it. Restrained was the lust to kill, for patient were they in their preparation. Humans with their pathetic little minds could not understand events as they were, as much as they did not understand the nature of reality or the insignificance of their role in it.

Amy overcame the paralysis of fear and tried to stand. But its response was quicker, snatching her ankles in one hand and yanking her towards it. Her naked belly slapped its naked chest, then it lifted her off the ground by the vice-grip on her ankles. Its head lowered to her upturned crotch and she began screaming again.

Savouring the moment, it breathed in the pungent scent of the prey, smelling the arousal now laced with terror. A victim ripe for the taking.

Bruised and bleeding, Vincent tried to shake off dizziness and find his feet. He sought to extend his left arm to grasp a trunk and felt an intense, burning pain. Looking down, he saw his forearm broken at a crazy angle and soaked with blood.

Then he heard Amy screaming and saw the monster holding her aloft in the moonlight about ten metres away. Its head was buried between her legs.

Something snapped.

Vincent charged across the campsite towards the creature. Barely conscious of his actions, a smoking brand from the campfire found its way into his right hand en route.

Though Amy twisted against the beast and punched its body, it would not relinquish its hold. Suspended upside down, her heart pounding in her head, she was helpless. The world became blurred with tears and pain.

She felt a sudden jerk as the beast kicked out at something behind it. She glimpsed its clawed foot striking Vincent in the face as he advanced. There was a sickening crunch and he collapsed.

Time to silence this interruption.

It released the female to fall into a crumpled, weeping heap. "STAY!" it commanded with a voice like coarse razors, reinforcing the point by pressing its index finger against her head.

Then it pivoted to the male in a broken, bleeding heap.

Vincent lay in the dirt struggling with agony, when he felt claws close around his throat. He could only cough and bleed as the creature lifted him to bring him face to face.

Demonic red slits stared at him from a slavering wolfish face. Folds of hairy flesh curled back from its blackened gums, revealing a malevolent smile of savage teeth.

End it now.

Then he saw Amy over the beast's hulking shoulder. He saw her grab her handbag and some clothing from among the tent remains and run...

Vincent felt a sense of relief that he should die to save Amy's life. Nothing else mattered now. Looking death in the eye, he raised a thumb in salute.

"Pretty good!" he said grinning.

Still holding Vincent under the chin, the demon slammed his body into a nearby gum tree. Delirious with pain, Vincent felt his ribs crack and prayed for a quick death.

Pinning Vincent to the tree with one arm, the beast swiped across his exposed belly with the other. Blood and bile bubbled out of his mouth as he felt its claws slicing through his flesh. Cutting him open like a can, it doubled back on its arc through his abdomen to drag out his intestines and hold them up to his face.

"*Pretty! Hahaha!*" it boomed.

The end was upon him. Vincent smiled at his slayer and spoke through a gurgle, "I'm dead but she'll get away."

It laughed again and dropped him to the ground. His entrails piled onto him. Feeling the approach of oblivion, he closed his eyes for the last time...

His last memory was a rasping whisper in his ear like a knife in the dark, "*I can smell her for miles... I WILL find her.*"

MONDAY 11:35 PM

He awoke in darkness a third time.

Where am I?

Somewhere, a cruel voice answered, *"Home."*

Who is that?

Again it answered, *"Your true calling."*

What's going on?

A third answer, *"We have returned."*

Then there was light, revealing an earthen chamber with dark recesses. Before him leered a huge wolf-faced creature that stood upright in purple bloodstained robes. Its piercing red eyes flashed with malice.

Screaming, he ran into darkness, not caring where except away from the horrible visage. Then he was falling, blinded by eternal night.

Somewhere above him, a voice called...

"Henry! Remember!"

Darkness.

Murmurs in the gloom. Red eyes flicker. Hairy figures wait. Guttural groans resonate. A pungent stench stifles the smell of blood. Claws scrape against stone. Restless. Eager.

Torches burst aflame, shedding a sickly light that flickers through palls of fetid smoke. Illuminated is a chamber massive beyond description, its cavernous walls fading into murk at the limits of perception...

Filled with the *Dark Horde* beyond number.

As one unholy mass they begin to moan, a rasping discordant sonority that carries from one horizon to another. The *Dark Horde* in their many millions, cast their impious gaze upward to the central stone: a fifteen-metre monolith of agony and lust. A bloody pillar of stone with the likeness of knotted ebony flesh, barbed spikes gracing its vile surface like hairs, impaled on which hang the weeping bodies of ravaged humans.

Dominating the altar on which the Elders stand.

In purple robes of putrefaction, the Elders line the perimeter of a round platform etched with arcane symbology, its inscriptions shining like molten cracks in hardened lava. The great and terrible pillar pierces the platform at its centre, a monument to eternal torment.

The *Venomed One*, a scorpioid abomination six metres tall, stands alone before the pillar. Exultant, it raises a long barbed tail and massive pincers to the ceiling soaring overhead and throws back its head set with a mass of green eyes like mirrors. Its oversized mandibles quiver as it unleashes a heaven-smashing scream.

The world shudders. The pillar twitches.

As one almighty mass the *Dark Horde* begin to howl, an earthquake of lustful malice. As one they cast their malevolent gaze upwards, to the corrupted centre of the unholy service towering over them.

And as one they wait with fervent anticipation...

With each roar from their scorpioid leader, the uncountable chorus increases in volume and fervour, the air becoming so turgid with the malignant resonance that it seems solid. Never wavering, in unison, the demonic legions maintain their diabolical din.

Awakening to the sound of slaughter, the putrid pillar begins to pulse with unearthly life.

The *Venomed One*, a crimson-coloured juggernaut, now paces in a circle around the infernal spit-roast of humans that is the central column. With merciless deliberation, it considers each of the victims in turn. Some lie unconscious but breathing, others lie with eyes open, their minds blank with terror, and yet others lie as lifeless, dismembered lumps. Long spikes tear the humans' flesh even as they impale them, the horrid twitching of the pillar drawing fresh blood with each undulation.

Aroused by the sacrificial offering, thick purple ichor begins to drip down the sides of the monolith, hardening like some hellish candle.

The crimson juggernaut stops before its chosen first victim and roars with such deafening fury that it drowns the swamp of noise around it. Its huge pincer punches into the chest of a horrified male, sending forth an explosion of gore. The male screams in agony as the pincer closes around his heart, then is silenced as his torso is ripped apart. Roaring again, the grim task-master tears out the still-beating chunk of meat, beating in synchronicity with the pulsing tower. The *Venomed One* raises its prize in triumph to an ecstatic audience.

The scorpioid abomination turns to the gory centrepiece and impales the human's heart, fluids rushing down the pillar's sides as the pulp is mashed and ground. The *Venomed One* roars with thrill. The *Dark Horde* scream with ecstasy. The walls rock with the intensity.

Undulating ever faster, a dull ruby glow emerges from the bloody spire. Dark sappy fluids leak down its barbed sides with new passion.

The next victim is chosen, a savaged female whose swollen eyes struggle to open as she awakes from deep slumber...

Helpless to watch as her slayer smashes through her ribs to rip her heart out and show it to her.

The *Venomed One* laughs as it watches life fade from her eyes. Screaming in bloody glory, it slams her still-living heart upon the pillar's spikes, sending forth a new rush of hot blood. The fire within the column grows brighter, its beats more violent. Dripping ichor, moving with a life force of its own, it begins to smother and penetrate the helpless humans.

The *Dark Horde* are a sea of howling screams, drowning the tormented cries of raped human souls...

The executioner completes its gruesome task, systematically tearing the humans' hearts out and impaling them on the gigantic gorging phallus, which finally erupts in an orgasm of death, spraying hot squirts of ichor about the blood-soaked platform.

Exultant, the *Venomed One* roars and the Elders rush forward to fornicate with the human dead. Committing obscene acts of corpse violation, the Elders mix their seed with that from the pillar. The *Dark Horde* watching are a frenzy of howls amidst the sickening, carnal indulgence of mortal flesh.

The *Venomed One*, its thick frame spattered with sacrificial blood, faces the ejaculating obelisk of necrophilic orgy and scoops dark purple lumps of rapidly hardening mess from its oozing orifices. In doing so, the Elders cease their unclean acts to stand back and unleash blood-curdling howls, thronged all around by the lamentations of the *Dark Horde* beyond count.

Their leader is silent as it moves around the circle of Elders, handing each a lump of ichor, moulded into the crude likeness of a human heart, beating with supernatural life.

It returns to the centre of the platform and joins the evil chorus with its own head-crushing roar. The Elders move forward to deposit the replacement hearts within the chests of the violated dead, chanting morbid hymns to awaken the dark within them, invoking a dark new life to begin...

The *Venomed One* screams with enough intensity to kill a man and the infernal fluid covering the corpses begins to sizzle, seeding new life and making the butchered bodies unnaturally whole again.

The created *Halform* open their eyes for the first time on their new world. Their lungs fill with tainted air to disgorge chilling howls of corruption, united with the universe of voices around them.

The *Venomed One* speaks with a voice like thunder, carrying over the abysmal din, *"LET US MAKE MAN IN OUR IMAGE, ACCORDING TO OUR LIKENESS."*

DAY THREE

11th April, 1989

TUESDAY 1:39 AM

Whispers.

Voices in the dark called Amy's name. The hot wind of their breath tickled the fine hair on her neck and licked her ears.

Teasing.

She had fled the campsite, crashing and stumbling through thick and thorny undergrowth, her mind fixated on flight. After what seemed like only a few minutes, she'd recovered enough to realise that she wasn't being pursued. Suddenly terrified for Vincent, she double-backed towards the campsite, knowing that Vincent's car was also there... As a baleful moon shone overhead through grey slivers of cloud circling like sharks.

Running back through cutting branches, she approached the campsite and saw through the cover of trees, a scene of ruin. Flickering in the ember light of the fire lay tatters of tent, belongings and intestines. The car, a yellow Datsun Sunny, was gutted, its steering wheel torn free and cast aside. The forest was cold and silent, like a tomb.

She sank to her knees, crying, overcome with anguish.

And then something stirred behind her...

Laughing.

Things became a blur of fear and confusion after that.

Screaming... Running... Something chasing... Falling onto stinging nettles... Hot breath upon her... Running again... Colliding with trees... Bleeding and sore, but still running... Galloping crashes through the forest behind her... Feral grunting as it drew nearer... The rancid stench of its hot breath... Claws ripping at her back and legs... Ribbons of clothing and flesh... Somehow still running... Ever the demon at her heels...

Until she could run no further. And collapsed.

, , ,

And now, hearing voices, she stirred awake. A dark prickly forest pressed down on her, infested with crawling bugs and other horrors she didn't want to imagine.

Something hairy ran across her leg.

She leapt up screaming and from behind came a voice grating like rusty nails, *"You cannot run from deeeaaath."*

She spun to see the towering bulk of the demon in moonlit silhouette. Piercing red eyes flickered from the shadows.

Her mind left her and the world became a long, dark tunnel. At the end stood a black figure with eyes of fiery crimson. The power of its fixating stare compelled her into submission. Her body resisted efforts to move. Her mind abandoned efforts to think.

A cruel rasp, *"Accept your faaate."*

It moved closer.

Its wretched face was clear now. A wolf-like snout swollen with teeth, extending back to a hairy black head set with red eyes that burned with malice. Its demonic visage rose over her, enveloping her with its shadow.

Screaming, she started running again.

Again, it followed...

Every step a struggle... Every breath a battle... Every move it shadowed... Crying for help... Praying for salvation...

Falling in desperation... Somehow finding the strength to rise and stumble on... Blood throbbing in her ears and bleeding from her cuts... Crashing through endless forest as unyielding as her pursuer...

Aching, exhausted, her pace slowed to a crawl... And yet ever it maintained a cruel distance of a couple of metres behind her...

Gloating.

Finally, she could run no more. She turned to face her attacker.

It stopped, its slavering maw widened to a grin. The time had come.

Through sobs she screamed, "WHAT ARE YOU? WHAT DO YOU WANT?"

It licked its lips. *"I am deeeaaath and I want yooouuu."*

A pathetic gesture of resistance, she raised two fists and scanned around for something, anything, to use to defend herself. But there was nothing...

It was over.

It leapt forward to grab her throat. Its claws closed around her neck and lifted her from the ground. Her windpipe crushed, her hands fought to wrest free the vice grip, her legs kicked the air.

It caressed her face with its tongue, smothering her with drool. Helpless she was, but to bunch her face in horror.

Its eyes met hers. *"Taaasty."*

Then there was a violent crack as her neck snapped.

TUESDAY 7:06 AM

It was still dark.

Howard stretched his arms and yawned as he craned his head to read his digital clock.

It was time to get up for school. Strange that it was still dark though... But that was probably just because the curtains were closed.

Strange shapes crowded the murky shadows – only the Treasure Island poster facing him was distinct. It glowed in the pale moonlight, the pirate's eyes luminous and haunting...

Staring directly at him.

Howard hid under the bed covers, his pulse racing. He dared not move or breathe, lest the pirate become aware of his presence. His chest ached with the force of his pounding heart. He began to fear that even his heartbeat was audible and would reveal him.

After a tense silence, he began to hear voices:

"Howard's so lazy, he's always sleeping in. Why did I have to have such a lazy brother?"

"Yes I know. He should be up by now. Never mind, at least I have a daughter I can be proud of."

Howard recognised the voices, but was still confused. It wasn't even that late in the morning! Whatever were mum and his sister talking about?

He decided he would make a dash across the room for

the light switch, braving the darkness and the pirate's wrath. Light brought safety, but he had to be quick.

Summoning the courage, he flung off his doona and leapt from his bed. He landed on something sharp and cried in pain. Panicking, he rushed towards the light switch and tripped on toys scattered in his way. He fell against the bedroom door...

And it slammed shut.

The darkness seemed greater now, unbearable.

Trying not to think about the glowing poster behind him, or the pain in his feet, face and hands, Howard lunged for the light switch, but his fingers only met a bare surface. Frantic, he ran his palms along the wall...

Then came the sound of bestial laughter behind him.

Shuddering in terror, he found the light switch and flicked it on.

Nothing happened.

The sound of laughter behind him became louder.

He grabbed the doorhandle and tried to yank it open. His sweaty hand slipped free and he realised that the laughter was coming from the closet to his left. Shaking with fear, his head turned to the source...

As the closet began to open.

Too shocked to scream, he wiped his hands on his pyjama shirt so he could open the bedroom door. An eerie red light began to spill out of the closet, revealing a towering, muscular form crammed within.

The bedroom door opened onto a dark hallway. At one end was a closed door leading to the lounge where he could detect light and the happy voices of his family. He was safe if he could only reach the lounge. Monsters never attacked in the light or when adults were around. He ran into the hallway...

As something heavy landed behind him, growling.

His scream frozen in his lungs, he ran at the lounge door down the hall. He grabbed and twisted the handle, but crashed into the door with his momentum.

Something loomed over him, poised to strike.

Still unable to scream, he flung the door open...

His mother and sister sat on the couch facing him in plain view. Engrossed in the television, they made no reaction.

Then something grabbed his ankle.

His leg was pulled back with such force that he face-planted into the carpet. He felt teeth dislodge and a burning sensation in his nose. Then something began to drag him back into the hall as he tried in vain to resist by grabbing onto the doorframe.

Tears flooded his eyes as he saw through a blur his family laughing at something on TV. How could they not notice him? Surely they could see the monster dragging him away? Surely they heard the noise?

But his mother and sister didn't even look in his direction. He tried to scream again, but failed. He banged the walls with his fists, desperate to attract attention, but could make no sound.

His fingernails raking the carpet, he was dragged back into the laughing darkness.

There was no escape. Howard turned to look at his captor...

And into the fiery red eyes of a hairy monster baring savage teeth, thronged by many more behind it, their red eyes lit up like candles.

, , ,

Howard awoke screaming so loud, his eardrums almost burst.

His mother Julie rushed into the room moments later. "Howard! What's wrong?"

Reality washed over his consciousness, comforting. Daylight streamed in through the curtains. The monsters were gone now.

"I had a nightmare about the monsters again."

TUESDAY 9:13 AM

He was late.

Brian turned into the carpark of Howqua Hills Police Station on Main Street and parked his 4WD patrol next to two others. He sighed as he grabbed a briefcase and stepped out of the vehicle. Light drizzle fell, dusting Brian as he made his way towards the front entrance.

Standing in the foyer was Sergeant Douglas McDougall, chatting to Constable Annette Baker, the fat bitch, at the reception counter. Down the hallway behind Annette, Constable Robert Harrington was quite literally scratching his arse.

Brian made eye contact with Douglas and Annette, ceasing their conversation. "Busy day, huh?"

Douglas turned to Brian. "Actually we were discussing the job, something I have much to talk to you about."

Brian looked at Robert watching from the hallway. "And Robert, what are you doing apart from excavating your anus?"

Annette winced. Douglas turned to look at Robert who blushed and dipped his head.

Robert looked up. "I was just–"

A phone began to ring from one of the offices.

Robert continued his sentence, "about to go answer that phone."

Annette huffed and looked at Brian. "And so, Mr Efficiency – why are *you* late?"

Brian turned to Annette, glaring at her through his eyebrows. "Some of us have work to do. I would think that includes you."

Douglas interrupted, easing the tension, "Is there any more news on your meeting with Dr Dawson?"

Annette stormed off to the kitchen whilst Brian answered Douglas, "Not since I phoned you late yesterday. The discussion I had with Dr Dawson was helpful in terms of understanding the crime but not solving it."

"Do you have a hard copy of his brief with you?"

Brian smiled. "Of course."

At that moment, Brian and Douglas were rejoined by Robert. The pair paused to look at him.

"Just letting you know Brian, I've got Sasha on the phone," Robert said.

"Tell her I'm not here yet. I'll call her when I get a moment."

Robert wrung his hands nervously. "Ahhh, I've already told her that you'd just arrived."

"Fuck, that's all I need." Brian sighed. His eyes fixed Robert like daggers. "I'll talk to you about this later."

Brian brushed past them both as he headed for his office. Douglas raised his eyebrows to Robert.

"Where the hell have you been?" was the first thing Sasha said.

"Busy," Brian replied. "I was about to call you, but I got sidetracked. I only just got here."

"From where? I thought you were coming home last night."

"From Melbourne. I stayed overnight at my parents' house. I had a few things to take care of."

"Well, you could have at least called to let me know where you were. I've hardly slept worrying about you."

"I'm sorry."

"If you were sorry you would have called."

Brian said nothing.

"Anyway, Julie wants you to mind Samantha and Howard tonight. Apparently she's got some dinner party."

"But she didn't think to ask whether I was free tonight, did she?"

"If I had any idea what you *were* doing, I might have been able to tell her, mightn't I?"

Brian hesitated to respond before saying, "Well, I'll call her anyway, sort something out."

"So what *are* you doing tonight?"

"Looks like I'm minding the kids, doesn't it?"

"Good. I'll see you tonight then. We'll get pizza, as I can't be bothered cooking." She hung up before he could answer.

"Yeah, love you too," he said as he put the phone down.

Brian looked up to see Douglas waiting outside his office.

"Can you spare a few minutes?" Douglas said.

Brian nodded with a sigh.

Douglas gently closed the door behind him and asked, "Is everything okay?"

Brian leaned back on his chair and produced a fake smile. "Sure! My partner and ex-wife are both pissed at me. I'm running around like a headless chook trying to track down a killer loose on the town, whilst simultaneously trying to manage this department and keep the fucking media happy without telling them anything that might alarm the population more than they already are. And to top it off, I've got a migraine that refuses to leave me the fuck alone."

And that's not even the half of it.

"Things are just dandy!" Brian said.

Douglas sat in a chair facing Brian's cluttered desk. "Has anyone ever told you that you can be a sarcastic prick sometimes?"

"Nah, never."

Douglas took a deep breath...

Whatever did Julie see in you?

Douglas checked his watch. "Anyway, let's get down to business, shall we?"

They were interrupted by the phone ringing on Brian's desk.

Brian hesitated. "Er, that's probably Dr Dawson now. He said he'd call about this time."

"I see."

Brian rose from his chair and stepped over to the door. Opening it, he proclaimed, "I'll come and see you shortly and we can go through the details then. There may be more to add after this phone call. Is that okay?"

Douglas nodded solemnly as Brian ushered him out.

"Don't worry, Douglas, your time will come."

Brian rushed back to the phone.

Douglas' unheard response was ominous, "So will yours, Brian."

"Senior Sergeant Derwent speaking."

"Ohhh finally! I've been trying to contact you since Sunday!"

"Oh hi, Julie. I was just about to call you."

"You always say that, Brian! Maybe Sasha believes you when you say that, but I don't."

"I–"

"I don't care what your excuse is, Brian. I'm just calling to tell you that I'll be dropping off Sam and Howard tonight around five thirty."

There was no point in arguing.

"Fine."

"I know it's fine. I've already organised it with Sasha. At least *she's* reliable. Which is surprising considering her age."

Don't get me started. If you weren't such a bitch, maybe we'd still be together.

"So was that all then?"

"Yes, I'll be picking them up tomorrow after school."

"Okay."

"And don't give them McDonalds. I go to the trouble of cooking healthy meals for them every night, so the least you can do is the same."

Nah, just Pizza Hut.

"Yep," he answered.

"Okay, bye."

He hung up and sighed.

Brian cast his gaze over papers strewn across his desk and began to arrange them into sensible piles.

Then the phone rang again...

"Hello, my name is Samuel Cartwright. I'm a reporter at National Nine News."

Oh fuck, here we go.

"I understand that you're the police officer in charge of the Howqua Hills Station?'

"Yes."

"And that you're involved in the investigation of the Weston murders?"

"Unfortunately, yes."

"Is now convenient for you to answer a few questions regarding what you know about the incident?"

"Not really."

"Perhaps we can arrange for a better time? Ideally I'd like to come and speak to you in person."

"Look, can I call you back? I'm really busy right now."

"Yeah, that's fine."

"Good." Brian hung up before he could continue.

Almost immediately, the phone rang again.

"Um, it's Samuel Cartwright calling back. Sorry to trouble you again sir–"

"What is it?"

"Ah, I didn't get a chance to give you a number to contact me on."

"Fine. What is it then?"

Brian let him recite the number he had no intention of writing down. They'd contact again anyway.

"Okay, thanks." He hung up.

The phone rang again.

I don't believe this shit.

"What now?"

"Er, is that Sergeant Brian Derwent? It's Dr David Dawson here."

"Oh, sorry David! I thought it was this pesky reporter who keeps holding up the line."

"Yes, I did try a couple of times just before and your line was busy. You didn't divulge anything of note, I trust?"

"Of course not."

"I mean I knew that you wouldn't, but it doesn't hurt to make sure."

"We're all on the same side here, David. Protecting the public interest."

David laughed. "So how are things back at the office anyway?"

"It's been one bloody thing after another."

"Yes, I can imagine."

I doubt it.

"Anyway Brian, I'll be brief as I'm sure you're very busy–"

"You got that right."

"I need to see you again, quite urgently I'm afraid. Some more information has come to light that I need to discuss with you in person as soon as possible. I.e. today."

Brian ran a hand through his hair. "Can't we discuss this over the phone?"

"It's not secure. I have reason to believe that your phone could already be being monitored."

"What?"

"Look Brian, you really must get down here as soon as possible. I wouldn't even tell anyone that you're coming down. Something is going on that I don't understand. I fear that you're the only one who can help."

Fucking great.

Brian sighed. "Okay, I'll get down there as soon as I can."

"How soon?"

"Um, I've got a few things to sort out here first, which will take a couple of hours. So let's say I'll come meet you for about three pm?"

"That'll have to do, I guess."

"Yes, it will."

"We'll see you then, Brian. Be careful."

What was *that* supposed to mean?

"Okay, David. See you then."

Brian hung up and collapsed back into his chair.

I should have stayed in Melbourne. At least down there I was away from all this shit... And I got a decent night's sleep.

Now I'll have to contact Sasha and Julie again to tell them plans had changed.

Fuck it, I'm going for a coffee and a ciggie first.

Brian rose and staggered out of his office. As he was leaving, his phone began ringing again.

Let them call back if it's important.

Brian headed for the carpark round the back, the refuge of smokers in this modern era of the smoke-free workplace.

Douglas, not far away, heard Brian's phone ringing.

This time, he answered it.

*"Hello and welcome to today's coverage of
this exciting match between Alex can't-
play-for-shit Norton and the reigning
champion, Bruce Power."*

It was morning recess and the boys of Unit H had gathered
to watch the table tennis game between Alex Norton,
ranked third on the Unit ladder, and Bruce Power, currently
undefeated. Bill Tramly, impersonating Gibbo of the *Wired
World of Sports* send-up, was commentating with a canister
of spray-on deodorant as a microphone prop. The score
stood at 18 to 3 in Bruce's favour and Alex now saw why
Didge, ranked second, refused to play Bruce.

"Shut up, Bill," Alex said. "I need to concentrate."

Bill and the rest of the gallery fell silent, watching,
waiting... All except for Danny, who sat at his desk in the
corner, unnoticed.

Bruce licked his lips and raised the ping-pong ball in
preparation to serve. Alex was poised for reaction on the
other side of the table, bat in his right hand, eyes fixed on
the white globe in Bruce's fingertips.

Bruce tossed the ball and cut it with his bat as it came
down. The ball launched across the net, landed short and
spun sharply sideways away from Alex's left.

Alex lunged across, barely managing to get a backhand
to the elusive target, and sent it back high over the net.

Grinning, Bruce smashed the ball down from its trajectory. It ricocheted off the table and at Alex's face.

Alex ducked instinctively and the ball crashed into the bookcase atop one of the desks behind him, bouncing back again almost as far as the table tennis table.

"19 – 3," Bruce announced.

"Spectacular action!" Bill added.

"I said shut up, Bill!" Alex raised his bat in threat.

Bill went deadpan long enough for Alex to turn back to the game, and pulled a mocking face at Alex as soon as he looked away.

The audience muttered before lapsing into quiet ahead of Bruce's next serve. Bill exchanged smiles with some of them.

Bruce hit the ball gently over the net to Alex, teasing him with an easy return shot.

Alex gritted his teeth and smacked back the ball with heavy top spin at the right corner of Bruce's half, nearest the net.

Bruce reached past the table's corner and lobbed the ball back, teasing once more.

Alex grunted as he bashed the ball to Bruce's left, spinning the ball wide and trying to set up the point.

Bruce leapt around the table and returned the ball at full stretch. The crowd gasped.

The shot was deep and directly at Alex. Too quick for him, he could only fend the ball away. Horrified, he watched the ball sail back high over the net...

Bruce feigned another smash at the ball, then changed his angle at the last moment and tapped the ball over the net.

Alex, bracing for the smash, had backed away from the table. Too late, he saw the ball fall short. He flung his bat across the table in a desperate attempt to hit the ball before it bounced twice and somehow return it, but the bat missed and the point was lost.

"20 – 3," Bruce said laughing.

"By gee, by jingo, by crikey, it's match point!" hollered Bill.

"I fuckin' told you to shut up, Bill!" said Alex.

"Oooooo... He's gettin' cut!" Scuza said from the sidelines. Others joined him in laughter.

Alex sighed and shook his head, before returning his attention to the game. Bill was poised with microphone in hand to call the end of the match.

Bruce licked his lips again and served, curving the ball through the air at Alex.

Alex swatted the ball before it landed, but a moment later it was back on his side, curving the opposite way and forcing him across court.

Teeth clenched, he smashed the ball at the far corner, but again and again the ball returned as again and again he smashed it back. Bruce played each shot with robotic perfection.

"Man, what a rally!" cried Robbo.

Alex continued the onslaught, as Bruce's returns became less ambitious, weaker. Alex began to smile.

Then Bruce clipped the net and the ball rolled down onto Alex's side: an impossible shot to recover.

"I win," Bruce said.

Bill leapt to the fore. "And that is game, set and match, folks! Fabulous stuff! We hope you've enjoyed this exclusive coverage of this fantastic match where once again Alex I-need-to-concentrate-even-though-I'm-shit Norton is defeated by the *reigning champion* Bruce the-machine Power!"

Robbo updated the leaderboard with yet another victory to Bruce, whilst others congratulated Bruce or laughed at Bill's antics. Danny, bent over his desk, didn't raise his head.

Bill dashed to Alex. "We now cross live to Alex Norton for comments on his defeat." He shoved the mock microphone into Alex's face.

Alex backhanded the canister Bill held. "Piss off, Bill."

Bill turned to his audience. "Okie dokes, it seems that Alex Norton doesn't wish to speak on camera. Apparently the humiliation of losing 21 – 3 is just too much for the big man, haha! Anyhow, stiff shit, we'll now cross to the winner."

Alex shook his head and headed into the pantry. Others laughed. Ben and Scuza took up places at the table tennis table.

Bill rushed to Bruce. "And here he is, the champ himself! Never mind the screaming hordes of chicks wanting you to sign their tits, Bruce, whadaya have to say for the fans watching at home?"

"That's my deodorant," Bruce said as he snatched Bill's prop from him.

Bill laughed and patted Bruce on the shoulder as he walked away. The crowd dispersed. Ben and Scuza began playing.

Danny was broken from his doodling when the ping-pong ball smacked into his neck, leaving a bright red mark. He jolted with fright.

"GOT 'IM!" Ben shouted, laughing with Scuza.

Danny stared at his desk, fidgeting with trembling hands.

"DANNY!" Scuza screamed. "PICK THE BALL UP!"

Danny tensed, hesitating to respond.

"I SAID PICK THE FUCKING BALL UP, GEEK!"

"Yeah, pick it up, geek!" Ben chimed in. "You touched it last!" Scuza and Ben laughed together.

Danny reached down to pick up the ball near his foot. Without raising his head, he tossed it to Scuza.

"Next time do it when I tell you, geek!" Scuza turned back to Ben and they both laughed again.

Suddenly, Mr Neilson strode into the room, ending the laughter. He ignored Scuza and Ben as he walked over to where Danny sat.

"Danny. Dr Russell is here to see you. He's waiting at the San now and expects to be with you for an hour or more. Which teacher is your next class meant to be with?"

Danny glanced up at Mr Neilson. "Um... Mrs Connelly," he droned.

"Right. I'll let her know then. You best get going."

Danny slowly began to pack up his desk.

"Hurry up now, Danny. You don't want to keep him waiting."

As abruptly as he arrived, Mr Neilson left.

Danny finished arranging his things and rose to leave.

Scuza grabbed his arm and leered into his face. "You say anything to anyone about the Unit and you're dead, geek."

A dark cloud began to descend.

TUESDAY 10:48 AM

Round two... And this time things would be different.

Dr Bernard Russell sat at a desk in Matron Susan Inglis' office re-reading his notes whilst he waited for Danny's arrival, sipping a cup of Earl Grey tea. Outside was still, classes had resumed. A chill wind wailed under grey swollen skies.

The normal protocol of investigation, including medical analysis and consultation with the boy's parents, had failed to identify the source of Danny's malady. A change in tactics was required.

Bernard looked up to see Danny sitting across from him.

"Oh, you're here!"

"Yes, Bernard. I am."

Bernard smiled and reached for the tape recorder on the desk to switch it on. Danny's eyes met his with a steady gaze, his hands resting in his lap. The wind moaned at the window.

"So how are you feeling today, Danny?"

"Fine." He smiled.

Bernard took a deep breath. "That's good," he said nodding slowly.

Mental note: Subject displays the same initial behaviour as on the previous occasion. Unorthodox methodology is warranted in order to delve below surface psychological symptoms.

"How are you finding it being back at school?"

"Fine."

"Mr Neilson tells me that the boys in your Unit have been bullying you... Would you like to discuss that?"

Danny shrugged. "There's nothing worth discussing about it. It's just a bit of teasing, that's all. It's nothing I'm singled out for, we all tease each other."

"That's not the impression that Mr Neilson gave me."

"You'll reach your own conclusions, Bernard, but I suggest your most reliable source is the horse's mouth... I.e. me."

Mental note: Subject seems resistant to prying and is dismissive of there being anything wrong. Remains unperturbed by the seriousness of past events. Possibly indicative of Bipolar Mood Disorder, Paranoid or Schizoid Personality, or even Multiple Personality Disorder. Time to execute Plan B.

"Danny. I'm going to suggest trying something different. It's a special technique often used to increase awareness of one's own mental processes and enable greater control over them. It's a state of self-awareness where you'll cease to be aware of what's going on around you, a bit like being so absorbed in a book or a movie that you don't hear your name called."

"In other words, you want to hypnotise me."

Retain composure. Do not feed hostility or negativity. The subject's trust is imperative to the therapy achieving its objective.

"I'm not going to do anything that will harm or endanger you in any way, Danny. At all times you will be in control, like a dream which takes the course you choose, ends whenever you choose and where you will be safe at all times. It's quite fun really."

"You put such a good spin on it, Doctor."

Bernard laughed awkwardly. "Have you ever had a wondrous dream that you wished would never end, where something profound about yourself or the world was revealed to you, and yet once you awoke you could no longer remember it?"

Danny yawned. "It really doesn't matter what I say, does it? You're determined to sell me this idea of yours. So come on, finish your spiel."

Bernard leaned forward. "Danny. I can't do this alone. I need your help and trust, otherwise it won't work. We're both trying to achieve the same thing."

Danny folded his arms and cocked his head. "And just what would *that* be?"

"Understanding... And with understanding comes control."

"If only you knew."

Well soon, Danny, I will.

"Your subconscious mind has the power to reveal things that otherwise would remain hidden. And it is empowered to protect you at all times, even in dreams. I want to teach you how to harness this power, how to explore things about yourself with your subconscious mind, and how to solve any problems that you may have. This experience will belong to you, Danny, and it will be something that you can use in any way you decide."

Danny grinned. "You obviously don't subscribe to the notion that it's better to let sleeping dragons lie."

"No harm is going to come to you, Danny. You have to trust me and let go all resistance. Do I have your cooperation? Will you let me help you?"

Danny smiled into his eyes. "No, I don't trust you and frankly I don't even like you. But I can see you won't be dissuaded from your folly, so let's get this over with."

This better work, dealing with this obnoxious kid, was becoming a nightmare. At least he'll be easier to manage under hypnosis. Assuming, he even submits to hypnosis.

"Okay now, I'm going to stay right here and talk you through the steps you need to take to reach your subconscious. All you need to do is close your eyes and follow my instructions. When I'm finished, I will say 'Open your eyes' and you will be back in the present. Do you understand?"

"Ohhh, I do." Danny smirked.

"Okay then, let's begin..."

, , ,

Danny now sat in a deep trance before Bernard. His breathing deep and regular, his body relaxed. Bernard rolled up his sleeves.

"Picture yourself, Danny, entering an elevator at the top of a very tall building and pushing the down button. As the elevator descends floor by floor, you go deeper and deeper into trance and relaxation. I do not know nor does your conscious mind know, just how far down you need to go, but your subconscious mind does. When your subconscious mind knows that we have reached the right depth, I want you to push the button to stop the elevator and open the doors."

After a pause, Danny jolted. "Wh-Where am I?"

Already his manner and mode of speech had changed dramatically. Interesting...

"You should now be able to see down a hallway leading to a clean and spacious lounge. Can you see that?"

"Um. Yeah I can but–"

"I want you to walk down the hallway to the lounge. In there, you'll see a nice, comfortable couch."

"There's something else down here as well!"

Bernard frowned. "What do you mean, Danny? Do you mean there's someone else down there?"

"Yes! There's a few of them!"

"No, Danny. There's no one else down there at all. I want you to visualise that you are safe and alone and that your subconscious is not going to create anything that could possibly scare you."

"They're laughing at me! But I ran down the hall into the lounge and closed the door."

"Okay, maybe there's a lock on the door that you can use to ensure that you have peace and quiet."

"Yes there is. It's a safe room."

Roll with it – what's important is that Danny is in the lounge now and the metaphor can proceed.

"Okay, now on the wall to your left or right is a chalkboard."

"Yes, there is... And it's got something written on it!"

"Well, at the bottom of the board is a tray with chalk and a duster. I want you to take the duster and–"

"It says: Bernard, please help me. I am trapped in endless darkness." Danny's breathing became frantic.

I'm not sure how long I should let this continue. Obviously the subject has significant trauma buried in his subconscious. Perhaps I shouldn't have allowed him to go so deep.

"Danny, I want you to erase the writing on the blackboard and imagine it clearing your mind as you work. I want you to visualise that you are safe and free from intrusions or distractions."

"But it has a name under it!"

Curious. Could this be another personality, subliminal in Danny? Perhaps this was the personality that needed 'help'.

"What is the name, Danny?"

"Um, it says... Henry Wilcox."

Henry Wilcox? That's not possible, is it? Henry Wilcox was a schizophrenic client of his about ten years ago, who was roughly the same age then, as Danny was now. Random coincidence? Or did Danny and Henry somehow know each other?

Let's try making contact with this Henry, but let's also be careful not to jump to conclusions.

"The chalk at the bottom of the board is very special, Danny. We can ask it questions and it will write the answer for us on the blackboard. I want you to clear the board with the duster and ask the chalk where we can find Henry."

"Okay," said Danny.

There was a pause and then Danny began to whimper.

"What's wrong, Danny? Tell me."

"The chalk only wrote one word... Hell!"

Enough was enough. Time to bring Danny out of there.

"Alright, Danny. I think it's time we went somewhere else. We'll come back here later when you're feeling more comfortable."

"But the demons are outside! I can hear them scratching at the door, trying to get in!"

Demons? My suspicions were right. The psychosis had remained all along.

Outside, the wind gained intensity: a forlorn howl.

"There's another door behind you, Danny, that you can take. It will take you down a *safe* corridor back to the elevator and away from anything that your mind can create to try and scare you."

"But there isn't another door!"

"Then you need to look harder. Visualise the door in front of you and see that you can open it."

Danny screamed. "The demons are breaking through!"

We'll take the quick way out then.

"I want you to fly through the walls, Danny, as if they weren't there. Fly up and back to where you started. The closer you get, the more awake you'll become. When you reach where you started–"

Tears streamed. "But I can't fly! Ohhh they're horrible! Like big werewolves with red slits for eyes!"

Henry Wilcox used to talk about the same thing. Suggestion perhaps? Definitely something to be investigated later. Now it was time to employ some suggestion of my own.

"Danny, I want you to repeat after me: The demons can't hurt me. They're not real. They're all in my mind."

Unresponsive, Danny's wailing coincided with the rising wind.

"Danny, listen! Repeat the words: The demons can't hurt me. They're not real. They're all in my mind."

Danny fell silent.

Then his eyes opened, fiery and glazed.

A voice unlike Danny's rasped, *"Ohhh Bernard... We are real."*

Bernard rushed round the desk to Danny and gripped him by his shoulders. "The demons can't hurt me! They're not real! They're all in my mind!"

Again, Danny rasped, *"We come for you too, Bernard. And there's nothing your psychobabble can do to save you. Hahaha!"*

The phone began to ring, fighting to be heard over the wind.

"That's for you." Danny smiled.

I thought I told them that the session was not to be interrupted under any circumstances. Especially now of all times.

Bernard turned away to answer the phone.

"Hello?"

A demonic voice taunted, *"The Devil sings. Leviathan stirs. Armageddon awaits."*

The line went dead.

When Bernard looked up, feverish with terror, the office door was wide open...

And Danny was gone.

⸖   ⸖   ⸖

It would be almost an hour before Bernard left the Matron's office. Stony-faced, briefcase in hand, he strode out to his car...

Speaking to no one.

TUESDAY 1:00 PM

A white Holden Torana, apparently abandoned.

Sergeant Douglas McDougall sat in his 4WD patrol, squinting through rain at the discovery. The vehicle lay under a yellow wattle tree, fifty metres down a dirt road from Frank Weston's house on the outskirts of Howqua Hills. Blossom covered the bonnet and Douglas wondered how long the car had been there...

And why it hadn't been noticed before.

Douglas stepped out into the drenching storm. The scrub around him shook as if in terror, invaded by a chill, relentless wind.

Shoeprint-shaped puddles lay in the mud, leading from the car towards Frank's house. Douglas stepped carefully around the scene, peering into the car.

It was unlocked and looked empty save for discarded food wrapping. Douglas noted the numberplate and returned to his patrol.

He opened the driver's side door and reached for the two-way UHF radio fitted to the dashboard. He flicked it on to open a channel with D24, the Police Communications Division. The nearest D24 network control was in Wangaratta, an hour's drive away.

"VKC Wangaratta, this is Howqua Hills 151 requesting a vehicle registration check."

A voice replied over static, "Okay, Howqua Hills 151. What's the registration?"

"Registration AES-775."

"That's AES-775?"

"Yes."

"Okay, won't be long."

Beneath the baying wind, Douglas heard twigs snapping. It came from a stand of trees close to the far side of the vehicle he'd found.

"VKC Wangaratta, this is Howqua Hills 151 again. I'll call back in ten minutes."

"Okay, I should have the details for you then."

As Douglas approached the Torana a second time, the storm abated... Only to be replaced by the fetor of filth and excrement. He paused to cover his nose.

What is that smell?

A sickening crunch sounded from the trees ahead, its source hidden.

Douglas drew his pistol. "This is the police! Who's there?"

Only the storm seemed to answer, "Dooouuug."

Now I'm hearing things!

He crept closer and the rancid stench increased.

Another crunch. Then a snap. This time the trees moved a little.

Douglas broke into a run, wheeling around the Torana and into the copse of trees, pistol ready. In a few frantic heartbeats, the sound's source was revealed...

Amongst broken branches lay a gutted wallaby, twitching in agony. Red splashes meshed with bile and faeces from its split intestines. The reek was overwhelming.

"Ohhh. It's just a joey!"

The creature turned its bloody head towards Douglas, making a strangled mewing sound.

Douglas wiped the rain from his face. "That's quite a stink for such a small animal!"

He regarded his gun a moment and then the adjoining properties about a hundred metres away. He frowned and started to probe the bush around him.

He picked up a branch that was as thick as his arm and stepped around the wallaby to stand at its head. Curling his nose in disgust, he turned his head away as he struck.

A soft thomp sounded as he hit the wallaby's head. It began to thrash and mew with renewed strength.

He clubbed it again and again with frantic abandon. It whined dismally, refusing to relinquish its hold on life.

Douglas ceased his efforts and stepped back from the convulsing beast.

Die damn you!

It mewed back in agonised defiance, kicking its broken legs.

Douglas looked around and spotted a lichen-covered rock the size of a watermelon a few metres away.

He squatted to lift it and heaved it over to where the wallaby lay. He raised the boulder above his head and cast it down to crush the animal's skull...

It moved and mewed no more.

"Finally!" Douglas sighed, wiping his muddy hands on his trousers. He took a moment to appraise the stinking carcass.

What could have inflicted such a horrible attack and was it related to the murders in any way? Hmm, that'll be a job for forensics, I think.

He walked back to the 4WD police patrol and switched on the radio. "VKC Wangaratta, this is Howqua Hills 151."

A scratchy voice answered, "Yes, Howqua Hills. I have the information you requested."

Douglas prompted "And that is?"

"Registration AES-775 is for a white '72 Holden LC Torana, expiring 10th October 1989, registered to Henry Wilcox of Fitzroy North, Melbourne."

Douglas took notes, commenting "I see."

The voice continued, "Henry Wilcox, date of birth the 18th of February 1966, was reported missing by his mother late yesterday."

"Really? Can you fax those details through to Howqua Hills. I'll take care of it from there."

"Sure."

"Thank you very much, VKC Wangaratta. That will be all."

Douglas flicked off the radio and looked with a smile at the sun emerging from behind a grey head of cloud...

Unaware of the hulking black figure looming behind him.

TUESDAY 3:07 PM

"There's someone here now, so I'd better go."

Brian stood for a second time in the lavish reception of the VIFP. The receptionist, a young woman with hair too auburn and too much make-up, kept him waiting whilst she finished her phone call.

A little girl, maybe five years old, sat on a couch facing the entrance, staring at him. Brian adjusted his collar and smiled in her direction.

It was not returned.

"Okay, I'll look forward to seeing you tonight... Don't worry, I'll pick up some wine on the way home... Okay, sounds lovely... Oh, and don't forget to bring the photos! Ok sweet, I really better go, someone's waiting... Ok, love you, byeee!"

The receptionist looked up at Brian. Brian flashed his badge and talked mostly to the wall beside her, "Senior Sergeant Brian Derwent with an appointment to see Dr Dawson."

"I'll just buzz him for you."

She picked up the phone again and dialled an extension. "Hello David, Sergeant Derwent is here to see you."

She hung up and announced, "Dr Dawson will come and meet you here so please take a seat. He won't be long."

Brian nodded slightly and sat in one of the plush chairs. He sighed loudly and stared into space, ignoring a glass cabinet displaying Ned Kelly's inquest papers from 1880 to his left.

The little girl moved from the couch to stand in front of him.

"What are you doing here?" she said.

Brian looked into an unyielding gaze framed by childish innocence. He smirked. "I'm just here to see a friend."

She pouted and put her hands on her hips. "You're lying!"

The receptionist interjected, "Cayla! Don't talk to the man like that!"

Cayla called back without looking away from Brian, "But he's lying, mum. He's not here for *friends*."

Brian returned her gaze. "Cayla, why would I lie to you?"

She screwed up her face. "Cos you're a cop!"

Brian laughed. "Yes, I *am* a cop. And that means I help people like you, Cayla."

She didn't move. "So what are you *really* here for?"

Dr David Dawson emerged from a doorway, unshaven and wearing his trademark white lab coat.

Brian rose from his seat and stepped past the child.

"Hello, David."

David looked elated. "Good to see you, Brian!" He thrust his hand into Brian's and shook it with enthusiasm. "I'm glad you could make it again at such short notice. I really appreciate it."

"That's–"

David continued, "Do you feel like stepping out for a coffee? I was thinking we could go chat somewhere less formal."

Brian shrugged. "Um, I guess so. I–"

"Excellent! I'll just go get my jacket. I'll only be a moment."

David turned and rushed back through the doorway from which he had appeared. Brian exhaled slowly.

You do that David, you fucking git.

His thought was broken by Cayla's voice at his side, "Why won't you answer me?"

He turned to look down at her. "Because I already have."

Her mother called, "Cayla honey, come over here and leave the man alone. You can do some drawings with mummy."

The joys of the modern workplace. They'll ban smoking but letting children run loose is fine.

Cayla lowered her voice so as not to be heard by her mother. "We're gunna get you, you know."

Before Brian could respond, Cayla turned and ran to her mother. He frowned.

What a little shit of a kid!

,　　,　　,

"This ought to be a good spot."

Brian, cappuccino in hand, looked at the table David pointed to. Isolated, it lay in a quiet corner of the café, its lacquered fake wood top complemented by cheap indoor chairs.

Brian shrugged. "It'll do."

David sat opposite Brian with his cup, scanning the rest of the café and the street outside. As Brian sat down, David leaned forward. "I think we should be safe here, but just keep your voice down all the same... There may be someone listening."

Brian frowned. "David, what the hell are you talking about?"

David sat back and sighed. "Well–"

"The *short* version."

David nodded. "Okay yes, the short version."

"And this better be worth my coming down here."

David grimaced. "Yes, I felt I had no other option, which you'll come to understand once I explain it to you."

Brian gave David a sceptical look.

"You remember everything we talked about last time?"

"Yes, yes, get to the point."

"Well, it's already happened... The cover-up. Only it's much worse than I feared."

Brian raised his eyebrows. "How so? What's happened?"

David leaned forward again. "Sometime last night they removed all of the evidence, Brian... *All* of it. They got into my lab and the autopsy ward and took everything: the bodies, the samples, the photos, reports, computer files... Everything!"

"Who's they?"

"I have my suspicions... Whoever it was, knew exactly what they were looking for and seemed to have no trouble getting in. Which I think can only mean that one or both of John Taylor and Chris Gamble from my lab must have done it or helped someone else. Only they had the access and knowledge of where everything was."

"And where were they last night allegedly?"

"They were both working back late and deny any knowledge of the events. Apparently they left about 1 AM when everything was in order and no one else was here apart from the shift clerk and the security warden."

"Have you spoken to the clerk and warden?"

"Yes I have, and they both said that they didn't notice anything unusual. But as you know, the Institute is a big place, so the culprits would have had plenty of opportunity."

Brian squeezed his face in his hand and took a deep breath.

He looked up at David. "Have you reported this to the police?"

"I contacted D24 first thing and got someone down here to have a look. They took our statements and dusted my lab for fingerprints, which is now sealed off as a crime scene."

"Well, surely they'll take care of this?"

"You'd hope so. However, I'm not so sure... John and Chris have been acting weird ever since this happened and-"

"Weird? What do you mean?"

David paused to consider his answer. "Secretive about their own movements yet keeping an eerie vigilance over mine."

"Like-"

"Even the police that came here, Brian, they seemed, er, uninterested. You might think it's just paranoia, but there definitely seems to be something strange going on... And they're all in on it!"

Brian raised an arresting palm. "Whoa! Slow down there, Dave. For a start, just because an officer seems uninterested doesn't mean that he's plotting against you!"

"Yes, yes, you're right." David cast his gaze out of the window, fidgeting.

Brian forced a laugh. "So you've made me come all the way down here again just to tell me this in person? Because you think that your phone might be bugged and even the café down the road isn't safe because someone may be watching!"

"Brian! Brian, I'm-"

"Haha! And you think that even the police are in on some conspiracy! David, for all you know, I could be in on it too!"

David's expression was sombre. "If I can't trust you Brian, then I can trust no one."

"What about the Coroner? Is he in on it too?"

"The Coroner has as yet only been informed of a delay with the final autopsy report."

Brian snorted. "So what is it that you'd have me do anyway? I've already been summoned back to Howqua Hills and this so far has been a complete waste of my time."

"Brian, we're dealing with an alien attack!" David looked nervously around him. "We agreed about the likelihood of a cover-up and now we're seeing it happen!"

Brian folded his arms. "You're not answering my question."

"Well, I was hoping you could. I had hoped that you'd be able to do something or at least offer some advice."

Brian rose from his chair as he smirked. "Didn't you pick the wrong person!"

David looked dismayed. "You're not leaving, are you?"

Brian adjusted his belt and pulled out his wallet. "Of course I am. I've got enough things of my own to deal with. Sergeant McDougall is expecting to meet me at Frank Weston's house at six thirty, which means leaving now."

"I should have known you'd be of no help."

"Exactly," Brian said as he drew out a ten-dollar note. "This ought to cover the drink; you can keep the change."

David slumped in his chair. "Thanks."

Brian smiled. "Pleasure."

David stared ahead into space and Brian placed a hand on his shoulder. "I'm sorry to hear about what happened, but it's not my place to act. That's what D24 and the state police are for, so I'll let them do their job."

David's eyes didn't move from the vacant space in front of him. "Sure."

Brian leaned over to speak in David's ear. "But just for the record, I actually believe you that we're up against something we don't understand and that no one can be trusted. If you want my advice, do what I'm gunna do: Take a holiday and get away from all this shit!"

David looked dejected as Brian left.

TUESDAY 4:24 PM

He had no choice.

Danny walked up the hill from his Unit towards the dining hall, clad in only a white T-shirt and shorts, shivering against the rain and wind. Others jogged past him, eager to meet friends up there, start the run or just trying to keep warm.

Outside the dining hall, a herd of humans gathered, students and their teachers, as the time approached four thirty, when their race was due to start. They stood in the chilling rain, rubbing their arms and legs for warmth. Some chatted and others scanned the clouds for a sign of respite...

But none saw the Dark Horde.

Danny sat alone on a wooden bench along the side of the dining hall, making circles in the white sand with his foot. The cross-country runs used to be scant relief from the ordeal of H Unit, but now there were the voices...

"It doesn't matter where you run, Danny, we will always find you."

Mrs Moffatt ascended the steps at the front of the dining hall wearing a blue tracksuit. She turned to the gathering and motioned for them to be quiet.

"I know it's raining, but it's only light and expected to clear soon, so today's long run is still going ahead. Isn't that good!"

She was answered with groans.

"Today we're doing Hermit's Knoll run. It's a twelve-kilometre run and it's a new route that was first run last year. I'll go over the course again for those who weren't paying attention at lunch time and didn't check the map up here on the notice board."

She pointed with a wooden ruler at a map next to her. "The run goes from here, down the hill and past the Wood Shed. Go out the school gate and up the driveway towards Mueller Road. When you get to Mueller Road, you'll turn right and follow it along for a couple of kilometres, before turning down a track that'll be marked with the usual orange tape. Follow this track 'round for a bit, and then you'll go over a steep hill about halfway along."

She smiled at the sound of more groans from the audience. "This, folks, is Hermit's Knoll. From there the track winds back and past a junction where you *don't* keep going straight ahead, but turn sharply right to head back towards the school. The track crosses Carters Creek a bit further on and following the track up the other side, you'll see that it joins onto the standard course where the stiles are over the fence into the horse paddock. From there it's just a simple matter of following the standard course home."

Danny wasn't listening to the directions. He never did. It was much easier just to follow those in front of him.

"One final thing. It is raining and most of this course is on dirt tracks, so it'll be slippery in some places. So take it easy, especially when going downhill like you will when you leave here."

The humans moved to a line drawn in the sand. Some pushed to the front, others did last minute stretches and some just talked.

The time had come...

Danny saw the others lining up and slowly followed. He stood at the back of the throng to avoid attention.

Mrs Moffatt stood beside the line that bulged with poised runners. She held up the starting pistol. Heads turned to look at her or bent low, eyes and ears straining to judge the moment to start.

Adjusting an earplug, she pulled the trigger...

And like a river bursting its banks, the masses surged forward. Five hundred odd feet trampling down the dirt road leading past the main wood shed, through the gates and out of the school grounds.

The usual show-offs began the race by sprinting away, savouring the few moments they led the pack, before burning themselves out and finishing behind the first hundred.

Danny ran with the tail of the group, in his usual company of the overweight, asthmatic and physically inept. He surrendered his body to the gravity of the hill, letting it carry him like a leaf floating downstream. A slave of will, Danny followed like all the others.

The human herd began to stretch out as they settled into their running rhythms. Fleshy frail creatures struggling to obey orders, their knees wobbling and jarring with their descent.

The lead pack was past the basketball courts and the Wood Shed as the last runners reached the bottom of the hill. By the time the stragglers reached the Wood Shed, the leaders were beyond the school gates and halfway to Mueller Road.

Danny ran in a slow jog at the end of the field. His chest burning, his breath became laboured and a stitch began to aggravate his left side. He made to stop and walk...

But his legs would not respond.

Some alien force dragged him onward, compelling his legs to keep moving... A force he feared was all too familiar.

Danny ran on, moving past the others around him who had stopped to walk like he wished. His face flushed and his side aching, he felt like vomiting but still his body refused to relent. Now positioned behind three-quarters of the pack, he saw some of his fellow Unit members up ahead.

The beast within kept calling...

Danny continued to move further upfield, stranger to this new determination. Of his Unit he passed Mark, then Price, then Mike and the others he ran with.

Some ignored his passing and some turned their heads in amazement, whilst others sneered things like "Are you running away again, Danny!" or "Is your mummy waiting for you at the end!"

Danny ran on past them. The voices, the pain and even the world faded into unconsciousness. It was easy to forget who he was.

He reached Mueller Road and broke into a sprint as he turned down its length, shackled and helpless to this strange drive. He shoved his way past others who normally beat the shit out of him, surging beyond their reach before they could respond. He dashed past the drink stops without slowing and leapt easily over a fallen tree at the side of the road that others avoided.

"That was Danny Malone!" said a stupefied Mrs Farell to the principal Lucas Prescott at the drink stop.

Nearing the track turn-off now and in the upper half of the runners, Danny's limited body finally gave out on him. His knobbly legs buckled and he went crashing to the hard asphalt. There was a horrible ripping sound as the tarmac tore at his hands and knees.

Nathan and John, the two runners he had just passed, almost followed him down. Jumping clear, they both stopped.

"Shit, Danny! Are you alright?" John said as he moved to Danny's side to help him up.

Blood flowing down his leg from one of his knees, Danny forced himself up and pushed John away with lacerated hands.

Nathan pointed at Danny's gory knee. "You better go back to Mr Prescott."

Danny seemed not to hear them, they couldn't even be sure that he saw them, he simply turned and ran on again, leaving a trail of blood in his wake.

Inhuman and unstoppable.

The road became an open path, then a muddy trail winding through Wattle trees towards Hermit's Knoll. Branches swayed above, dumping wattles, leaves and rain on those below.

Danny, now abreast of three-quarters of the field, didn't hear the cries of those he passed. There was only the wind in his ears.

Danny coursed up the steep hill and careered down the other side, leaping over boulders and past an ever-thinning field of other runners. His feet slipped a few times on the muddy descent but he retained his footing and the momentum carried him onward.

The ground flattened out and continued through wet scrub until reaching the turn off. Danny charged ahead into the undergrowth the other side of the path, oblivious to the barbed blackberries and stinging nettles there to mar his passage...

Then his head hit something hard and the world went black.

, , ,

"You're a failure."

Danny's head throbbed with pain, his hair sticky as it clung to his face. His body leaden, he lay immobile in the mud. His eyes stuttered open, but he could only make out splashes of red adorning him. A chill voice whispered in his ear.

"We should kill you now."

Danny managed a forlorn whimper, "Then do it!"

"Haha! You think we'll reward you with charity? No Danny, you will suffer. We will torture and rape you until your body is so mangled and broken that you cease to be recognisable as having once been human. We will reduce you to what you started your pathetic existence as: protoplasmic jelly. And then Danny, you will be re-created... As one of uuusss."

"Wh-Why are you doing this?"

"A puppet does not question its master. It knows only to obey. Now rise!"

As if by strings, Danny was lifted to his feet, scattering flies that crawled over the exposed meat of his torn knee. Searing pain scored his head. His upper body hung in the air like a crucifixion.

"Wh-Wh–"

Danny suddenly pivoted and ran at a tree to his left. Unable to stop himself, he impacted face-on against the unyielding trunk. The crippling force felled him instantly. He felt a burning sensation in his nose as fresh blood began to spill down his face.

"Haha. Dance puppet!"

Once more he rose against his will and threw himself at the tree. Again the collision floored him. Blood washed his eyes and his nose was a pulpy mess squashed against his cheek. Unable to resist, he rose again and again to keep hurling himself at the tree.

"Please! Please stop!"

"Even death is denied you, Danny. There is only one way it will stop."

"I'll do anything! Just please stop!"

His head jerked towards the stub of a broken branch, poising to slam eye-first onto the protruding spike.

"Obeeey."

Danny thrashed at the branches around him, but still his head remained poised for impalement.

Between choked sobs, "I obey! I obey! Ple-e-e-eeeaaassse!"

"You will not fail again."

Danny flung himself at the spike. He felt it pop his eyeball before driving into his brain... Obliterating consciousness.

TUESDAY 6:31 PM

No one was there.

Brian looked through steady rain on his windshield at Frank Weston's house. In fading daylight he saw white police tape extending around the modest weatherboard building and down a dirt side road to encompass a white Torana lying there. Neither the building nor the vehicle showed signs of activity. There were no other cars or people to be seen.

Fucking typical.

Brian sighed as he picked up his two-way radio...

"VKC Wangaratta, this is Howqua Hills 150."

The only reply was static.

"VKC Wangaratta, are you there?"

Again, only static.

He threw the handpiece at the dashboard and flung open the car door. He stepped out of the patrol into a large puddle.

Brian looked down at the muddy water splashed over him...

One fucking thing after another.

A strange mewing sound reached his ears, somewhere close. Brian turned to determine its source as the noise emanated again from a copse of gum trees near the Torana.

That's it.

Brian stormed over to open the trunk at the back of his

4WD patrol. Inside laid an equipment belt with a pair of steel handcuffs, a baton-sized torch and a pump-action shotgun. He took them all.

Shotgun ready, he approached the copse of trees from which the noise came. Incessant rain soaked him, adrenalin flooded him.

The distressed mewing continued. Brian slowed his pace as he reached the trees and peered inside...

Twitching in pools of brown and red were the mutilated remnants of some marsupial animal, its body torn asunder, its head a flattened pulp. And still it made that horrible sound.

Brian raised his shotgun. "I haven't got time for this shit."

Twigs snapped in the grass behind him.

He spun around to look across a muddy paddock at a line of gum trees a hundred metres away. He used his torch to scan the area. Trees and scrub waved in the wind and rain, but he could see little else. Satisfied, he turned back to the mewing...

Lightning struck nearby, revealing a host of hairy black figures crouched among the trees Brian had surveyed, their red eyes lighting up the scrub like spot fires.

Brian used the torch to guide his shot at the animal's head and pulled the trigger in time with the coming thunderclap. The animal's head disintegrated in an explosion of blood, bone and brain.

Probably shouldn't have done that... Fuck it.

Brian looked up at Frank's house, a beacon of calm amid the howling storm.

He ran his torch over the abandoned Torana. Unlocked, its rubbish-filled interior revealed little of interest. Stepping through mud, he approached the house.

Hmm, maybe I should try the radio again.

Brian returned to his car and picked up the handpiece hanging from the dashboard.

Still only static.

Rain continued to lash him as the wind screamed in his ear. Then he realised the wind was also coming from the radio...

Calling his name.

Shotgun firmly in hand, he started again for Frank's house.

Under cover of wind, rain and darkness, something followed.

He strode across the wooden porch, passing a saturated green couch, to the front door. He rapped on the door with the brass knocker and stepped back.

Only the raging storm answered. He shrugged and tried the door knob...

The door swung open to reveal a short grimy hallway adorned by posters of rock bands, cars and girls. It led to a cluttered lounge on his left and around a corner to the right. There was a filthy stench he could not identify, and yet somehow, it was familiar.

Carefully, Brian stepped inside the building and leaned around the doorway leading into the lounge with shotgun raised.

No one.

Beer bottles, food wrappers, dirty plates, videos and porno mags lay strewn about the lounge: a scene of bachelor excess. Exits the other side of the room were a doorway into the kitchen, where the familiar stench was strongest, and a door to the backyard.

He stepped past the refuse of the lounge to look in the kitchen...

And into the red demonic eyes of a huge wolf-like beast.

It stood hunched against the middle of the kitchen ceiling, arms ending in savage claws outstretched as if to greet him.

"I've been waiting for you."

"Really," Brian answered as he fired both barrels of his twelve-gauge shotgun point-blank into the creature's chest.

The blast knocked the monster backwards as the pellet spray shredded its flesh. Its ribcage shattered with the force, ripping the vital organs within. Screaming in agony, it crumpled to the ground but managed to keep its eyes defiantly fixed on Brian.

"You cannot kill what is already dead."

Brian laughed, pumped the shotgun to reload it and lifted both barrels to the demon's face. As the monster lunged, he fired again.

Its head exploded in a spray of purple and grey, painting the walls and floor the other side of Brian. The beast fell still.

"Your face is already dead!"

Think I'll have a cigarette after that effort.

Brian lit up as he admired the carnage stretched before him...

Then footsteps could be heard on the front porch.

Brian reloaded his shotgun and flicked the cigarette he'd only just started into the carcass at his feet. He crept back into the lounge...

Another of the demons was there, lunging for Brian as he emerged from the doorway. It grabbed the barrel of his gun as it fired, taking out a large section of wall and a hanging clock.

Shit, two of the bastards! I'm gunna need more ammo!

The demon loomed over him as it ripped the shotgun from his grasp. Brian launched himself at a nearby window.

Brian hit the window hard enough to break through the

flyscreen and glass. Splinters cut his forearm and fell around him as he landed hip-first onto the concrete driveway that ran down the side of the house.

A slavering head emerged through the broken window, roaring.

Ignoring the pain in his arm and side, Brian surged to his feet and down the driveway to the front of the house...

Waiting for Brian was Sergeant Douglas McDougall and his sidekick Constable Robert Harrington. Both had their pistols aimed at his chest.

"Don't move, Brian!" Douglas ordered.

Brian stopped, raising his hands. He glanced over his shoulder... Nothing followed.

"What the fuck is going on?" Brian said.

"You're under arrest, Brian, for the murder of Barney and Frank Weston. And if you resist," Douglas smiled, "we'll shoot you."

TUESDAY 7:48 PM

"You won't break me... You won't take me..."

The lyrics of Judas Priest blared from the stereo next to Jason as he wrestled the joystick playing *Double Dragon* on his Commodore 64 computer.

"Cos I'll fight you under blood-red skies."

Jason roamed alleyways and sewers, slamming and bashing hundreds of enemies, in his quest to clear the streets and ultimately rescue his woman. A quest made easier using a cheat to give him infinite lives.

Then the phone rang, summoning him back to reality.

Jason left the couch and the game he'd already finished four times to answer the phone.

"Hello?"

He ran a hand over his shaven head. "Aaron! Where the hell have you been?... I went 'round to your house last night and you weren't there. I haven't been able to get onto anyone. It was like you, Bruce and Vino had all disappeared!"

Jason rocked back in surprise. "Well shit, sounds like a story! Um, d'you wanna come over now? I'm not doing anything and the oldies are out somewhere 'til about ten."

Jason nodded, "Yeah, cool man. I'll see you soon then. Just give me, say, ten minutes or so 'cos I gotta go take a shit."

Jason laughed, "Yeah mate, a real beauty!"

,   ,   ,

The doorbell rang.

Jason strode up to the door of the neat four-bedroom home and pulled it open...

Aaron stood there like death. Matted hair fell across a pale unshaven face. Bloodshot eyes stared at Jason from worn sockets.

"Holy shit, Aaron! You look fucked!"

Aaron answered grimly, "I am."

"Well, come in and sit down. Tell me what's happened."

Jason began to lead Aaron down the hall towards the lounge before pausing at the doorway to the kitchen.

He turned to Aaron, who was following him like a shadow. "D'you wanna drink?"

"Naaah, it's alright."

Jason shrugged and turned back for the lounge.

They sat on leather couches either side of a coffee table occupied by Jason's computer.

Jason squinted at Aaron. "Your eyes look fucked!"

"They are," Aaron replied, prodding an eyelid...

His eyeball popped out of its bloody socket to hang down the side of his face.

Jason leapt back on the couch. "Fucking hell, Aaron!"

Aaron calmly pushed the eyeball back into its socket. "Naaah, it's alright. It's just a lazy eye."

Jason cringed with revulsion. "You've gotta be out of your fucking mind, Aaron! You gotta get that treated!"

"Maybe..." Aaron smiled, looking at Jason with his one good eye. "Or maybe I'll just take yours!"

Aaron dived at Jason. Jason kicked his leg up to catch Aaron with his foot as he sailed towards him. Aaron's arms stretched out, fingers seeking Jason's eyes.

This can't really be happening, can it?

Struggling to hold Aaron off, Jason saw a thick purple scar around Aaron's neck... Splitting to leak a viscous purple fluid.

Jason was speechless with horror as he reached for a vase behind him.

"GIMME YOUR FUCKIN' EYES, CUNT!" Aaron screamed as his 'lazy eye' slipped out again to dangle freely.

Jason grabbed the vase and brought it down on Aaron's head with smashing force, drenching him and the room. Oozing hot purple fluids, Aaron collapsed onto Jason, pinning him against the couch.

Jason squirmed free of the horrid embrace, leaving Aaron's still body on the couch. Hyperventilating, he wiped his trembling hands on his shirt and stepped back... Speechless.

Aaron's head lolled around to face him. "Haha, tricked ya!" He slowly rose from the couch, smiling.

Jason looked around for something to use as he backed towards the hall. "What the fuck's wrong with you, Aaron?"

"I just want your eyes!"

Aaron launched himself at Jason with outstretched arms. His face connected with Jason's fist in mid-flight. Aaron crashed sideways into the wall, impacted heavily and slid down to the carpet, leaving a purplish smear.

Before Aaron got up again, Jason ran into the kitchen and grabbed the biggest knife he could find. He ran back into the hall to see Aaron standing with one hand on the wall for support, his head resting gruesomely on one shoulder, the exposed sinews of his neck leaking down his chest in spurts... Still he smiled and began advancing towards Jason.

"Back the fuck off, Aaron!" Jason reinforced the point with the blade he brandished.

"Or what?" Aaron gargled through bubbles of blood. "You'll kill me?" He stepped closer.

Holding Aaron at bay with his knife, Jason back-stepped to the front door.

Aaron stopped to watch Jason leaving. "It doesn't matter anyway, you're all fucked."

"What do you mean all? Do you mean the others too? Are they dead?"

"Nup. None of them are. Just fucked. Like you will be soon."

Jason opened the front door and stepped outside. He slammed the door behind him and dashed to his car...

He only realised once he'd started his silver Valiant Charger and floored it out of the driveway that he'd left his wallet behind.

Too late.

Not thinking where, he sped off, reaching the town's outskirts before thought and a cold sweat began to seep into his consciousness. His mind a menagerie of panic and pain, he pulled over on a deserted roadside, unable to control himself and the car any longer...

And began to cry.

TUESDAY 8:56 PM

"We got another one."

Sergeant Douglas McDougall put down his steaming cup of coffee and looked up from a desk strewn with newspapers and reports. Constable Robert Harrington stood at the doorway to the office, wringing his hands nervously.

Douglas frowned. "Another?"

"Yeah, this one says he was attacked at home by a friend of his that's returned from the dead. His name is Jason Lloyd and he says the attacker is still in the house where his parents are due to arrive soon. He's waiting in reception now. What should we do?"

Douglas rose. "They've certainly been busy." He sighed. "Well, arrest him for the murder of his friend and put him in one of the holding cells. We'll deal with him later. Right now, we've got Brian to interrogate." He grimaced.

Robert nodded and turned to leave.

"And Rob," Douglas called.

Robert looked back at Douglas. "Yes?"

"I suggest you're gunna need to sedate him. Inject him with enough thiopental to put him out 'til morning."

, , ,

Douglas entered a small, windowless and sound-proofed room containing two armless chairs either side of a lacquered table. Brian sat in handcuffs facing the door, staring at Douglas.

Douglas shut the door behind him and drew a deep breath. Sitting down, he looked at Brian with a smirk and folded his arms. "I've been looking forward to this."

"I'll bet," Brian spat.

Douglas smiled back at his former colleague.

"Aren't you going to tape-record this?"

"Won't be necessary," Douglas answered. "What transpires here won't ever be admitted in any court."

"I thought you would have tried to maintain a semblance of proper procedure. But obviously you don't even care for that."

"No Brian, I don't. I only care that you do exactly what I say."

"Ha! And what makes you think I'm going to cooperate with a slimy fuck like you?"

"Come now Brian, be reasonable. We're both adults here and you're not doing yourself any favours."

"Be reasonable? You arrest me without a scrap of fucking evidence and you expect me to be reasonable? I know you're in on this and obviously the rest of your arse-licking officers are too, so go fuck yourself."

Douglas sighed and shook his head disapprovingly. "It really doesn't matter what you do, Brian. They can't be stopped."

"Then why even bother talking to me, if it makes no difference?"

A note of irritation crept into Douglas' voice. "Because I'm offering you the choice I was never given, the choice to join us."

Brian snorted. "Get fucked."

"Join us and you can have all that you desire. Alternatively, you can refuse and leave me no option but to have you, your family and that dumb slut you call your girlfriend killed."

Brian launched himself forward. He crashed over the table onto Douglas, knocking him backwards off his chair. Brian's handcuffed hands grabbed Douglas' throat as Douglas tried in vain to wrest them free.

"And what's to stop me crushing the life out of you now like the worm you are?"

Douglas could only choke in reply.

"If it doesn't matter what I do, then I might as well... Then we'll call it even!"

Brian's fingernails dug into Douglas' windpipe, drawing blood that glowed purple under the muted fluorescent lighting.

At that moment, Constable Harrington rushed into the room, wielding a syringe. Whilst Brian and Douglas struggled, Robert plunged the needle into Brian's arm.

Brian pivoted to slam his boot into Robert's knee. Robert cried in pain and grabbed his knee, releasing the syringe now planted in Brian's shoulder. Still choking Douglas, Brian followed up on Robert with a kick to the head, knocking him backwards.

"You spineless leech," were the last words Brian uttered before he collapsed unconscious to the floor.

Douglas coughed and rubbed his wounded neck. "What took you so long?"

Robert, fretting over his own wounds, paused to answer. "I thought you had the situation under control."

Douglas stepped forward to knee Robert in the groin. Robert doubled over in agony.

"The next time you fail to provide backup when needed Robert, I'll execute you myself."

"Yes, sarge," Robert managed to splutter.

"Now put Brian into one of the cells until tomorrow. Hopefully he'll be more reasonable with the light of day."

Robert winced as he limped over to Brian's body and began to drag him by his feet out of the room.

"And before you're done, Robert, handcuff his hands *behind* his back. I don't want any repeat performances."

TUESDAY 10:09 PM

Ready.

He stood on the wooden veranda outside the Unit.

Angry.

He looked in at the life of H Unit that he hated and was soon to destroy.

Deadly.

He loaded his gun and slammed the breech home, gritting his teeth.

Let the carnage begin.

The door opened and a short, skinny, brown-haired boy stood at the entrance a moment before entering... Shotgun in hand.

Ben didn't look up from the table tennis table, "Hey Danny, can ya get me some snakes from me tuck box."

"I don't think so," Danny replied, levelling his gun point blank at Ben's chest and pulling the trigger.

The blast scattered Ben's innards across the room in small, bloody chunks.

Alex stood frozen on the other side of the table.

"Hey Alex, d'you want some Maltesers?" Danny said, turning the barrel towards him. "Well, have some lead instead!"

Danny unloaded another pellet spray, striking Alex in the face. Fragments of flesh landed in the dormitory beyond, others splattered against the wall and stayed there. Alex slumped to the ground in a widening pool of his own blood, his head a featureless mess.

"Hmm, not enough choke," Danny commented, adjusting his weapon.

Danny stepped over to Alex's body and put another blast through his nose, sending a parade of multi-coloured marbles dancing across the wooden floor.

Now Danny turned to enter the pantry...

Damien was there, like he suspected, raiding Danny's tuck box, like he always did.

Damien just had time to look around from his position crouched over the box, before Danny slammed a boot into his face. Sending blood, spittle and teeth flying, Damien crashed against the wall, unconscious.

Danny followed up by ramming the nozzle of his weapon into Damien's neck.

Damien stirred once, gurgled twice, and then was dead.

His work done here, Danny left the pantry. Now carrying an automatic rifle, he headed for the sounds of life coming from the dormitory...

Between two rows of beds that lined the long room, four of them were kicking a football that barely missed windows and lights.

I don't believe my luck.

Mike stood closest to Danny, his attention on the incoming football...

Which would never reach him.

Danny struggled to contain his shuddering rifle as it discharged a furious volley of silvery death. The volley of bullets sliced through Mike, walls, windows, beds and the football, which fell to the bloody ground in red strips.

Mark was next to Mike and dived for cover behind one

of the nearby beds, as did Didge at the other end of the dormitory. Clint, also at the far end, was not so quick...

And merciless, lethal fire tore into him where he stood.

Clint's corpse fell onto the shattered and blood-speckled window behind him. The upper half of his mangled body flopped backwards out of the opening: a grotesque expression of death.

Danny unleashed another burst of fire at Clint's exposed belly, severing his body. The truncated torso slid out of the window, dragging with it long loops of leaking intestines. Clint's disjunct lower half flopped sideways to the ground.

"This is fun," said Danny, blood-smeared, cradling his toy.

On cue, Didge stuck his head up over the bed he hid behind...

To see Danny staring down the gun sights at him...

Who did not hesitate to kill.

An onslaught of bullets slugged through Didge's head, shattering his skull and scattering grey chunks of brain. The force of the strike lifted him off his feet and dumped him on the bed behind.

Mark crouched in-between beds not far from Danny, not daring to move. He heard determined footsteps approaching and closed his eyes, praying for salvation.

Danny reached the aisle where Mark crouched, shaking with terror.

Danny looked down on him with contempt. "Any last words?"

Mark pulled his body into a tight ball, squeezing his teeth and eyes shut.

Then the gun fired again and he knew only darkness.

"Guess not," Danny said with a shrug, before moving on...

Danny stepped into the togs room and saw with a smile that Scuza was here, his back to Danny, bent over one of the low benches, polishing his boots.

Danny drew a long machete from his garments and plunged its wicked blade into Scuza's back.

"Hey, Scuza, have some blood to polish those boots!" Danny taunted as Scuza screamed in agony and the knife emerged out the other side of his abdomen.

"Remember that time you told me I was too wimpy to even hurt a fly?" Danny grunted in Scuza's ear, lifting Scuza against him by the hilt. "Well, I've learned to kill now. And let me tell you it's a *real rush!*"

The knife twisted inside Scuza, cutting up through his stomach. His screams ended and Danny let him slide off the blade to fall in a bloody heap on the floor...

Danny stuck his head into the bathroom and saw Robbo was there, brushing his teeth.

"Have you got gills, Robbo?" Danny said as he entered.

"What the fuck do you want, turd face?" Robbo swore at him in flecks of toothpaste.

"VENGEANCE!" Danny shouted, running at Robbo.

Before Robbo acted, Danny had one hand threatening to break his arm behind his back and had the other hand forcing his head into the basin that was rapidly filling with boiling water. Such speed and strength, Robbo had never known.

"Do you say you're sorry now, Robbo?" Danny mocked as the scalding water swept around the edges of Robbo's freckled face. "Do you take back all the shit you've given me over the years, all the insults, all the beatings?"

Robbo desperately tried to struggle free, but Danny's grip was strong as his will to murder. Robbo could only gurgle in pain.

"Say you're sorry! SAY IT PUNK!"

Robbo's reply was lost beneath a wave of water.

"I CAN'T HEAR YOU!" Danny taunted. "SPEAK CLEARLY, YOU FUCK!"

Robbo emptied his lungs, trying in vain to sound words that merely emerged as bubbles.

Phlegm and tears merged with the scalding water now surging down Robbo's throat, running its course of ruin. Danny continued to yell, "I STILL CAN'T HEAR YOU! SPEAK LOUDER, SHIT-HEAD!"

His head submerged in the overflowing basin, Robbo went into a fit of coughing. In throes of death he vomited blood and bile, unable to stop from reflexively inhaling it back again.

Eventually the convulsions subsided and Danny released his grip. Robbo's lifeless body slumped to the floor, his face a mess of red, blue and green.

"Such a shame," Danny said, shaking his head.

Turning away, Danny saw that one of the doors to the toilet cells was closed: its occupancy confirmed by a 'pfft' sound.

Redrawing his machete, Danny rammed it into the toilet door near the lock. With a loud crack, he forced the door open...

Within, Bill sat prone, trousers crumpled at his ankles. He looked up at Danny, blood-spattered and grinning with a long heavy knife in one hand.

"Danny? What the hell are you doing?"

Danny replied by lunging forward with his blade at Bill's exposed scrotum. There was a sound like sheets ripping and then a soft plop as Bill's disembodied testicles landed in the toilet bowl.

"Who's the one without any balls now, Bill?"

"SOMEONE HELP ME!" Bill screamed as he pulled his knees up to his chest and tried to ward Danny off with outstretched arms.

"I wouldn't worry about the loss," Danny reassured him. "You'll be dead in a few seconds anyway."

Danny struck again, stabbing his knife through Bill's forehead, pegging him against the cistern behind.

The cistern ruptured, washing blood down Bill's shirt and onto the tiles below.

"Let's go check the boiler room!" Danny said to himself, tingling with anticipation...

Price and Derrick were there, kneeling on the concrete floor as they chopped wood for kindling to light the boiler.

"That's not how you split it!" said Price in frustration, his back turned to Danny as he entered the room.

"No, but this is!" interrupted Danny, lifting an axe lying against the side wall.

Price turned to face Danny as Danny brought the axe down onto the crown of his head and cleaved it in half.

Derrick, staring at Danny through blood-spattered glasses, jumped back onto his feet, incredulous. "What's happened to you, Danny?"

"Question is," Danny grinned, "what's gunna happen to you."

Derrick bolted for the door leading outside, but Danny was too fast, swinging his axe at the back of Derrick's retreating knees.

The sharpened axe-head bit into Derrick's flesh, slicing bone and causing Derrick to buckle backwards. His head hit the concrete, sending his glasses tumbling. Through a blur of red, he looked up at Danny, now standing over him.

"Why, Danny?" was all he had time to utter before the blunt side of the axe impacted on his head, flattening it against the floor.

Danny paused to scrape a bit of red pulp off his shoe, before stepping outside...

On the slope outside the Unit, under the gaze of floodlights, Bruce and Jamie were working together with a hacksaw on a stubborn log.

Bruce looked up as he wiped his brow. "It's the geek."

Danny approached, the wolf to the sheep...

Bruce took a few menacing steps towards Danny. "Fuck off, geek."

Danny shook his head, coming closer.

"You're really asking for it, geek. Now FUCK OFF!"

Danny moved to within Bruce's striking range, glutton for punishment... Or to punish.

Bruce raised a fist and in response, Danny raised a revolver to his face, pulling the trigger.

Bruce's head exploded backwards as the large calibre bullet ripped out the back of his skull, fanning gore over a wide area.

Danny looked down at his pistol. "Not bad, the old Smith and Wesson."

"YOU'RE FUCKED NOW!" Jamie screamed, eyes bulging from his sockets.

"You think?" Danny answered with a smirk.

Jamie came at Danny with a low gut-punch, but by the time he swung, Danny wasn't there. Danny had moved beside Jamie in an instant and kneed him in the stomach. Jamie doubled over with a groan as his breath left him.

Before Jamie could recover, Danny hit him again, bringing his heel down onto his spine. Jamie slumped to the ground.

"That's for calling me, geek!"

Danny slammed his boot into Jamie's groin, drawing a muffled cry of pain.

"That's for always telling me what to do!"

Jamie lay writhing, trying to blink away the dirt that filled his eyes, but could do nothing more.

"And this is for making me eat shit!"

Danny jumped above Jamie's head and came down on it so hard, that it split open against the rock, spilling its seeds.

All was calm around Danny now. His vendetta was complete.

Then he heard the sound of something growling... Nearby.

Danny turned to the source to see a large black wolf emerge from a stand of gum trees, fiery crimson eyes flashing in the mottled light. He stood transfixed as it dashed across his path and was gone...

Leaving him with a strange, warm sensation in his belly.

⁊   ⁊   ⁊

Danny woke from the dream then and realised his fate. Not comprehending how he was back in the Unit he so despised and feared. He lay on his bed, his hand immersed in a bucket of cold water, drenched in his own warm urine, surrounded by the merciless laughter of his fellow Unit members: he helpless, they heartless.

He was back in the real world.

A single flame, a single set of eyes. A single voice, a single purpose...

> "I am darkness, I am death.
> I am light, I am the breath.
> I am creation, all possibility.
> I am destruction... Entropy.
> I am your enemy, your darker twin,
> The voice of evil, calling from within.
> But I am outcast, I am hated.
> Alone I have suffered, but I have waited.
> Until the time, of my return,
> To claim what is mine, the world to burn.
>
> I bring you misery, insanity and rage.
> I herald the beginning, of a dark new age.
> You cannot resist me, for you are only man.
> You cannot defeat me, nor understand.
> On winds of revenge, my spirit flies free,
> Merciless my power, to destroy all that be.
> Every barrier broken, every chain, every ward,
> Now feel the fury, of the Dark Horde."

DAY FOUR

12th April, 1989

WEDNESDAY 6:16 AM

I really need to go to the toilet.

And try as he might, the thought wouldn't leave.

Howard lay under crumpled, sweat-soaked sheets considering his dilemma. Desperate was the need to urinate, but fear of the dark crushed his resolve. He didn't even dare open his eyes.

Maybe I can wait it out until sunrise... It'll be safe then.

I hope I don't wet the bed.

He returned to sleep's warm embrace, sanctuary from the night... And biological urges.

＞　＞　＞

What seemed a moment later, Howard awoke again, the pressure on his bladder worse than ever. He could wait no longer.

Semiconscious, he flung off the bed covers and swung his body over the side of the bed.

The pirate in the poster on his bedroom wall stared down at him... Vigilant.

In a daze, he ran to his door, opened it and bolted into the hallway. He imagined figures moving in the dark behind him and raced for the toilet door. He ripped the door open, flicked on the light and slammed the door shut behind him.

Safe.

Able to hold on only seconds longer, Howard rushed to relieve himself...

As shadows danced to the wind outside.

Howard finished and prepared himself for the dash back to bed.

Then coarse laughter began to emanate from down the corridor...

If I go now, I can make it.

Summoning courage, he opened the door onto the hallway. Darkness lurked outside, cloaking figures in wait.

Howard ran the gauntlet of the darkened corridor, trying not to look at the red eyes following him from the shadows at the far end.

Imagining monsters in chase, he charged back into his bedroom, slamming the door behind him. His light was on, bathing the dark in a feeble yellow light. He leapt onto his bed and hid under the covers, too scared to move or even breathe loudly.

The sound of demonic laughter reached his ears. It came from the poster facing his bed.

Howard curled himself into a defensive ball but still the mocking sound continued...

And then the bed began to move.

Something was straining at the thin sheet that Howard lay on; what felt like a claw ran down the side of his back.

Howard opened his eyes again to a room filled with an unclean red glow. He leapt from the bed as a hairy taloned appendage tore through the flimsy fabric where he had been a moment ago.

"Weee comeee to claim yooouuu."

Howard turned to the source of the voice, the poster. A twisted visage gazed down at him, crimson eyes flaring, flanked by tendrils of smoke.

Howard ran from the room, screaming for mother.
Laughter followed.

Focused on flight, Howard ran the length of the corridor to his mother's bedroom at the far end, where he would be safe from the monsters.

He surged into the master bedroom shrieking "MUUUM!"

And only then did he take in the scene before him...

His mother lay in a pool of blood on the bed amidst a swarm of flies, her clouded eyes framed by a mouth agape in dead silence.

Screaming in horror, Howard shook her violently, unable to believe. Her head rolled over to face him, spilling a torrent of fat squirming maggots from her lifeless lips.

The walls shook with laughter: a maddening panorama of malice.

"Where's your mummy now, little boy?"

⸢   ⸢   ⸢

Howard's sobbing screams subsided as the room swirled into view. Still shaking his mother, he saw now that she was alive and that he'd only been dreaming. Pre-dawn twilight filtered through the curtains, heralding the arrival of a new day.

He had escaped.

"What's happened, Howard?" Julie said, instantly awake.

"It's the nightmares again! They're real, mum!"

"Oh Howard, they're not real, they're just bad dreams! They can't hurt you. Can't you see that?"

"BUT THEY ARE REAL! YOU DON'T UNDERSTAND! Every night they come and try and take me! They won't leave!" Howard began to choke with tears.

"Howard, I've had enough of this!" Julie rose from the bed as she grabbed Howard's wrist. "I'm going to show you just how real these silly little fantasies are."

Don't you remember what mummy taught you when she tucked you in and kissed you sweet goodnight?

Monsters weren't real, they didn't exist. It's all in your mind.

Don't you trust your mother? Why would she lie to you, your own mother?

There are no monsters, Howard.

Believe.

Julie dragged Howard to the doorway of his room and released her grip on him as she pushed open the door...

Howard's untidy room greeted them, devoid of red glow, torn sheets or animated posters.

"You see." Julie turned to Howard, keeping her voice down so as not to wake Samantha next-door. "There are no monsters, Howard." Then slower and more deliberately, "*No monsters.*"

"But, but they were here just a moment ago."

Julie strode to the clothing cupboard and flung it open, revealing a lifeless interior. "No monsters in here."

Howard pointed to the wall. "What about the poster?"

"It's just a poster, Howard!"

Howard persisted. "Look behind it."

Julie sighed as she lifted the poster from the wall. Only white paint lay underneath. "Nothing there either."

"What about under the bed? They were there too."

Julie crouched down and called out under the bed, "Are there any monsters hiding under here?"

Only silence answered.

Julie stood up again, pulling the sheets back to reveal a bare mattress. Satisfied she had scoured the room, she turned back to Howard. "There are no monsters here, Howard, or anywhere else. *They don't exist.*"

Howard ran into his mother's arms as tears began to flow once more. Soothing, she stroked his hair and said over and over, "No monsters Howard, no monsters."

No monsters Howard, no monsters.

No monsters Howard, no monsters.

No monsters Howard, no monsters.

The words became a rhythm, the rhythm became a mantra, a mantra echoing endlessly inside his mind, dispelling the darkness.

No monsters Howard, no monsters.

There were no monsters. It was just a dream, just his imagination, just his mind playing tricks on him.

No monsters Howard, no monsters.

Listen to mummy. She knows best, she knows what's real and what's not. Listen to her, her words, her wisdom.

No monsters Howard, no monsters.

Howard began to whisper the words with her now, joining in the chanting game, blindly believing.

No monsters Howard, no monsters.

No monsters Howard, no monsters.

No monsters Howard, no monsters.

With clenched fists, he drove away the voices of the night, purging their memory as if they had never existed. Fantasy and wild imagination were banished to their rightful place.

No monsters Howard, no monsters.

Awareness of the room around him returned and with it, the warm embrace of his mother's arms, her wide and loving smile drying the tears on his face.

He was safe now.

WEDNESDAY 8:14 AM

Time to get into it.

Cracking his knuckles, Sergeant Douglas McDougall entered the sound-proofed interrogation room, a bandage around his neck. Brian sat impassively at an empty table, handcuffed behind his back. Constable Robert Harrington stood by the doorway, baton in hand. Douglas and Brian exchanged a steady gaze.

"Good morning, Brian."

Brian grunted.

Douglas walked to stand before a chair opposite Brian, smiling down at him. "Close the door please, Robert."

"You're not even getting your lackey to fetch a syringe this time." Brian said to Douglas. "Trying to keep up appearances, hey?"

Douglas stepped towards him. "I'm glad you're handcuffed behind now, Brian."

Brian didn't flinch.

"Makes it a lot easier to do this." Douglas smacked his fist into the side of Brian's nose. Brian lurched sideways as blood began to trickle down onto his shirt.

Brian coughed and spat bloody phlegm onto the floor next to him. He raised himself to turn to Douglas. "Does it make you feel a man to know that this is the only way you can beat the shit out of me?"

"Does it make you feel a man to know that I'm going to kill you because you won't cooperate?"

Brian took a deep breath and exhaled slowly. "I'll cooperate."

Douglas raised his eyebrows. "A change of heart, Brian? That's unlike you."

"I'll cooperate providing you set me free and leave me and my family alone. Otherwise no deal."

"You do everything I say or I *will* kill you. That's the deal."

Brian took another deep breath. "Okay."

Douglas' face was beaming. "Excellent."

Rubbing his hands together, Douglas took a few paces away and turned to face Brian. "First of all, let me tell you-"

"First of all, tell me why you're even bothering to recruit me," Brian interrupted. "When according to you, it makes no difference?"

"Let's just say it's important for operational security."

Brian snorted, blowing bubbles of blood out of his nostrils. "For the fucking aliens? Or you?"

"You cannot understand how fortunate you are to be given this opportunity."

"How's it feel to be their puppet? Always knew you were a spineless sheep looking for a new arse to lick."

Douglas clenched his teeth and turned to the statuesque Robert. "Robert, pass me that baton, would you?"

Robert robotically passed his baton to Douglas.

"Who else have you got in your arse-licking cult?"

Douglas' hand tightened on the baton as he advanced towards Brian.

"Forensics? Homicide? What about the media?"

Douglas slugged Brian across the face, splitting his lips. Brian spat more blood and laughed back at Douglas.

"Do you want to die?" Douglas said.

Brian smiled. "Nah, I wanna join. What do I do?"

Douglas smashed the baton across Brian's face again. "Shut up and I will tell you!"

Brian smirked. "But why are you so keen for me to join?"

Douglas leaned forward into Brian's bruised and bleeding face. "If you knew why you were so important, then I'd definitely have to kill you, which I'm going to do anyway if you ask one more question!"

"Is it because I actually have the balls to stand up against you arse-lickers?"

Douglas drew his pistol on Brian...

Then there was a knocking sound at the door.

"Oh, for Christ's sake! Didn't I say that there were to be no interruptions!" Douglas cursed. He gestured at Robert standing next to the door. "Get that, will you."

Robert nodded and opened the door, revealing Constable Annette Baker, distressed and shaking.

Her cries flooded the room. "Constables James and Lisa are under attack and need our help!"

Douglas turned from Brian to the door. "What the hell are you babbling about? Where are they?"

"At Frank Weston's house. They've turned on us, Douglas!" Annette panted. "They've already killed Constables Barry and Peter!"

Douglas planted his face in his hand. "Shit! Why does this have to happen now?"

Brian shifted forward in his chair.

Douglas looked up at Robert trembling and Annette white-faced. "Look, you two will have to go and check this out now whilst I deal with this here. Let me know what you find."

Robert nodded and Annette spoke up. "But there's no other officers on duty. There's no one else to mind the station."

"Well, then get someone here."

Annette lowered her voice, "Douglas, there *is* no one else."

"Well, call Benalla. Call D24 in Wangaratta. JUST GET SOMEONE!"

"Okay." Annette cast her eyes to Brian. He returned a smirk.

Robert and Annette scurried off, closing the door behind them. Douglas returned to his subject...

Just as Brian launched from his seat to slam the top of his skull into Douglas' face.

Douglas toppled backwards and Brian landed on top of him. Brian reached for Douglas' pistol and a desperate struggle ensued.

The gun fired and Brian pulled free from Douglas and scrambled to his feet. Brian held the pistol behind his back in his handcuffed hands, pointing it side-on at Douglas who lay writhing at his feet, his stomach soaked with purple blood.

"Even when I'm handcuffed and outnumbered, you're no match for me, Douglas."

Agonised, Douglas raised himself up on one arm.

"I was never gunna join. You should have killed me when you had your chance."

Douglas vainly raised a palm in resistance, "Listen, Brian–"

And then the gun fired again.

"Cos I won't make the same mistake you just did." Brian finished, stepping over Douglas' now lifeless body to get his keys...

, , ,

"CONSTABLE KLOPSKI, ARE YOU THERE?" Annette shouted into the headset.

Annette looked over at Robert and shook her head. "I'm not getting anything."

"I'm not getting anything either. There's no signal on any band."

"Maybe something's wrong with our transmitter. Try calling D24."

There was the muffled sound of a gunshot from the interrogation room.

Annette frowned. "That's the second one. You better go check that out, Robert."

Robert hesitated.

"I'll call D24. Now you go."

Robert nodded, his hands trembling as he started off down the corridor towards the interrogation room. Annette dialled a line to D24...

But the line was only static like every other.

, , ,

Robert stepped carefully down the corridor, pistol outstretched. Ahead on the right side lay the door to the interrogation room. Beyond the corridor reached a t-junction where a holding cell could be seen, currently occupied by the young man that came in last night. There were no signs of activity from this direction.

Robert reached the closed door to the interrogation room. Pistol in one hand, he gently turned the doorhandle with the other...

The door swung open to reveal an apparently uninhabited room. A pool of purple blood had collected on the floor amidst the scattered arrangement of the desk and chairs. The blood trailed out of sight to the corner behind the door. He stepped forward...

"Don't move," said Brian quietly as he placed the barrel of his pistol against the back of Robert's head.

Robert twitched with fright and froze.

Brian stepped back into the interrogation room and closed the door behind him, revealing Douglas' bloody corpse in the corner.

"Please don't kill me, Brian. I was only following orders."

"That all depends, Robert," Brian said as he deftly disarmed Robert and put him into handcuffs, "on the colour of your blood."

Brian shot him in the foot. Robert fell to the floor in agony.

"You deserved that anyway," Brian said.

A purple trickle emerged from the side of Robert's shoe.

Robert struggled to his knees. "Please, Brian! It's not my fault! They made me become one of them!"

Brian levelled his gun at Robert's head. "Now it's your turn to answer questions. Tell me what you know and how I can stop them. Then I might let you live."

Robert began to cry. "They make us *Halform* so that they can blend in with you. But *Halform* are not like them – they do not die as we do!"

Brian cocked his pistol. "Now I know you're lying. I've already killed one."

Robert shook his head. "No, Brian. You didn't!"

The door flew open. Annette's bulky frame stood in the doorway holding a shotgun. Brian stood in her firing line, his weapon aimed at Robert.

"Drop it, Brian, or you're dead," Annette said.

Brian looked over his shoulder at Annette... And sighed.

"You've got three seconds to drop your weapon. Then I shoot."

Brian hesitated, glancing around the room.

"One... Two..."

Brian dropped his pistol. Annette and Robert both relaxed.

"Now kick it over," Annette ordered.

Brian grimaced in reluctance.

"Three seconds to die, Brian, counting one..."

Brian's lips pinched together as he booted the pistol at her. It flew across the room and into her thick shins with a fleshy thud.

"I ought to shoot you for that," Annette said without flinching.

Brian shrugged as he looked over at Robert rising slowly to his feet and backing away.

Then Annette bent down to pick up Brian's pistol...

You stupid bitch.

In the time it took for Annette to reach past her torso, Brian had crossed the room to take a running kick at her lowered head. His foot smashed into her face, throwing her backwards in a spray of spittle, teeth and purple blood. She landed on the other side of the corridor, whilst the pistol landed near his feet.

Purple, eh?

A bloody smile cracked Annette's lips as her eyes opened onto the barrel of Brian's pistol staring down at her.

"I cannot–"

She ate the first bullet before the next two struck her forehead, silencing her.

Brian regarded the mangled remains of Annette before him and Douglas' corpse in the corner of the room. Satisfied they moved no more, Brian turned to Robert whimpering against the wall...

"What do I do with you?"

WEDNESDAY 8:41 AM

Consciousness assembled slowly...

A horrid stench of unclean beasts. A pervasive red glow, the borders of which flickered with moving figures. Minds in whispered conversation: *"We cannot take him... He slips from our grasp."*

⁊   ⁊   ⁊

The cold, hard reality of the room materialised into being around Jason. Leather straps bound him to a bed, digging into the flesh on his wrists and ankles. High on the wall facing him, sunlight entered through a small, brick-lined window blocked by iron bars. Dull grey brick walls surrounded him, tangled cobwebs hanging from their corners. Not far behind the dusty pillow his head rested on, he could make out the stout iron bars of his police cell.

What the fuck just happened?

The sound of keys jiggled in the lock behind his head.

Jason stretched his head back to see an officer, slightly built and boyish-looking, slide aside the bars to his cell. Smiling, the officer limped through the entrance and looked down at him.

"What the fuck is going on?" Jason demanded.

Giggling, the officer drew out his pistol and pointed it at Jason's head.

"Aaahhh! For fuck's sake, what are you doing?"

The officer giggled again but said nothing.

I'm going to die!

Then there was a voice from the corridor behind them, "I knew I should have killed you Robert, you slimy fuck."

The officer called Robert turned to the voice without taking the gun off Jason. "If you shoot me Brian, I'll shoot him."

Brian's answer was nonchalant. "Fine."

Jason interjected, "Hey! I haven't done anything! I don't even know how I got here!"

Neither of them answered Jason.

"Tell me how you got out of those handcuffs before I kill you like the worm you are," Brian said.

"I believe I can answer that," came a third voice further away and deeper than the rest.

Two shots from different pistols fired in quick succession and Jason heard bodies crashing to the ground. The officer nearest him was one of them.

Then everything was still.

Jason angled his head around, but could see only walls and ceiling. His heart hammered in his brain.

Tell me I'm fucking dreaming!

Wait... Someone's moving. And it's not the officer who'd fallen next to me...

I can't believe this is happening! I'm fucked! I can't do anything!

Down the corridor, someone burst into laughter and declared, "Douglas, you fuck! You shot your own man, haha!"

A dull thud sounded from the proximity of the speaker, followed by a low groan.

"I dunno how you got back up, you determined bastard,

but I'm gunna make sure that *this* time, you don't get up again."

A rasping reply, pained and furious, "I'm already dead, Brian! And I'll–"

The gun sounded twice more. Silence followed.

Excruciating silence. Seconds passed in agonising, surreal slow-motion... Unrelenting.

Then came the sound of approaching footsteps...

The middle-aged face of an officer emerged into view. Solid, a little unshaven like himself, with intense blue-grey eyes.

The officer smiled. "It's your lucky day!"

"Worst fucking day of my life! Um... What is going on?"

The officer bent down to retrieve a pistol from the body at his feet, pausing to check the body wasn't moving.

He rose and looked back at Jason. "I wish I knew. Have you used a gun before?" He held out a pistol to Jason, even though he was still bound to the bed.

Jason frowned. "Yeah... I do have a shooting licence. But–"

"Good, 'cos you may have to use it if you wanna get out of here alive."

Jason forced a laugh. "Well yeah, I would like to get out of here alive. But tell me what's going on first. I need to know!"

"Look, I don't know either. All I can say is that some major supernatural shit is going on and we're getting out of here."

Jason nodded with a look of confusion. "Riiight."

Brian began to loosen the straps immobilising Jason. "Once we get to safety, we'll be able to talk. But right now we're not safe. It's only a matter of time before someone or *something* comes here looking for us."

Jason didn't ask any more questions after that.

WEDNESDAY 10:57 AM

Seeking.

Bernard drove down the highway to Melbourne, passing sodden paddocks dotted with glum cattle and trees. Rain hissed like static on the windscreen, dulling his senses but channelling his thoughts.

The therapy session with Danny Malone was almost precisely this time yesterday. And yet Bernard still struggled to make sense of it...

Either he himself was suffering psychosis, or these demons Danny perceived were real.

He clearly heard that unearthly malicious voice at the end of yesterday's session, simultaneously issuing from Danny and the phone Bernard held. Yet the recording he made bore no trace of any such voice, an unexplained anomaly considering it detected the background wind.

And as horrifying as it all was, it was also familiar...

Henry Wilcox, a former schizophrenic patient, spoke in that same horrid voice whilst under hypnosis and was of a similar age then to Danny now. He was also the same patient that Danny referred to in yesterday's session...

Henry's hallucinations and delusions were compelling in a way that even now, almost ten years later, Bernard loathed to contemplate. At times, notably the last time he saw Henry, he actually shared the hallucinations: an untenable situation. He terminated future appointments with Henry and sought psychiatric help for himself. He lost contact with the Wilcox family and two years passed before Bernard practiced again. In the years since, memories of events faded and were easily dismissed as fictional.

But now, by some cruel machination of fate, the *Dark Horde* as Henry called them, had returned to haunt Bernard: driving him to seek answers.

Bernard made contact with Henry's mother Mary this morning... And learnt that Henry was reported missing only two days ago and had left what appeared to be a suicide note on tape.

He immediately left for Melbourne to see her.

, , ,

Shortly before midday, Bernard reached Mary's house: a modest home on a quiet street in Ivanhoe, ten kilometres north east of Melbourne's centre.

It was still raining.

Bernard parked his car on the kerb and looked up at the neatly presented brick-veneer house with a patent dread...

What horrors hide within these walls, waiting to be revealed?

Bernard grabbed his briefcase and stepped out into the rain with his umbrella open. Strong winds lashed him, drenching his suit and seeping chill into his bones.

He followed a paved driveway lined with rose bushes to the front door, noting that curtains were drawn across all the windows.

Curious.

He pressed the doorbell and stepped back. He stood awkwardly in the rain a few moments before ringing again with greater insistence.

But only the wind howled in reply.

Bernard chomped his mouth as he considered his options. Nonchalant, he shrugged and tried the doorhandle...

It was unlocked. Bernard stepped back, frowning in thought.

What should I do now? Surely I should enter? That's why I tested the handle, isn't it?

His heart racing, Bernard opened the front door, adrenalin honing his senses...

An orderly lounge greeted him, featuring an olive velvet sofa and chairs around a dormant fireplace. A bitter stench stained the air and past the kitchen on the other side of the room, chanting could be heard, interspersed with animalistic grunts.

"We are as one, as many are we..."

Bernard called out, "Hello? Is anybody home?"

"Become one, once more be..."

Too horrified for rational thought, Bernard strode forward towards the sound, leaving his briefcase and umbrella by the door...

I have to know.

"We are as one, as many are we..."

As Bernard crept past the kitchen and into the dining room beyond, an empty mug crashed from the dining table onto the carpet. He jolted in fright but there was no perpetrator to be seen.

Chants and grunts issued from a tape in a stereo against the wall facing him. Half-eaten butter and bread lay on the table next to a box of tissues. A glass side door overlooked a still garden and the door to the rest of the house was closed.

Maybe it was just sheer random chance that I happened to enter at the moment the mug overbalanced... I hope so.

"Hellooo? Hellooo?" he called again.

Only the tape answered, *"Become one, once more be..."*

The recording stirred unwelcome memories, releasing hidden terrors of his inner psyche...

Time to turn that blasted tape off.

Bernard moved to the stereo and was shocked to see that the tape had already stopped and yet the sound continued unabated, driven by some unseen force.

In blind panic, he turned off every stereo switch he could find. Silence ensued and relief washed over him...

Then the phone rang.

Bernard spun around to stare suspiciously at the phone ringing on the cluttered kitchen bench behind him.

Surely I should get it? I am here lawfully after all.

With a sigh, he relented.

"Hello, Wilcox residence."

"Good morning sir, this is Senior Sergeant Brian Derwent of Howqua Hills Police Station."

"Oh, thank goodness!" Bernard wiped sweat from his brow.

"Whom would I be speaking to?"

"Dr Bernard Russell. I'm just visiting here and–"

"Ahhh, you're Henry Wilcox's former psychiatrist, right?"

"Yes, that's correct. How did you come to know that so readily?"

"You were on my list of people to contact regarding Henry Wilcox. Are you there with his parents now?"

"Well, I had arranged to meet Mary Wilcox here, however I have just arrived to find the house abandoned–"

"Shit."

"With some strange recording, I believe Henry's, playing on the stereo."

"What do you mean by strange?"

"Um..."

At that moment, the stereo leapt back into unearthly life, this time in that horrible demonic voice he knew only too well...

"Weee are as oneee, as manyyy are weee."

Bernard shuddered so violently he almost dropped the phone. "Like that! Can you hear it? It's playing of its own accord!"

"Becomeee oneee, once moreee beee."

"Actually, I can only hear you."

The voice intensified, *"WEEE ARE AS ONEEE!"*

"It's getting so loud I can hardly hear you!"

"AS MANYYY ARE WEEE!"

"Look, whatever's going on, I think you'd better get out of there."

"Agreed!"

"BECOMEEE ONEEE!"

"Can you meet me at Ivanhoe station *tonight* at 9pm?"

Bernard replied, "Did you say Ivanhoe station 9pm?"

"ONCE MOREEE BEEE!"

"Yes, it's vitally important that we speak as soon as possible."

Then the front door slammed. Heavy breathing followed.

"Something's coming in the front door!"

"Then run!"

And run he did, dropping the phone and bolting out of the glass side door...

As laughter chased his heels.

WEDNESDAY 12:01 PM

The final battle.

He rolled over the bunker and surged in, machine gun blazing, a merciless destroyer, obliterating all in his way.

One of the enemies leapt from a bush nearby. It was Jake with a thick wooden stick – a fearsome bazooka – on his shoulder and preparing to fire.

"Ah-ah-ah-ah!" Tom went, sweeping across Jake in an arc of imaginary bullets.

Jake stood unmoving and fired his deadly weapon back. "Bqwa!"

"I shot you first!" Tom protested, lowering his stick.

"Did not!"

"You're a cheat, Jake! I shot you first and you know it!"

Running footsteps approached. Tom turned to face them...

"Ah-ah-ah-ah-ah! Got ya!" Paul boomed as he shot Tom. "Start counting!"

Jake turned to Tom. "Okay you got me, Tom. But we're both counting now, hahaha."

"YOU'RE STILL A CHEAT!" Tom shouted as he ran off counting, trying to put as much distance between him and the other two as possible.

Jake and Paul looked at each other.

"You counted to twenty yet?" Paul said.

"Haha yeah, near enough." Jake grinned.

"Let's get him."

Suddenly, two others joined them from across the oval: Howard and Arthur, carrying half-eaten sandwiches and fruit.

"Can we play?" Howard said.

Paul screwed his face with sudden hate. "Arthur can play, but we aren't gunna let *you* play! Your dad's a murderer!"

"HE IS NOT!" shouted Howard.

"What did you say that for, Paul?" Jake said. "His dad's going after the murderer with your dad!"

Paul spat and leered at the shorter Howard. "My dad, not your dad, is the boss of the police now. And he told me last night that your dad is the killer!"

"I'll kill you!" Howard said as he hurled his sandwiches at Paul.

By the time Paul said "Missed!" Howard had followed up his attack.

Paul pulled away from a punch glancing his cheek. Another one Howard threw caught only air as Paul stepped clear. For a moment they faced off against each other with clenched fists.

Arthur stood petrified.

Jake grinned and began chanting, "Fight! Fight! Fight! Fight!"

"C'mon, killer!" Paul taunted.

Howard ran at Paul blindly, doing windmills with his arms. Jake laughed as Paul easily stepped clear of Howard's wild swings and crash-tackled him side-on to the ground. Paul landed on Howard and immediately began throwing punches of his own at Howard's head.

Arthur finally acted to defend his best friend, rushing in to pull Paul off Howard by the shoulders. Paul landed one more thump into Howard's face before relenting and allowing Howard up. Howard was covered in dirt but seemingly unhurt save a fat lip.

"Are you okay?" Arthur said, putting a hand on Howard's shoulder.

Howard didn't take his eyes off Paul, who returned the stare. "Yeah."

Tom had wandered back with Jeremy, the only other ones playing. "What's going on?" he said.

Jake looked over at the new arrivals. "Paul and Howard are having a fight and Howard's losing haha."

Paul taunted Howard again, "C'mon wimp, have another go!"

Arthur stepped in front of Howard to block his view. "Howard! Give it a rest, will ya?"

"C'mon, fight!" Jake hollered.

Arthur turned to Jake. "No more fighting!"

Tom spoke up, "Yeah c'mon guys, we'll get in trouble."

Jake laughed. "If Howard isn't already! Just look at him!"

"And Paul," Arthur reminded him.

"Maybe we should play something else," Tom suggested.

"Let's play chasey!" Jeremy said.

"I'm not playing with him!" Howard pointed at Paul.

"No one was asking you!" Paul retorted.

"C'mon guys, shake and make up." Arthur dragged Howard and Paul's hands together.

Jake looked disappointed, but Tom and Jeremy encouraged the idea. Eventually the combatants shook hands limply.

"Say sorry to Howard for what you said, Paul," Arthur said.

Paul smirked. "Sorry."

"And say that you didn't mean it."

"I didn't mean it."

I don't believe you one bit, Paul, and I hate you more than ever. But I guess I'll let it drop for now and get on with the game. We'll settle this later...

"Yeah, okay," Howard muttered.

"Alright everyone, put your foot in," Jeremy said.

Arthur, Tom, Jake and Paul put a foot forward into a circle around Jeremy's foot.

Paul looked at Howard. "You playin', wimp?"

Jake laughed and Howard shot back, "You're the wimp!"

"STOP IT GUYS!" Arthur shouted.

Howard sighed and put his foot into the circle opposite Paul. Jeremy crouched down to tap their shoes in a clockwise fashion as he said a rhyme:

"There's- a- party- on- the- hill- would- you- like- to- come?"

Jake's finger stopped on Paul's boot.

"Yes," Paul said.

"Then- bring- some- friends- and- a- bottle- of- rum."

Jake stopped on Arthur's foot now, who recited, "Can't afford it."

"Then- get- lost."

Jake finished on his own shoe, so he was out. With five left now, he started the rhyme again.

"Nah, that one takes ages, do this one," said Jake, "Ip- dip- dog- shit- stuck- on- your- shoe- and- you're- it!"

Jake's finger was pointing at Paul's foot.

"I'm it," Paul said smiling.

The boys scattered across the oval away from Paul who stood covering his eyes. Jeremy called over his shoulder, "AND COUNT TO FIFTY THIS TIME!"

"FIFTY?" Paul shouted back, but his voice was lost to the wind.

Paul counted to twenty, before deciding that would do

and opened his eyes. He saw Tom, the slowest runner, heading for the shelter shed on the other side of the oval.

As a predator moving in for the kill, he began his pursuit.

Tom reached the asphalt near the shelter shed and slowed to a walk to regain his breath. He looked behind him to see if Paul had finished counting yet...

Straight at Paul a few metres away, charging at him like a hungry beast.

"Shit!" he cursed and he started running again for the shed only twenty metres away.

Paul pushed his body to its limits trying to reach Tom before he reached the shed, but Tom just beat him.

He skidded past the entrance to the corrugated iron shed as Tom called from inside, "You can't get me in here! It's barley!"

Paul conceded the point that Tom was safe and left to search for other victims...

Howard was heading for the shelter shed too, going the long route via the adventure playground. His bruises ached and all he wanted to do was sit down. The shed meant barley and a chance to recover. He could go to the sick bay but didn't want to draw attention to himself. He wasn't a wimp. He was tough, like his dad Brian, and smarter than stupid Paul and his dad.

As he approached the entrance to the shed, a familiar mantra began to repeat in his head:

No monsters Howard, no monsters.

Then Paul stepped around the corner, blocking his path to salvation.

Howard took a step back. "Are you it?"

Paul sneered, "Not for long!" as he launched himself at Howard.

Howard bolted for the adventure playground. Paul gave chase, determined to run him down.

His face and chest burning, Howard ran through the crowded playground, past the slide, zigzagging through swings and ducking under the monkey bars. Icy wind howled in his ears and the beast followed relentlessly, murder in its throat.

The mantra in his head grew ever louder, now mocking:

No monsters Howard, no monsters.

As the beast drew ever nearer.

The mantra in his head became a mangled hybrid of guttural roars, all chanting in unison:

No monsters Howard, no monsters.

He fought to exorcise the demonic voices, as his lungs fought for breath and his body screamed for respite. With the beast in relentless pursuit, he ran on towards the basketball courts.

No monsters Howard, no monsterrrs.

Suddenly Paul slapped him on the back. "You're it!"

Howard slowed to a stop, defeated.

The monsters had won.

Paul laughed like a manic beast and dashed off across the busy playground. Howard's head and shoulders slumped forward in exhausted defeat.

Then the voice of the School Secretary blared from the loudspeakers nearby, "Would Howard Derwent please collect his bag and go to the reception office *immediately*. Thank you."

⁊   ⁊   ⁊

Waiting for Howard in the otherwise vacant reception office was a tall, gaunt man in police uniform... Paul's dad,

Sergeant Douglas McDougall. His brow was furrowed, his thick black moustache framing a grim expression.

"Don't be alarmed Howard, but I need to take you with me now."

Howard stopped before Douglas' imposing edifice. "Why, what's happened?"

Douglas took Howard by the hand, pulling him towards the carpark outside. "I'll have to explain on the way, there's no time now."

"Am I in trouble?"

Douglas smirked as he led Howard out to the waiting 4WD police car. "Not yet."

Held in the strong man's grip, Howard was unable to pull away. He saw that they were alone in the carpark. "What do you mean, not yet?"

Douglas reached the vehicle and produced a pair of handcuffs, which he slammed on Howard before he could move. Ignoring Howard's cries, he opened the backdoor of the 4WD and pushed him inside. The backdoor slammed and Douglas climbed into the driver's seat.

Howard saw through tears Douglas smiling at him in the rear-vision mirror.

"Now you're in trouble," Douglas said.

WEDNESDAY 2:08 PM

*Under foreboding skies, dark with malice,
the humans gathered...*

*Like a colony of ants. Insects blind to their presence, hidden in
the shadows, just as they were blind to their design or destiny.*

The Oberon Grammar students at Timberhome
assembled on the flagstone courtyard outside the dining
hall, preparing to disembark for their weekly hike. Lucas
regarded his flock from his lofty principal's office, quietly
sipping his tea. He was proud of the confident, able
creatures they had become, now capable of packing,
hiking, camping and cooking independently.

Almost two hundred and twenty five young adults, save
for a handful of sick, diligently emptied their hiking packs
for the outdoors staff who checked they had the essentials:
map, compasses, hiking instructions, torches, water
bottles, tents, pegs and poles, sleeping bags and mats,
cooking equipment, raincoats, spare clothing and
toiletries. The students were then issued food, toilet paper,
soap and plastic garbage bags for waterproofing, which
they happily divided among their hike-groups of six,
packing everything back into their packs. Lucas marvelled
at their diligent cooperation like efficient components in a
prodigious machine.

Unaware what awaited them...

Matron Susan Inglis, a well-dressed mature woman with

auburn hair tied in a bun, emerged from the sanatorium nearby and approached him.

"Good afternoon, Lucas." She smiled.

"Good afternoon, Susan. How fare the students in your expert care?"

She swallowed. "Well... Tracy of N Unit and Matthew and Stuart of D Unit have gastro, and Tim Hamilton will be in the San for another week before both his arm casts can come off."

Lucas nodded. "And what about the other boy... What's his name?"

"You mean Danny?"

Lucas laughed awkwardly. "Yes, Danny Malone. He's still okay to be hiking today, is he?"

Susan sighed. "Well, he is in perfect physical health according to Howqua Hills Hospital and the checks I did this morning but..."

Lucas furrowed his brow. "His mental health?"

"Yes. I mean I guess he's okay to be hiking, but I think that there's something not quite right with him."

"What do you mean?"

"I can't quite put my finger on it, but it's almost as if he's recovered too quickly. He's a new person suddenly, happier than he's ever been. It just seems I dunno, too weird."

Lucas shrugged and smiled. "Well, all of God's creatures were created unique. Danny's just different from the other kids and if he's healthy and happier than he's ever been, so much the better!"

"Yes, but I think even the psychiatrist was weirded out by him."

"Weirded out by him? I didn't get that impression when I spoke to him yesterday afternoon. He told me that Danny had recovered."

"Yes, but to me, and I know this sounds strange, but Dr Russell seemed strangely I dunno, dismissive yesterday all of a sudden. He left suddenly too."

Lucas shrugged again. "Oh well, maybe he's just a busy man. I think everything will be okay, Susan, and there's no real reason to expect anything else."

"Yes well, I hope you're right." Susan grimaced. "Anyway, the Hike Masters know about it and they'll have anti-psychotics to give him if needed."

"Sounds good, Susan. You're doing a fantastic job as usual."

They both turned their attention to Jodie Moffatt, the physical education teacher, as she began to brief the students from the dining-hall steps: "Okay school, we're going to make a start whilst we have a good break in the weather. But first I'll go through the route again, especially for those of you who haven't familiarised yourselves with the map that's been up here on the notice board since last week."

The congregation quietened and the speaker continued:

"As you know, we're doing the Eagles' Peaks hike. It's a fairly easy hike, especially since the second day is a day hike where you'll return to the same place you camped on the first night."

John of I Unit stood next to his mate Nathan and pumped the air. "That's mad! I love day hikes!"

Nathan smiled. "Who doesn't?"

As Nathan looked back at John, he saw Danny of H Unit a short distance away. Danny was sitting on his pack, away from the others in his hiking group, chin in his palms and staring at the ground...

Danny's knee had almost completely healed. Only a purplish bruise remained in evidence of the gory wound he had yesterday.

Mrs Moffatt went on, "We take the track going up past Oldham Weir to where it meets the Howqua track at the foot of Bald Hill, which we then follow uphill to Warrambat saddle. From there we take the south fork, which will be marked with the usual orange tape, past Red Hill and then downhill following Black Dog Creek towards the Howqua River following the orange markers. Once reaching Howqua River, you'll see the campsite next to Fry's hut."

"Fry's hut? Oh mad!" John said.

Nathan wasn't paying attention. He was staring at that knee...

It's not possible for it to have healed so quickly, is it? I'm sure I saw Danny cut it open yesterday – the flesh was hanging off!

"We won't be using Fry's hut, of course; it's across the other side of the river anyway. But there *is* a woodshed nearby, with plenty of wood for us to use. Tomorrow we head off bright and early, for Eagles' peaks. I'll brief you tomorrow morning on the route before we leave."

Danny looked up with bloodshot ashen eyes to see Nathan staring at him and spoke in a harsh voice, "What are *you* looking at."

Nathan shivered and looked away reflexively.

Did Danny's lips even move?

Mrs Moffatt clapped her hands. "We'll start with Units I and J this week, since it's their turn to go first."

Nathan's hiking group and the other hiking groups from his Unit hauled their packs on and began to make their way towards Mrs Moffatt and the track beyond.

"Time to roll like Jewish foreskins!" John said, giving Nathan a playful jab.

Nathan needed no further encouragement, suddenly determined to put as much distance between himself and Danny as possible...

And so the exodus began.

WEDNESDAY 2:53 PM

Amused by the humans' folly, they watched...

Fragile, helpless creatures, blindly stumbling towards their demise.

Yet sooo arousing.

Nathan hiked with the other five members of his hiking group: John, Kev, Richo, Mouldy and Spaz. They slowly hiked up the bracken-lined track leading from the school past the Weir, which was overgrown with blackberries and stinging nettles, to Warrambat saddle. A little ahead and far behind them stretched a long chain of the other hike groups and staff...

Like a trail of ants.

At Warrambat saddle, the track met others at a clearing walled by grey weepy Peppermints. Above, the sun shone defiantly over the heads of grey cloud. A signpost stood at the edge of a muddy puddle announcing various destinations:

Mount Warrambat summit to the east 1.1 kilometres, Fry's Hut 4.9 kilometres to the south and a 4WD road led west 8.3 kilometres to Lower Howqua. On a mossy rock at the foot of the signpost was a blue Tupperware container. John opened it and signed the logbook inside for his hike group.

"Man, I need to re-adjust my pack," Richo said as he slung his hiking pack, half the size he was, from his slight frame onto the ground.

"Bit heavy, Richo?" John laughed.

Richo unclipped the hood of his pack and began to pull out the plastic-bag wrapped contents. "It's all weighted on one side. It's fucking killing me."

Spaz looked on vacantly, Mouldy studied trees and Kev sat down on a rotted stump that sported a couple of fungus discs on its side. A couple of metres from Kev, a magpie foraged through leafy debris, unperturbed by his presence. Staff and other hike groups passed them by, notably some of the hot chicks from Unit O.

Nathan looked worried. "C'mon guys! Everyone's passing us! Let's go."

"Yeah alright!" Richo snapped. "Just give us a fucking second, will ya."

Nathan sighed with impatience.

"What's the hurry, Nathan?" said John.

"I just wanna get there, that's all."

Kev suddenly jumped from the stump he was sitting on, frantically brushing large black bull ants from his legs and buttocks. "Ah fuck, that hurts!"

John, Mouldy and Spaz laughed.

Kev stepped clear of the swarming ants, rubbing his hip. "One of those little bastards bit me!"

John checked the wound and smiled at Kev. "You'll be alright."

Nathan and Mouldy gave Richo a hand organising his pack and Spaz just stood there in a daze occasionally moving to shoo flies.

Getting close now.

"Is everyone right to go?" Nathan asked, looking down the path behind them at the next group of advancing hikers.

Kev and Mouldy nodded and started down the trail

marked with orange tape to Fry's Hut. Richo rose wincing as he hauled his pack on. John walked next to Nathan, and Spaz dawdled along behind, trying to read the map as they walked.

Closer...

"C'MON SPAZ, CATCH UP!" Nathan yelled.

Spaz looked up to see his group twenty or so metres ahead of him. He tucked the map into his waist, secured by the wide belt of his pack and jogged forward to catch up.

"You can look at the map later," Nathan said.

"Just don't lose it," added John.

The track wound its way through a dense forest of gum trees and bracken, staying mostly level as they passed Red Hill, before following Black Dog Creek down a gully to where it met the Howqua River.

In the shadow of the mountain ridge, the forest was much cooler and wetter, blanketed by heavy dew. Manna Gums towered over them, bark hanging off their ebony trunks like flesh peeling from the bone. The air, thick with the smell of eucalyptus, was strangely still, like a breath held.

Nathan paused a moment to look up at the trees...

Wonder where all the birds have gone?

The group hiked on through the silent landscape, minds too laboured to talk or to admire the serene beauty around them...

Oblivious.

The track became overgrown with ferns, rocks and fallen trees. There was no sign of the orange markers or the other hike groups.

Kev was at the front and stopped to look back at the others. "Are we going the right way?"

"I dunno," Mouldy answered. "I was following you, Kev."

"Oh, that's fucking great, isn't it," Nathan said.

Richo seized the opportunity to remove his pack and rest.

"Well, let's check the map," said Kev. "Who's got it?"

"Spaz had it last," John said.

Everyone's gaze turned to Spaz...

"I didn't have it last, did I?"

"Spaaaz! You spaz! Haha!" said Richo, sitting on his pack and pulling a muesli bar out of his pocket.

"Spaz, you idiot!" said Nathan. "You were looking at it before instead of where you were walking!"

Spaz made a goofy grin. "Oh yeah."

Nathan clipped him over the head in frustration.

Then something large crashed ferociously through the trees nearby. It passed quickly, heading in the same direction they were...

Unseen.

"What the fuck was that?" Kev said.

"Kangaroo, I hope," John answered.

Richo stood shaking. "Bullshit it was a kangaroo! Sounded more like an elephant!"

"Not that we have any of them here," Kev said. "Whatever it was, it's going the same way we were."

Nathan raised steadying hands. "Well, we need to establish whether we were even *going* the right way."

"I reckon we were going the wrong way," Richo said.

Nathan turned to Richo. "Well, nice of you to tell us that *now*, isn't it, Richo?"

Richo raised his pitch. "Oh, fuck off! You were following too!"

John stepped between them. "C'mon guys. Let's figure out where we're supposed to go." He turned to Spaz, who was looking in the direction of noise they'd heard. "Spazzy. Where did you put the map?"

Spaz rummaged through his pockets, getting more agitated the longer he searched. With everyone's reproachful gaze on him, he took his pack off and began to search its contents.

"Hey, that's right," Nathan pointed to the now unclipped belt of Spaz's pack. "I saw you put the map in your belt there."

Spaz made another goofy grin. "Oh yeah, I did too."

Nathan squeezed his face in his palm. "Spaz, you're a *fuckin'* idiot!"

Spaz scanned the ground in the vicinity: a vain attempt.

Nathan looked at the others and shook his head. "He's fuckin' lost it. I don't believe this shit!"

No one said anything.

Distant thunder erupted. The sky grew darker.

Nathan spoke again, "Whose idea was it anyway to give this fuckin' retard the map?"

Kev started to rub his arms. "It doesn't matter now, Nathan. I say we start going back. This has to be the wrong way."

"Nah, we seemed to be following a track." John said. "I reckon we might as well keep going for a bit and see where this one leads. It'll probably join back up with the right path further on."

"Not with that fucking thing out there!" Richo protested.

"Richo, we have to go that way *anyway*," John answered him.

"Well John, why can't we see anyone else here?" Kev said. "We must have missed a turn."

"Look, how about John goes up ahead to see where this path leads and whether it joins back up. The rest of us will wait for him here," suggested Nathan.

"Nah fuck this, I'm not waiting," said Kev. "I'm gunna head back the way we came. This is bullshit!"

"Kev, I'll only be a few minutes and you know we're not supposed to split the group," John said. "Just wait here, will ya?"

Kev sighed and rolled his eyes. "Alright then. Be quick."

John threw off his pack and started jogging down the track, disappearing into the forest soon after...

It began to rain.

,　,　,

The five of them sat in sombre huddles among sodden puddles. Steady rain fell, dripping off the limp skin of trees and soaking through their raincoats and into their bones. They called out for John a few times, but had no reply.

"How long's John been?" said Richo, his teeth chattering. "I'm freezing!"

"At least twenty minutes," said Mouldy.

"Maybe I should go up ahead and see where he is. He might have hurt himself," suggested Nathan.

"He might have found that thing," said Richo.

There was an uncomfortable silence.

"Shit Nathan, we might as well all go," said Kev.

The others agreed: no one wanted to be left alone.

Lightning flashed nearby them, sending strobes across the gloomy sky. The rain got harder, driven by wailing gusts.

They set off down the slippery path in pursuit of John. Weaving through bracken, boulders and the leering branches of Manna Gums, they reached a grassy clearing after a few hundred metres. It disappeared into a thick, churning fog ahead.

Kev stopped to look back at the others, raising his voice over the wind and rain, "Can anyone see a path here?"

"Nup. But that fog's weird!" said Richo.

Nathan called out for John again: a forlorn hope.

Spaz wandered away to a discrete tree. Despite cold, unresponsive fingers, he managed to open the front of his pants and began to relieve himself.

Something stumbled through the bushes behind him, incoming.

Spaz pissed on his leg as he craned back over his shoulder...

And saw John standing there smiling.

Spaz relaxed. "John! You scared the shit out of me!"

"Wanna see something really mad?"

Spaz finished and turned to face John. "Like what?"

"C'arn, I'll show ya." John tugged Spaz's raincoat sleeve.

Spaz hesitated. "We better tell the others you're here. They're still looking for you."

"Naaah, they'll be alright. This'll only take a moment. Don't worry, it'll be worth it. It's mad!"

"Oh, ok then," Spaz said and followed John into the churning mist...

Spaz felt like he'd stepped into a dream. His head spun trying to comprehend the sudden darkness, the heavy sound of chanting, the burning torches, the fornicating bodies...

A great crowd of people danced naked and bleeding with hundreds of hulking, hairy, dog-faced creatures, groaning, screaming and growling in a sadistic orgy of blood. Central to them was a figure in purple bloodstained robes upon a blackened pedestal, chanting.

One of the towering beasts turned to fix its red demonic gaze on Spaz and licked its lips.

"See, I told you it was mad! Haha!" John said.

WEDNESDAY 5:05 PM

"Honey, I'm home!"

Brian called from the open doorway of his house. His new accomplice Jason waited outside in the driveway, sweating in the driver's seat of his silver Valiant Charger.

After escaping Howqua Hills Police Station in Jason's car, the pair of them went to get loved ones, but neither Brian's partner Sasha nor his ex-wife Julie that his two children lived with, were home. Jason's parents weren't home either, leaving Brian and Jason alone to face the world. Struggling to contain the panic enveloping them, fellow victims became comrades in times of turmoil. With everything that mattered in their lives at stake, they had no choice but to fight.

They checked into a motel to examine the police files they grabbed as they escaped. The files on the Weston killings pointed to the involvement of Henry Wilcox: a twenty-three year-old man from Melbourne with a history of psychiatric illness. His mother reported him missing two days ago and his abandoned Torana was found yesterday at Frank Weston's house on the outskirts of Howqua Hills. Brian phoned the office of forensic pathologist Dr David Dawson, but there was no answer, and when he called Henry's parents' house, he got Henry's former psychiatrist, Dr Bernard Russell, instead. Desperate to make sense of events, Brian organised to meet him in Melbourne that night, hoping to find David too.

Back in the present, there was no reply, or any signs of activity inside his home. Brian stepped into the hallway of the house...

As a groan issued from behind the closed door of the master bedroom to his immediate right.

Brian pivoted to face the sound. "Sasha?"

Another groan came in answer.

Don't think. Just be ready to do what you may have to do.

Brian reached for the doorhandle with one hand and drew his pistol with the other...

"Is that you, Brian?"

Brian quickly holstered his pistol. "Yes it's me, Sasha." He opened the door.

Sasha was sitting up in bed next to the phone, her long brown hair tumbling down the front of her faded pink T-shirt. A filthy fetor lingered...

The familiar fetor of foul demon-spawn.

She smiled. "It's so nice to see you!"

"Is everything ok, Sasha?"

"Yes, everything's fine! I was really tired from work today, so I was just having a lie-down for a bit."

Brian glanced around the corners of the room. He turned back to her. "So everything's fine?"

"Yes! That's what I just said, honey! Why, are you surprised?"

Still that smell...

"Um, yeah maybe. Has anyone called?"

Sasha shook her head. "Not a soul... Look, I know you've been really busy and stressed with work–"

"Yeah I–"

"And I'm sorry I haven't been nicer to you lately and more understanding."

Brian raised his eyebrows. "Well, thanks!"

"You're having such a tough time at the moment with everything, the last thing you need is someone nagging you about what's going on and what you're doing, when even you don't know!"

Brian laughed. "You *do* understand!"

"Of course, honey! I love you!"

A moment's hesitation. "I love you too, babe."

She reached forward and embraced him. He felt the warmth of her body against his cold skin, the soothing aroma of her perfume, the softness of her breath.

Hang on. Isn't this all a bit *too* easy?

"You're not mad at me anymore, then?"

"No honey," she murmured.

"That's good." Brian gave her another squeeze and stepped back. He looked her in the eyes. "But why the sudden change?"

She returned his gaze. "I haven't changed."

Outside, the sky darkened as grey clouds rolled in on stormy gusts to cover the setting sun.

Brian looked over at the dressing-table nearby. He turned back to her. "Sasha. I'm going to do something which is going to seem a bit strange, but trust me on this one, okay."

Sasha wrinkled her brow. "What are you going to do?"

Brian stepped over to the dressing-table and opened the main drawer. He pulled out a pin from the sewing kit there and turned to face her. "Just need to test something. It won't hurt."

"Brian, what the hell are you on?"

Brian moved towards her, pin in hand.

Sasha leapt from the bed towards the door.

Brian lunged across the bed and grabbed her right wrist. "I'm sorry, Sasha. But I have to do this."

Brian held onto her wrist as he pricked her finger.

"For fuck's sake, Brian! What's wrong with you?"

Please God, let it not be her too.

A bubble of blood began to form on her fingertip...
Purple.

Unmistakeably purple.

Still holding her wrist with one hand, he drew his pistol
with the other, his hands shaking.

It has to be done.

"BRIAN! WHAT THE FUCK ARE YOU DOING?"

"What has to be done. I'm–"

Sasha swiped the phone from the bedside table and
twisted past Brian's aimed pistol. The gun went off as she
smashed the phone on his head as hard as she could.

Brian slumped on the bed, releasing his grip on Sasha.
She tried to wrestle the pistol from him, but he quickly
recovered and pulled back.

She staggered to her feet, facing him, incredulous. Her
right arm hung limp and bleeding from a gaping bullet
wound in her shoulder, drenching her shirt. "You just tried
to kill me."

Tears welled in his eyes as he raised the gun again, but
she was quicker, bolting out the door.

"HELP! HELP! SOMEBODY HEEELP!"

Sasha ran out of the front door and into Jason coming
the other way. "My God, you've been shot!" he exclaimed as
he grabbed her.

Sasha turned and pointed with her good arm at Brian
advancing behind her, pistol in his hand.

"HE'S TRYING TO KILL ME! HE'S FUCKING CRAZY!"

"She's one of them, Jason! Look at the colour of her
blood!"

Across the street, a mother desperately dragged her
curious children inside. Other households called the police.

Jason shielded Sasha from Brian's aim. "What? Her blood's not purple!"

Brian saw the perplexed looks on their faces and the worried faces of his neighbours peering through windows... He'd made a terrible mistake.

Sasha's blood wasn't purple after all. He'd just tried to murder his own girlfriend. Publicly.

Brian dropped his gun and sank to his knees in anguish, sobbing into his hands.

I can't take this anymore.

Now Jason had his gun, the one Brian had given him, out but lowered. He stood between Sasha and Brian. "Thanks for rescuing me, but I ain't staying around for this shit. And besides," Jason looked at Sasha trying to stop the blood flowing from her wound, "I think I better get this lady to hospital."

Brian didn't look up. "Yeah, ok."

Sasha and Jason said something to each other that Brian didn't hear. Then Brian felt Sasha spit on his face.

"I never want to see or hear from you again unless it's to put you in jail, you fucking psycho!"

Brian didn't move. "Fair enough."

"I'll be getting all my stuff tonight or tomorrow, and I'd better not have to see your face when I do."

"I was heading down to Melbourne tonight anyway."

"Try telling your police buddies that."

WEDNESDAY 6:13 PM

The darkness within whispered.

Then the darkness had eyes: piercing red orbs. Then a sleek wolfish head, lips curled into a macabre grin. Finally a hulking, upright body with arms ending in claws like fistfuls of rusty knifes.

The demonic beast stepped from the deep shadows of the suburban backyard, silent, graceful. As dusk became darkness, it gazed upon the red-brick house before it. Lights were on and through open curtains it saw an elderly couple eating dinner.

It paused to sniff the air and then bounded towards the backdoor.

, , ,

Herbert and Marilyn Derwent sat at a polished oak dining table in their comfortable house in suburban Watsonia, quietly enjoying a lamb roast. Beethoven's Moonlight Sonata played in the background, providing a gentle backdrop to the soft clatter of silver cutlery.

"So when did Brian say he was getting here?" Herbert asked.

Marilyn finished her mouthful before answering, "He said it'd be late if at all and for us not to stay up for him. He knows where the keys are, I s'pose."

Herbert nodded. "Yes, he'll be fine."

They continued eating. Outside, wind began to slowly build, drowning the sounds of Beethoven's Piano Sonata.

Marilyn paused. "I don't think he's coping well with the stress of his work though. I'm a bit worried about him actually. He was very terse on the phone when he–"

Suddenly there was a loud knocking, three times, on the backdoor.

Marilyn's arms dropped. "What is that?"

Herbert peered at the hallway door, from beyond which the sound came. "I better go see."

Herbert dusted his mouth with a cloth serviette and rose from the table. With Marilyn following, he went into the darkened hallway that led to the bedrooms, bathroom and laundry. He stopped at the door to the laundry and flicked the switch on.

An empty basket rested atop a dormant washing machine next to a water trough, bucket and mop. On the other side of the room were two doors: one for the toilet, the other the backdoor where they had heard the noise. Both doors were closed. The narrow windows either side of the backdoor showed signs of neglect but little of the dark outside. The only noise was the wind, wailing miserably.

Herbert turned to Marilyn and shrugged. "Guess it's nothing."

She frowned. "We both heard something."

He shrugged again. "Probably just the wind."

Outside, the wind dropped low enough to hear the clang of a metal rubbish bin.

"Maybe it's something trying to get into bins?" Herbert said.

"Well, maybe you should take a look."

Herbert picked up the mop next to him and stepped

towards the backdoor. Marilyn stood in the hallway as he turned the outside light on...

Light spilled over a concrete back porch strewn with rubbish blowing in the wind from an overturned metal bin. Beyond, the tops of trees could be seen, swaying against the cloudy moonlit sky.

"Ohhh, the bin's been knocked over!" Herbert said. "There's rubbish everywhere! I better go clean it up."

He unlocked the backdoor and stepped out into the night. Marilyn watched him for a moment from the hallway and then called out, "I'll get you a pan and broom."

Still holding the mop, Herbert looked around for signs of any intruder. Seeing none, he stepped back inside to replace the mop. He then returned outside to clean the mess, leaving the backdoor open.

He had picked most of it up by hand before Marilyn returned. She handed him the pan and broom. "Here."

Herbert began sweeping the remaining rubbish into the pan as Marilyn stood watching.

"Any idea what knocked the bin over?" she said.

Herbert finished quickly and looked up at Marilyn. "Nope."

Marilyn rubbed her exposed forearms and crinkled her nose. "Anyway, it's cold out here and that rubbish smells, so I'm going back inside."

Herbert followed her back into the hallway.

Marilyn stopped to ask him, "Did you lock the backdoor?"

"Of course!" He smiled and put his hand on her shoulder. "Don't worry love, we're quite safe."

Marilyn walked into the dining room. "We really should think about getting an alarm system, y'know," she said as she sat back down at the table.

Herbert joined her at the table. "Oh, let's not go through this again. I already told you I'm not going to live in a fortress. This isn't bloody America!"

"Please don't swear, Herbert," Marilyn said before digging into her meal.

"Sorry, Marilyn." Herbert pointed his fork at her. "But we are *not* getting an alarm system."

Suddenly, Marilyn's eyes widened in terror. A shaking hand across her mouth, she could only point at the doorway behind him...

"What's the matter, love?" Herbert asked as he turned around to where she was pointing.

Behind him loomed a hideous canine abomination. Two-and-a-half metres high, jet-black and hairy, its fanged snout agape, its terrible claws poised to rend. The stench of it smothered them like a pillow.

"Oh my God," was all Herbert managed to say before it grabbed his head, its palm pressed against his face. Then it lifted him from his seat.

Herbert flailed helplessly at the air, emitting muffled moans of agony, as the beast held his head in a vice grip that threatened to crush his skull.

Marilyn sat paralysed with incomprehension, saliva dribbling from her gibbering mouth. Herbert's scalp split with the pressure, dripping rivulets of blood down the beast's hairy arm.

It lingered in the moment, indulging itself in the sweet scent of suffering. It curled its lips to snarl at the drooling female whilst dangling the helpless male before it, slowly flexing its grip on the male's head, savouring the taste of terror...

Marilyn finally found her voice again, "Please God. Save us."

"*Mooortal praaayers to a mooortal God,*" it answered.

Marilyn screamed as long slimy black tendrils emerged from the claw that held her husband. Prehensile, they snaked their way from its palm down Herbert's shaking body, reaching his ankles in a few sickening seconds.

Transfixed, she watched as Herbert's now still body was sucked into an opening that appeared in its palm. It laughed at the horrifying sound of Herbert's body becoming pulp as it was drawn into the unearthly orifice.

And then before the quivering female could quiver any further, she joined him in endless darkness...

WEDNESDAY 8:11 PM

Minions of the dark gathered.

Around sullen campfires and under steady drizzle, the staff and students of Oberon Grammar huddled, the boys and girls separated by a safe distance of a couple of hundred metres or more. By now, even the stragglers had arrived. Soaked, hungry and tired, efforts were directed towards pitching tents and cooking, then eating and sleep. Across the river, Fry's hut could be seen, silhouetted against a murky sky, empty save for the rats known to reside there.

Alex, Ben, Bruce, Jeff, Andrew and Adam of H and G Units sat on logs around their fire, staring silently into the flames. Alex lifted his head from a mug of hot Milo and said, "Where's Bill and them gone?"

Bruce didn't look up. "Most of them snuck off to go do a séance."

Alex turned to Bruce sitting opposite him. "A séance? What are they doing that for?"

"Cos they're fucking idiots."

Derrick, Price, Sean, Simon and Hamish were gathered nearby around a hissing campfire that struggled in the light rain. Derrick paused from piling on wood.

"Where's Danny gone?" he asked.

The others only shrugged.

No one cared.

, , ,

Nightfall.

Figures crept under night's blanket towards the sanctuary of the wood shed. With only the occasional flicker of torchlight to guide them, they stealthily followed their leader through trees and puddles in darkness...

With such obedience.

They reached the door, covered by shadow and the fine wet mist that swirled around them. Bill turned to the others with him – Mike, Didge, Robbo and Gary – and whispered, "We got everything?"

The others nodded and Mike answered his younger brother, "Yeah."

Bill grinned and pushed the door into the wood shed open. "Then let the show begin."

Robbo screwed up his face. "Errr good on you, Bill! As if it's fuckin' gunna work, you idiot!"

Bill put a hushing finger to his lips. "Shhh, keep it down, will ya? When we get inside we can make more noise."

Mike put a hand on Robbo's small shoulder and looked down on him from a taller height. "It'll work, dude. You'll see. Me and Bill have done 'em before."

Without further delay, the boys entered the shed and began their preparations.

And they waited.

First they unfurled a blanket and hung it over the window facing the campsite to block the sound, but mostly the light, from their activities. Next they cleared an area in the middle of the leaf-strewn floor to spread out a contact-covered hiking map. In the centre of the smooth surface of the map, they placed an upturned glass. Around the edge of the map they placed small scraps of paper, representing all the letters of the alphabet and the words "YES" and "NO". Then they planted household candles, six in all, into the dirt around their makeshift ouija board and lit them. Finally they sat cross-legged in a circle around the board.

"Now we all have to hold hands, or else this won't work," Bill said.

"That's a bit gay, isn't it?" Robbo said.

Bill answered, "Trust me on this, Robbo, you won't regret it."

Gary spoke. "But really, Bill, what's to stop someone pushing the glass?"

Mike smiled at him. "You'll see it's real, Gazza. It won't take long."

Didge piped up. "D'you wanna make a bet?"

Mike turned to Didge and said sternly, "This stuff is real and something will happen. I know."

"Fuck off!" said Robbo. "Listen to this shit!"

"Are you scared, Robbo?" Mike said.

"Nah, why should I be? This is all bullshit, so what do I care?"

"C'mon Mike, if you're so sure something will happen, make a bet then. I bet ya nothing happens," Didge said.

"How much d'you wanna lose, Didge?" Bill said.

"I'll bet you and Mike fifty bucks each that nothing happens," Didge answered.

"And it doesn't count if someone could just be pushing the glass. Something freaky has to happen," Gary added.

Bill looked at Mike, who nodded back.

"Done!" Bill said, shaking.

"I just made a hundred bucks!" Didge declared.

Robbo clapped Didge on the back. "Easiest hundred bucks you'll ever make!"

"I'll say!" Didge answered.

"You haven't made your money yet, Didge," Bill said. "Let's get started or else the bet's off and you don't get shit."

And so on that fateful night, they began their séance, hidden from the watchful eyes of school staff. Outside the wood shed, wind and rain formed eerie flutelike acoustics, harmonising with the voices of the five boys, as they chanted:

"Spirits be with us."

Calling their name...

Minutes passed, marked by the candles that waned with their patience. Didge, Robbo and Gary shuffled with discomfort, dusting dirt from their backsides. Bill leaned forward to put his finger on the glass. "C'mon guys, you all have to put your finger on."

The others obeyed. Mike was trance-like, staring at the glass.

"Is there a spirit within this glass?" Bill said.

Moments passed in slow-motion as the wind frolicked outside.

Bill spoke again, louder, "*Is* there a spirit within this glass?"

More anxious moments, suspended in surreality...

"C'mon guys," Bill said. "You have to focus!"

"I'M FOCUSING! I'M FOCUSING!" Didge shouted as he leaned forward to bring his face centimetres from the glass.

Robbo and Gary laughed.

"Didge! Take it seriously!" said Bill.

"How can he?" said Robbo.

Didge sat back. "I *am* taking it seriously!"

Outside, a gust of wind rattled the door and the eaves of the wooden slabs that formed the roof.

Didge, his back to the door, jerked to look behind him. The others looked too, breaking the chain of hands. Except Mike, whose eyes hadn't left the glass.

Robbo burst into laughter. "You get a fright, Didge? It's just the wind, you fucking idiot!"

Didge pushed up the glasses sliding down his face and turned back around.

"Something's close," Mike said without looking up. "I can feel it."

"You can *feel* them?" Gary asked Mike. Meanwhile Robbo loomed behind Didge.

Mike looked at Gary and spoke with a strange assuredness, "*Yes.*"

"BURRHRHR!" was the sound Robbo made as he grabbed Didge's shoulders from behind and shook him violently.

Didge jumped up in panic, almost fell into logs stacked nearby and turned around to Robbo, who was now clutching his stomach in laughter. "JESUS FUCK MY CHRIST! Don't do that!"

Then the front door flew open and a chilling wind charged in...

Seeping into their souls.

In a moment, the candles were extinguished, leaving them in cold, dark silence. No one moved.

"Um, I think someone better close the door," Robbo said.

Then two eyes lit up near the top of the doorway, piercing red eyes staring from the icy darkness... The shape of convex slits. In the dull red light of those eyes, suggestions of the owner's towering body could be seen: dog-faced, hairy and muscular, bearing massive claws that caught the crimson light.

"*WELLLCOMEEE,*" it boomed in a rich, gravelly voice.

They had time to utter a plethora of expletives, before the window facing the campsite smashed inward. The screening blanket came ripping down as another of the dog-faced intruders stepped through the opening. Before they had time to react, the window on the opposite side of the ten-by-five metre hut smashed in too, as a third beast entered, leaving no exits available.

Robbo jumped towards the wood piled in the corner, Didge screamed and curled into a ball and Gary was motionless in shock.

Bill turned to Mike, "What the fuck have we done?"

Mike didn't move or answer. Darkness obscured his expression.

Such terror. Such helplessness. Time to play.

The demons rushed in, one grabbing Bill by his shirt back and flinging him at the far wall where wood lay piled a few metres deep. He windmilled the air a moment before impacting heavily against the logs. He ricocheted backwards and landed face-up on the floor, his head and chest covered in blood, unmoving.

The second demon, the one that had entered through the door, grabbed Didge by the throat and lifted him off his feet with one arm.

Robbo picked up a thin log that he swung like a baseball bat. "FUCK YOU!" he screamed at them, tears streaming down his face.

The demon holding Didge was closest to Robbo and it turned its terrible gaze to him to answer, "*Ohhh Robert. We willlll!*"

As it finished its words, its free hand grabbed the back of Didge's neck. Didge could only scream as the demon's sharp claws sliced through his flesh and gripped his spine. The demon snarled at Robert, revealing wickedly pointed teeth, before unleashing a primal roar as it yanked out Didge's spine with such force that it snapped and the severed vertebrae thrashed the air. Didge slumped lifeless

to the ground as blood spurted from his neck onto Robbo
and the beast he faced.

The third demon stepped on Gary's leg as he attempted
to dodge past for the window beyond. Gary squirmed in
agony beneath the crushing weight of the creature's foot.
Vainly he grabbed a nearby chunk of wood and tried to club
his assailant.

It laughed as it looked down at him...

The futile death throes of the trapped victim.

It swiftly grabbed his ankle and moved its foot over his
knee, still pinning him. Then it started to bend his knee
backwards, steady, unrelenting. In unbearable pain, Gary
desperately hurled everything within reach at the monster...

Savour the moment. Smell the fear. Taste the torment.

A horrific snap of splintering bone sounded as Gary's
knee gave way. His leg bent upward at a crazy angle, blood
from around the wound soaking his pants and the ground
he lay on.

"Ple-e-e-ase! Just kill meee!" Gary said, delirious.

The beast loomed over Gary as it gripped his other ankle
and stepped on his remaining knee. Its horrible, drooling
snout slackened into a smile.

"*Paaatience*," it said.

And then his other knee was violently snapped forward
too. He screamed a final time and then was still.

Pity they break so easily.

Through eyes blurred with tears, Robbo could see Gary
lying motionless on his back, knees pointing grotesquely
upwards in the hellish red glow.

The demon furthest from him sniffed Bill's bleeding and
limp body. Horrified into inaction, Robbo watched the
demon lift Bill up by his ankles, then grunt as it swung Bill's
body around in a circle, smashing his head against the edge

of the woodpile so hard that brains splattered in a wide arc from wall to ceiling.

Then Robbo noticed that Mike still sat cross-legged on the floor, staring into limbo, untouched by the carnage.

"MIKE! DO SOMETHING!" Robbo shouted.

Mike made no response.

And now Robbo had the attention of all three demons, their wolfish visages a menagerie of fur and blood, crowned by merciless red slits for eyes...

Closing in for the kill.

Swinging his baseball bat-sized log, Robbo rushed the beast nearest the open doorway. But in a fluid motion, it caught Robbo's wrist that held the log and twisted him down to the floor. His wrist cracked and his weapon rolled away.

Maintaining its grip on his arm, the beast braced a foot against his right shoulder and ripped his arm from its socket. Blood squirted in pulsing jets from the gaping wound as he convulsed helplessly in shock.

Then systematically, it tore each of his other limbs from his torso...

Mike heard his friends' chilling screams fade and felt their warm blood washing against his legs. The deed was done.

I'm so sorry, Bill. I'm sorry to all of you guys. I had no choice.

Then the stench of the creatures became intoxicating and he looked up to see that they were standing over him, blood-soaked, exultant.

One of the demons spoke, *"You have done wellll. You shall be rewaaarded."*

Mike restrained a smile. "Rewarded?"

"WITH A QUICK DEATH!" it answered as it struck the side of his head with its powerful claw.

He was dead in a heartbeat.

WEDNESDAY 9:10 PM

"So how do we stop them?"

Brian leaned forward as he asked the question, flicking cigarette ash into an ashtray. He sat over a beer with Dr Bernard Russell the psychiatrist, at a small table in the corner of Zagame's, a quiet bar and bistro on the main shopping strip of Ivanhoe. The establishment had only a couple of staff looking bored and a handful of patrons chatting over drinks. Pop from the 60s and 70s played in the background, preventing conversation from travelling.

This place seems safe enough, but there's a world of forces seeking to thwart me, including my own fucking police department, so how can it be safe? But more importantly, what choice do I have left? I have to keep fighting, to beat this demonic scourge and regain my life, or else die trying...

Otherwise, I might as well put a gun in my mouth now and blow my fucking brains out.

"We have to know what they are first," Bernard answered, looking at Brian steadily. "And frankly, we can't even be sure whether *they* are an actual physical entity, or no more than a disease of the mind."

"Well doctor." Brian blew a plume of cigarette smoke. "I've shot one and had another gouge my hand, so they're real alright. They bleed purple and infect humans with their blood, taking control of them somehow."

Bernard raised an eyebrow. "But what if your perceptions are merely symptoms of the disease? Hallucinations, as it were?"

"Then yours are as well."

"I know. That's what concerns me. We have yet to obtain physical, independent evidence of their existence."

Brian stubbed out his cigarette and sat back in his chair. "Dr David Dawson, the pathologist I spoke to here in Melbourne, had concrete evidence. He showed me their blood cells."

"Oh yes and...?"

"I've been unable to contact him since."

Bernard looked away into space. "Hmm."

"In a way, I guess, I could have done more to help him," Brian continued. "When we last met, he told me that all of the evidence he had accumulated on the case had gone missing and that his colleagues were acting suspiciously. He was beginning to believe that they were conspiring against him."

Bernard returned his gaze to Brian. "Similar to your experience at the police station?"

Let's not go there again.

"Um, in some ways, I guess... Anyway I told him that I was unable to do anything about it, that that was the responsibility of the state police and I haven't been able to get in touch with him since."

"Yes well, hindsight is always 20/20, isn't it?"

Brian folded his arms and said with raised eyebrows, "Is it, doctor? Should I know now what I should have done?"

Bernard held up his hands to ward Brian off. "An inappropriate choice of words for the situation, I'm sorry."

"Hmph," Brian said and took a large mouthful of beer.

"Anyway, I think that the key to understanding what's going on, Brian, is in understanding Henry's words."

"Go on," Brian said, his eyes not moving from Bernard's.

"During my time of consultation with Henry, he talked at length, usually under the influence of hypnosis, about these entities he called the *Dark Horde*.

"His description of these entities was similar to yours. Including the eyes, vividly. He claimed he had the power to bring them into this world, that he was their channel. And yet he was in constant fear of this power he believed he had. He believed that if he let them into this world, they would destroy life as we know it on this planet. And he believed that they could sometimes control him and that they would eventually succeed in making him let them in."

"Well, it looks like he *has* let them in," Brian said. "And that this *Dark Horde*, whatever it is, is real. So I ask again, *how do we stop them*?"

"Henry claimed that there was no way to stop them. That we could not kill them. And that to them, we are as ants are to us."

Brian sighed in frustration, finished his beer and reached for another cigarette, the last of a packet he'd bought only this morning.

"So you're saying we're fucked then. What's to understand?"

Bernard licked his lips and leaned forward for emphasis. "If he is their channel, it means they need him to get in."

Brian shrugged as he lit up. "So?"

"And they still do."

Brian scrutinised Bernard's expression. "What makes you say this?"

"It's something I gleaned from hypnotherapy sessions with Henry. The *Dark Horde* need to *maintain* a *living* link with this world in order to *maintain* access. I think this means that Henry is still alive."

"It's possible," Brian agreed.

"And that he's keeping a way open for them to reach this world," Bernard said.

Brian shrugged again. "So why not just kill him?"

"I believe they already have that covered. I believe they've been grooming specific others to take over, such as Danny."

Brian's head spun with the possibilities.

Bernard continued, "I believe it's also the reason why you're still alive. Because they need you too."

Brian's hand instinctively moved over his belt holster. "And just *how* would you know all this, doctor?"

Over behind the bar, the phone began to ring...

Bernard saw Brian's hand movement and smiled. "Because they need me too and hence I also still live. And this, Brian, they've told me to tell you... I'm afraid we're both pawns of the *Dark Horde*."

Brian shook his head as he drew his pistol and pointed it at Bernard underneath the table. "Believe me when I say I don't care anymore who I have to kill. I've already tried to shoot my girlfriend and half the officers I work with, so there's not much stopping me from shooting you."

Bernard smiled. "It's too late for that, Brian. And besides," he looked over at one of the bartenders standing at the phone by the bar, "that phone call's for you."

Brian followed his gaze, just as the bartender called out, "PHONE CALL FOR MR BRIAN DERWENT? IS HE HERE?"

Bernard attracted the bartender's attention with a jerk of his head at Brian.

Brian turned to Bernard. "You're a fool if you think I'm gunna answer that."

Brian didn't move. The bartender paused before speaking again to the caller.

"There really is no use fighting, Brian, it makes no difference," Bernard said.

Brian's face began to boil.

Try telling me that when I put a bullet in that fat gut of yours.

The bartender put the phone down and walked over to their table. "Excuse me, sir," he addressed Brian. "I hate to interrupt but–"

Brian turned briefly to the bartender. "No, my name is *not* Brian. You've got the wrong person." He turned back to Bernard, staring daggers.

Bernard laughed awkwardly and the bartender fidgeted for a moment before saying, "I'm sorry sir, but the caller, a young boy, said to say his name is Howard."

Brian's heart sank at the mention of the name.

"He says that his father Brian is here and that it's very important he speak to him. Are you sure it's not you?"

"You can't win, Brian. So just play the game," Bernard said.

Brian stormed over to the phone behind the bar. "Hello?"

"Hello, Brian," came a calm response. The voice was that of an adult man.

"Who is this?"

"We've yet to meet, but you know who I am."

"Are you gunna tell me? Or are you just gunna waste my fucking time?"

"You don't recognise me, but you'll recognise this..."

"Look pal–" Brian began.

Another voice came over the phone. Howard's. "Daddy?"

"Howard! What's happened?"

"I'm scared, daddy... The monsters have really got me. They're horrible, daddy and–"

"I'm coming to get you, Howard. I won't let them hurt you. Where are you?"

The adult male voice answered again, "Yes you are, yes we will, we're in Howqua Hills."

Brian reeled back from the phone, his pulse an endless drum roll in his ears. The bartender was now serving another customer, whilst Bernard remained sitting at their table, staring into space and stroking his white beard.

"Is this Henry Wilcox?" Brian said.

"Good guess. Surprised?"

"What the fuck are you doing with my son?"

"Oh not just your son, your daughter Samantha too."

"WHAT THE HELL DO YOU WANT WITH ME AND MY CHILDREN!"

"Actually, it's not just your children I've got here... Sasha, Julie and I wouldn't bother going to your parent's house tonight, 'cos they won't be there."

"WHAT THE FUCK DO YOU WANT? TELL ME!"

"I want you to come back to Howqua Hills now and be reunited with your family."

"Oh, I'll be doing that, YOU FUCKING ARSEHOLE! I'm gunna fuck you up too for this! WHERE ARE YOU?"

"Just drive back into Howqua Hills, you won't miss us, haha."

"WHAT HAVE YOU DONE TO THEM?"

"Nothing really yet. I was saving that until you got here, but don't keep me waiting 'cos I'll get bored."

Henry hung up.

WEDNESDAY 9:55 PM

Calm.

Lucas floated on gentle waves that rippled under a cool, soothing breeze: oceans of tranquillity stretching out to blue infinity. Consciousness immersed in transcendental timelessness, the outside world ceased to exist.

Seagulls flitted across the clear sky, catching the morning sun on their white feathers, flying in ones, twos, threes...

Now an exodus in one direction: north.

As Lucas watched the trickle transform into a flood, he felt panic seeping into his thoughts. Now the seagulls moved swiftly past him in huge numbers, flapping and squawking frantically.

A desperate flight.

Then Lucas became aware of something rising from the unknown depths below, something so huge that its dark form obscured the sea just as clouds cover sky. Incomprehensible, unstoppable...

Evil.

, , ,

Lucas' eyes flicked open as he became re-acquainted with his surroundings. His heart racing, he knelt alone in prayer on a square woollen hassock, in the front pew before the candle-lit chapel altar at Timberhome. In the darkness beyond the fifteen-metre-high windows of the prism-shaped chapel, Lucas looked onto the lights of the rest of his school, bordered by an expanse of eucalypt forest, stretching away down the hill.

Then in steady sequence, the lights along the tree-lined drive to Mueller Road and civilisation, began to go out. Approaching...

Ominous.

Lucas fled the serene sanctuary of the chapel and ran down to the central courtyard, around which the other school buildings clustered. Gathered in the light outside the dining hall, were Matron Susan Inglis and about twelve school children. Fear and exhaustion painted their faces. Among them was Danny Malone.

Susan turned to Lucas as he arrived, her eyes heavy with tears. "Oh Lucas, thank goodness you're here!"

"What's happened?"

"Something's attacking us Lucas, some kind of werewolf-like aliens! These children have run all the way back from the campsite to escape them and many at the campsite have already been killed! There's no answer from anyone at the staff village and to make things worse, I can't even get through to the police because the line's busy!"

Lucas was too stunned to speak.

Werewolf-like aliens? What in God's name is going on?

Then came a chorus of growls, its source somewhere beyond the far end of the dining hall. Then the dining hall lights went out. A heavy animal stench rent the air, foreboding.

"We've got to get out of here now," Lucas said.

"But what about the others?" Susan answered.

"Susan. We can't stay here." Lucas cringed at the guttural sounds approaching and looked across the school carpark.

"We'll take one of the minibuses and get these kids into town where they'll be safe and come back for others if we can, or at the very least we can send for help."

Susan shivered and rubbed her arms. "Okay, how about you take the kids and I go in my car? I'll get there more quickly then and can go to the police station for help."

"Agreed. Let's meet there."

The sound of breaking glass came from the dining hall. In the darkness alongside, a horde of hairy figures crept forward, their red slits for eyes catching the light of the full moon...

Menacing.

, , ,

Ignition.

With shaking hands fighting to steer the key into the lock, Susan started the engine of her red Ford Laser. She looked over and saw Lucas ushering the last of the children into the minibus...

And alien figures running in the gloom of the gum trees around the carpark. Encircling them.

First gear.

Susan stamped the accelerator pedal, slammed the gearstick into first and lifted the clutch. The front wheels spun on the loose surface of the carpark before gaining purchase. The car charged forward towards the dirt driveway on the far side that lead out of the school grounds. Lucas managed to wave goodbye as she passed.

Second gear.

Wiping sweat from her brow, Susan steered the car towards the exit. Something black and huge leapt between the two venerable Manna Gums flanking the exit. Then another.

Third gear.

The accelerator flat to the floor, Susan gripped the steering wheel in two fistfuls of white knuckles as she launched the car through the gap in the trees where the carpark exit was. She glimpsed red eyes watching her from the shadows...

Too many to count.

She accelerated down the hill and around the wide bends, unleashing a spray of dust as the car skidded sideways on each corner... Ever faster and closer to losing control.

Top gear.

At the bottom of the hill now and with the school gates a few hundred metres ahead, swarms of black figures began to leap across the road in front of and around her. Huge muscular beasts with piercing red eyes, covering the hillside like locusts.

Inescapable.

There was a loud crash and skitter of claws as one of them landed on the roof. Susan screamed, fighting to control the car and see the road. It smashed its claw through the passenger side window, showering her with glass. Another landed on the back of the car.

Susan screamed again and shook the steering wheel, desperate to dislodge them. Speeding on the dirt road at one-hundred kilometres per hour, the car swerved violently and pitched over sideways, rolling many times.

The world spun to a stop.

, , ,

Danny was the last to get into the minibus. All the seats in the back were taken. He hesitated at the edge of the open side door.

"Jump in the front, Danny," Lucas gestured to the front passenger seat as he rolled the side door shut. By the time Danny clambered into the front seat, Lucas had dashed around to the driver's side and jumped in too.

Susan spun her wheels as she passed them in her red Laser hatchback, disappearing out of the driveway soon after. He managed to wave.

Then he turned the headlights on and saw what surrounded him:

In the forest shadows at the carpark's edge, hundreds, if not thousands of the hulking demonic beasts lurked, their red eyes lighting up like stars in the night sky...

Creeping closer.

"DRIVE!" shouted the children from the back seats.

Lucas snapped from his brief trance and drove the minibus forward, struggling to pick up speed.

A futile effort.

They were halfway across the carpark when one of the creatures landed on the side of the minibus, not far behind where Lucas sat. Lucas strained to concentrate over the din of screaming children and the beast clawing at the window. As he neared the exit, it smashed the window next to his head.

Lucas steered the bus close to one of the gum trees flanking the exit, scraping paint, the side-mirror and the demon hanging on in the process. Torn from the side of the vehicle, the monster fell into the dust trailing from the back of the minibus and began to give chase...

Others followed.

The minibus leapt from the carpark into the driveway beyond. Lucas spun the wheel and careered down the dirt road to the bottom of the hill, thronged by the horde on all sides. Through a blur, he heard their blood-curdling roars, saw their swift movements and their awful faces leering at him from the moonlight.

Enjoying the thrill of the chase while it lasted.

The minibus surged out of the school gates, struggling to maintain a top speed of one-hundred kilometres per hour. The way ahead looked clear. Lucas dared to look in the rear vision mirror...

At the waves of black demonic beasts, fading into the murk behind. They seemed to be laughing.

My God, we might just get out of this alive.

Lucas raced down to Mueller Road and followed its mountainous bends towards Howqua Hills. The surfaced road sliced through the side of Mount Warrambat, its sheer mountain face plunging away on his left, adorned with Manna Gums and Peppermints.

A strange quiet fell over the minibus. Salvation was now only a few minutes away.

Danny broke the silence, "Thank you, Lucas, for taking us. You've saved us quite a lot of time and effort."

Lucas looked puzzled and glanced over at Danny. "Of course, Danny! I wasn't going to leave you!"

"Of course you weren't." Danny smiled back. "You may even be spared for your services, although I can't guarantee anything... They look pretty hungry, y'know." Danny directed Lucas' gaze to the rear vision mirror:

The cabin behind was filled with demons and not children at all. Their massive hairy bodies crammed the available space, the air hard to breathe for their heavy odour. They were laughing.

"I've got lots of friends now, Lucas." Danny grinned.

Lucas shrieked and drove the minibus at the cliff edge. In a couple of panicked seconds, he'd unclipped his seat belt and flung himself out the door, all as the minibus launched off the road and down the steep, forested mountainside. He landed on the road and rolled many times before stopping: shaking, bruised and bleeding.

Lucas lay shuddering a few moments, before forcing himself to his feet. He staggered to the roadside and looked down to see the wreckage of the minibus, smashed against a tree amongst scrub fifty or more metres down the slope.

Grimacing in pain, tormented to tears, Lucas turned and started running towards town...

, , ,

Soaked with tears and sweat, Lucas ran on down the lonely mountain highway, his tortured mind circling endlessly over the same questions:

What fell calamity had befallen humanity? What cruel cosmic forces had delivered such an indomitable evil? And what unspeakable act had he just committed?

He rounded a corner and in the moonlight saw the figure of a child standing in the middle of the road...

Waiting.

As Lucas approached, the shadows slid from the child's face and Lucas stopped, speechless in open-mouthed horror.

Danny smiled back at him. "We meet again."

Lucas struggled to speak, "B-B... How did you get here?"

"Don't underestimate me, Lucas. I can do lots of things now. I'm not a useless wimp anymore. Now I'm on the winning side."

Lucas began to make out the details of Danny's injuries. Through gaps in torn clothing and across his grinning face, numerous cuts oozed blood that seemed black under the feeble light.

"You've joined forces with *them?*" Lucas asked.

"They chose me, Lucas. And now I have more power and freedom than I ever could have imagined."

"What do they want?"

Danny's smile grew wider. "The fruits of humanity."

"Where do they come from?"

"I'm not actually sure. But regardless, it doesn't matter: they're here to stay."

"Somehow Danny, sooner or later they will be destroyed. Such evil cannot succeed. It is against God's design."

"Yes, that's a nice fantasy, isn't it. Good always triumphs over evil. A God exists to save us. Such fairytales you believe, haha."

"Once the word is out, they cannot hide. They will be hunted. They will be defeated. They will be destroyed."

Danny laughed long and loud. "You and who's army?"

"The world's! We will come together to fight for our survival. We have to. Perhaps this is our judgement day."

"You cannot even comprehend them, let alone defeat them. They can manipulate our minds with ease and control our perceptions, thus changing reality as we know it. And through them, we can too. That's how they blend in and what they've already been doing for aeons, accumulating power and waiting for the right moment to strike."

"I don't understand."

"No one can. Such things are beyond the human mind."

Suddenly, one of the demonic beasts burst forth from the bush lining the road. It landed next to Lucas on all-fours, shaking the earth with its force. Cruel red eyes stared at him from its wolfish visage.

"Behold the future," Danny said.

The beast reared up, brandishing long bloodstained claws and unleashed a thundering roar, exultant.

Lucas turned and ran on towards town. Head down, arms pumping, he didn't look back.

God give me strength.

But the beast merely watched him go...

Laughing at his folly.

WEDNESDAY 11:44 PM

The end of all.

All life, all hope, all belief in this cold, heartless world of lies, hate and greed. Gone. Gone with the world he had once known: his home, his family, his relationships, his job, his very being.

Yet the fury burned on within, an all-consuming fire propelling him onwards...

To victory or death.

Brian drove towards Howqua Hills in his blue Ford XF Falcon, oblivious to time. Manic, he drove at frantic speed, no longer caring for the law he had once fought to uphold. Everything rode on what he had to do now, in what might be his final act.

The last roll of the dice.

As Brian crested the rise into Howqua Hills, he was greeted by an ominous ruby glow over the town ahead. Gritting his teeth, shotgun across his lap, he urged his car faster, speeding into the heart of hell.

Fuck them all.

Brian reached the edge of the small town where Banner Road became Main Street and wondered what he had returned to. No houses were lit, no cars drove on the roads. There was only an eerie red permeating the town. In a few more moments, he could see the town centre...

And the source of the sinister light.

Where the Troopers' Monument once stood at the large roundabout in the centre of town, there now soared a luminescent fifteen-metre obelisk, bristling with horrible barbed spikes impaling the bleeding bodies of tortured victims, undulating slowly with nefarious life.

Crowding the ruby shadows cast by the unholy pillar, were swarms of hairy beasts, under which people lay slowly squirming in their final agonised death throes. An army of demons in an orgy of torture, rape and slaughter.

Towering over the flock near the column of pain, stood a six-metre scorpioid abomination, shining crimson in the infernal light. Its armoured body bore two massive red pincers, a long segmented stinger arching forward over its head, spiky mandibles like tusks and a mass of green eyes like a spider.

The massacre of mankind had begun.

Brian slowed the car to a stop a few metres from the writhing masses and stared hopelessly at the thousands of *Dark Horde* gathered before him.

Fuck.

Then came the sound of chanting, growing more distinct as the volume increased:

"We are as one, as many are we..."

Brian shivered in his car as he looked for the source of the sound.

Then the crowd parted to expose the road leading to the centre of the hellish congregation, as a chilling chorus repeated:

"Become one, once more be..."

Brian saw that about eight of the demonic beasts stood at the base of the pulsing pillar fifty metres ahead, clad in purple-embroidered robes. They raised barbed and bloody candles to acknowledge his arrival, as if they'd been expecting him.

Then from their midst, stepped a hooded man in matching robes.

There you are, you bastard.

Brian planted his foot, driving straight at the man in front.

One of the two of us is gunna die. Maybe both.

The robed demons easily leapt clear of Brian's oncoming vehicle, but the man in robes was slower... He hit the bumper bar on the driver's side and rolled across the bonnet to Brian's right.

Brian spun the wheel, sending the car sliding sideways into the wall of demonic spectators to his left. The beasts at the front fell backwards onto the ranks behind like a wave, but the elastic wall held and bounced back, cushioning Brian's car from the kerb. Brian took his foot off the brake and floored the accelerator...

As the windows down the left side of the car smashed, and the creatures there began to get a grip.

Brian's car lurched forward towards his purple-robed enemy that crawled on two broken legs twenty metres away. The demons surrounding him held onto his car, despite the broken glass that lacerated their hands and threatened to sever their digits. Two demons crashed into the bonnet, as others tore open his tyres.

Just a couple more seconds.

The car stopped moving, but near his target, Brian flung open the door and leapt out, shotgun drawn even as he landed.

The hooded man laughed back at him. A surreal moment passed when even the *Dark Horde* didn't seem to move.

Rushing in for the kill, Brian fired both barrels of his twelve-gauge pump-action shotgun from close quarters. A terrific blast erupted through his victim's chest, shredding robes, flesh and vital organs. The body slumped lifelessly in a pool of blood that shone purple in the car headlights...

Please let that be the end of it.

But the *Dark Horde* around him only laughed.

With shaking hands, Brian pulled back the hood of the man he'd just shot...

It wasn't Henry at all. It was Douglas McDougall. His death mask smiled back at him.

Brian stared down incredulous.

Why won't you fucking die?

Then a massive red pincer grabbed his throat and lifted him.

He craned his head to look into the alien arachnoid face of the scorpioid monstrosity looming six metres tall... Two large impenetrable green eyes sat either side of two rows of smaller eyes. Its slavering mandibles gibbering furiously and its crimson-coloured tail curled forward over its head towards him, ending in a barbed stinger, stained black with venom, the size of his head.

Without hesitation, Brian shoved the barrel of his shotgun into its cavernous mouth and pulled the trigger...

The top of its chitinous cranium exploded skyward as the lead spray tore through its head. Brian dropped to his feet as the almighty beast relaxed its grip and crashed backwards like a felled tree.

Shit, hey?

Pumping his shotgun to reload, he looked at the countless *Dark Horde* surrounding him... Growling.

Yeah, shit.

"BLASPHEMY!" bellowed one of the robed *Dark Horde* as it thundered into him from behind. One claw wrapped around his neck and another wrenched the shotgun from his grasp.

It's over. I failed.

The beast roared in fury as it raised Brian by his neck and slam-dunked him onto the spiked obelisk. Brian managed to pull his head down to miss one ebony spike a metre long, but another went through his right shoulder, ripping flesh and forcing the wound wide open. Pinned, his feet barely touching the ground, he could only scream in agony. His blood mingled with that of the butchered corpses at his feet and those impaled around him.

In the murk, he imagined he recognised some of them.

The pillar began to beat faster, aroused by the blood of new life.

Brian looked into the dead face of Jason, the twenty-something year-old he'd rescued this morning. His still body hung next to him, staked to the pillar by two spikes going through his torso, leaving dripping intestines spilling down his waist. A nauseating stench assaulted him.

Jason's eyes flicked open. He smiled as he returned Brian's gaze.

Do you know what it's like, Brian, to live in a world without death?

Brian pulled back in panic, wincing at the pain in his impaled shoulder, but could not escape.

His demonic attacker reared over him, red eyes flashing with malice as it flexed its terrible claws. Then it was crash-tackled from the side by another of the robed demons. Before it hit the ground, its attacker's savagely fanged teeth had torn out its throat.

The victorious demon now stood over the crumpled body of the other, purple ichor smeared across its maw and chest. It curled its lips at Brian and made a low, threatening growl. Are they fighting over the right to kill me now?

"JUST DO IT!" Brian shouted.

The demon stepped forward and grabbed Brian's head by the chin. Its sharp claws punctured his cheeks and drew blood as its rotten breath bore down on him...

"*Ifff ooonly*," it answered.

The robed beast turned towards another man-sized figure in gold-trimmed purple robes emerging from the demonic crowds. Brian followed its gaze...

The man-sized figure pulled back the hood of his robes. Cold, angular features behind an evil smile stared back at Brian.

The familiar face of Henry Anthony Wilcox.

"Glad you could make it," Henry said.

"Fuck you Henry, and your *Dark Horde*."

"Oh, come now, Brian – they're not that bad once you get used to them. And besides, why bat for the losing team?"

"Where's my family, you arsehole?"

Henry grimaced. "They're a little busy right now, I'm afraid. But once they're finished, you'll be able to speak to them... Though they may be a little, how shall I say?" Henry licked his lips. "Buggered."

"I'LL FUCKING KILL YOU, YOU BASTARD!"

"I know all too well, Brian, that you'd kill me if I gave you the chance. That's why I had your good friend Douglas McDougall pose in my place when you arrived. But now of course, you pose no threat," he paused to kick Brian's shotgun away, "so we can talk like the civil human beings that we are."

"YOU FUCKING SPINELESS COWARD!"

"Now, now, name-calling isn't being very civil, Brian."

"You can do what like with me. Just leave my family alone and let them go."

Henry shared a hearty laugh with his demonic audience, before turning to back to Brian. "Do you really think that you're in a position to negotiate? Hahahaha. Look at you now. You're impaled with no weapon and surrounded by an army of *Dark Horde*. There's no one here to save you, and you have no chance or way of victory."

"I'll fight you until my last breath."

Henry smiled as he shook his head gently. "Brian, Brian, Brian. You never give up... That's what I like about you."

"As long as I'm alive, I won't surrender to a worm like you."

"No Brian, you will, because you have no choice... But I'm not going to kill you, you're actually a lot more valuable alive. You are to become another channel, you see, which is only possible if you're still alive and have the chosen blood. All you have to do is submit to the will of the *Dark Horde* and be inseminated by the *Venomed One*."

"Go fuck yourself. I'll never become a sodomy slave of the *Dark Horde* like you."

"Submit and join us, Brian, and you'll be free to do whatever you wish with your beloved family. If you do not, I will torture, rape and butcher each and every one of them, right now before your very eyes."

Not if I kill you first.

Brian screamed in pain as he pulled himself up on the spike piercing his right shoulder. Bringing his feet up against the wet, fleshy side of the column, he tried to launch himself off the spike...

But the robed demon standing next to him was quicker. It dug its claw into his good shoulder, drawing fresh blood, and held him fast. The obelisk beat faster, spurred into new throes of arousal.

"*STAAAY!*" it commanded.

Henry clenched his fists. "Okay, enough of civility." He pointed to a couple of his robed demonic accomplices. "Bring out his family."

In a frenzy of anger, Brian struggled against the massive bulk of the robed demon immobilising him, in vain. Helpless, he watched as his parents Marilyn and Herbert, his partner Sasha, his ex-wife Julie, and his children Samantha and Howard were brought before him: bound, gagged and naked. He saw with horror their red bleeding bodies, their tormented expressions...

He went limp, falling back on the spike through his shoulder. Sobs racked his body.

Death would be better.

Henry put his hands together and smiled. "Okay Brian, your pick. Who's the first to die?"

"WHY ARE YOU DOING THIS!"

"Evolution does not have a purpose Brian, only an outcome. The *Dark Horde* are the new superior species. Their time has come."

"WHY ME?"

"You are chosen because you carry the channelling gene, rare among your kind and sought-after by the *Dark Horde*. But unlike other carriers, only you have shown the qualities that will make you a great leader in the fight ahead."

"WHAT, AND DESTROY EVERYTHING? NEVER!"

"Okay, I'll pick for you." Henry paced along the shaking line of Brian's family, held firm by demonic abductors. Henry stopped before the youngest: nine year-old Howard.

"You're it, Howard," he said.

Howard squealed in terror, desperately trying to shield himself behind his mother, but to no avail. Two demons held his arms and dragged him out before Brian.

"OKAY, I'LL DO WHAT YOU WANT! JUST LET MY FAMILY GO!"

Henry smiled. "I knew you'd see reason eventually."

"LET THEM GO!"

Henry stroked Howard's hair. "Yes, yes. Once you've made the pact, they are yours."

Brian cried as he looked at the mirror of his despair on the faces of his loved ones. "What else can I do?"

"Do you accept the *Dark Horde* into your heart and pledge your soul to them for eternity?"

Brian sobbed. "Yeees."

Henry swept his arm over the bleeding pillar of spikes soaring over them. "THEN BEHOLD THE ESSENCE OF ETERNAL RE-CREATION! OF LIFE EVERLASTING!"

The *Dark Horde* disgorged a thundering roar as the pulsing obelisk became brighter, its beats faster. The illuminated clouds above began to spin, pulsing with electricity in time with the pillar.

Bathed in the infernal red light, the many thousands of watchers began to sway to the beat, chanting:

We are as one, as many are we. Become one, once more be.

A maelstrom of wind and flickering comets of energy formed around the beating pillar, spiralling skywards into the whirlpool of clouds directly above. As the demonic chorus raised their chant above the rising tornado, the clouds at the centre of the whirlpool dissolved, revealing a starless void wherein lurked countless watching eyes...

The domain of the Infinite Ones.

The monolith erupted into a frenzy of ejaculation, showering dark purple ichor over the assembled mass. The ichor sizzled on contact with flesh and dripped down the pillar, hardening like hot wax.

Stupefied, Brian watched as the burning ichor that landed on him began to move like amoebae, seeking and penetrating every opening into his body.

His horrified screams were drowned by the universe of other screaming voices of pain and pleasure.

When is this fucking going to end?

Soooon, Brian. Soon you will be one with uuusss.

Brian felt the sentient ichor probing the inner regions of his body. He felt his impaled arm tingle and opened his eyes to see smooth purple flesh forming around the wound... And he looked around to see the sizzling ichor re-forming the butchered bodies about him.

Ouuurs soon but not yet. You still liiiveee.

His mind broken, Brian could only laugh at the sheer insanity of it all.

He watched as the ichor made that scorpioid monstrosity's head unnaturally whole again. Like time-lapse photography, its head was re-created in seconds. It swivelled its fearsome arachnoid visage towards him as it rose on two massive, taloned stumps for legs.

Bugger.

Gnashing its mandibles, the *Venomed One* stood before the demonic pillar, its mighty bulk towering over Brian staked at its feet.

It spoke with a voice like thunder, *"WE ARE THE DARK HORDE!"*

The audience answers, an avalanche of sound, *"WE ARE AS ONE! AS MANY ARE WE!"*

The *Venomed One* gripped Brian's wounded arm in one of its crushing pincers and tore him from the spiked obelisk. Its booming voice crashed through his pain, *"JOIN US IN BLOOD!"*

Again the audience echoes, *"BECOME ONE! ONCE MORE BE!"*

The *Venomed One* stabbed its barbed stinger into Brian's wound and injected its venomous ichor. Brian fell limply to the ground, unmoving.

Beyond pain, Brian felt only the world spinning as the

fluid seeded new life. Consciousness of who he was began to fade...

Henry, holding Howard racked with tears, smiled back at Brian.

"So this is how it ends, is it?" Brian said.

"No, Brian. This is how it begins."

Henry grabbed Howard's hair in one hand and dragged a long serrated knife across Howard's neck with the other. Howard screamed as red blood splashed down his chest and over his slayer's arms.

With legs like jelly, Brian struggled to his feet. His head a cocktail of confused thoughts, he saw his son flop to the ground, his screams becoming gurgles as his life drained away...

And he felt anger.

"I'm sorry I lied, Brian," Henry said. "It had to be done. Otherwise there'd be too much competition. He also carried the channelling gene, you see, but he was just backup in case you got killed. Now that you've joined, he's just a risk to have around."

Burning anger... Overwhelming.

Henry shrugged. "Don't worry, we can always re-animate him."

In an explosive instant, Brian launched himself at Henry, catching Henry in a headlock as he landed. "DIE!" he screamed as he rammed Henry's head into one of the barbed and bloody spikes.

The spike spilt the crown of Henry's skull like a watermelon, unleashing a red spray of blood and brains.

Killing never felt so good.

A frenzy of blows followed as Brian hammered Henry's head repeatedly into the spike, reducing it to splintered pulp.

Dressed in the flesh and blood of his victim, Brian turned to his captivated audience, raised his fists and roared with fury.

Overhead, in the nebulous space between the stars, there was an answer. A singular voice, expressed through countless different mouths, resonating in the ears, hearts and minds of all present:

Congratulations... Unmaker. Your initiation is complete. We are family now, united in blood. May your rage never die.

DAY FIVE

13th April, 1989

THURSDAY 2:26 PM

The gallery waited...

Stroking his moustache, a tall and gaunt police officer sat at one end of a long rectangular table before a packed media conference. Clearing his throat, he spoke into the microphones before him, "Thank you all for coming at short notice. I am Senior Sergeant Douglas McDougall and I'm here to update you on the investigation into the murders of Barney and Frank Weston on the 9th of April."

The entire gathering now had their attention on him. Observing this, Douglas continued.

"As I mentioned earlier, Detective Superintendent Warren Bailey from the homicide division of the Criminal Investigation Branch had to cancel his attendance at this briefing. So I will say what I can about the investigation and then field your questions.

"I won't go into operational details that could jeopardise the investigation, but I can say that we have made substantial progress on this case in the last twenty-four hours. We now have a suspect remanded in custody for questioning and whilst we haven't ruled out the possibility of others being involved, the evidence is consistent with a lone operation. This is good news for the community of Howqua Hills, whom I must say have been fantastic in coming forward with information to help us solve this case.

BREWIN

However, having said that, please keep the information coming, as any little bit can help."

Douglas paused to take a breath. "The motive for the murders is as yet unclear, but there have been no related incidents."

A reporter heckled, "Can you confirm or deny that the suspect is Henry Wilcox?"

Douglas smiled.

Let them think they're learning something.

"I cannot reveal that yet. Only when charges are formally laid, will the name of the accused be released to the public."

, , ,

"It's all bullshit anyway," said Vincent, looking at the wide television screen at the Royal Hotel in Howqua Hills.

Jason laughed as he turned to the other two, Aaron and Bruce, before turning back to Vincent. "No shit, Sherlock. You were pretty quick to figure that one out, shit-for-brains."

Aaron sculled the rest of his beer and smiled. "Least we can still get blind!"

Bruce laughed. "And you're getting more sex now, Aaron, than you've ever had!"

Vincent stared at his half-empty pint of beer. "I s'pose Henry wasn't that bad after all."

"Yeah, he's alright," Bruce said.

Laughing, they all answered: "For a dumb cunt!"

ALSO BY BREWIN:

Evermore: An Introduction
Gamebook Adventures: Infinite Universe *

* Available on iPhone/iPod Touch/iPad
through Tin Man Games